Scan the QR Code to Hear the Title in Anishinaabemowin

Noodin Me-koom-maa-senh

(Wind Witch)

[Document subtitle]

Nodin Me-koom-maa-senh

Anishnaabemowin

By

Carrie Leaureax

©jiibi-Kwe

Sheila L. Chingwa

***For the survivors
of the boarding schools.***

1

Wind Witch

Trigger Warning

Some scenes may cause discomfort.

Please seek professional assistance if needed.

For all the little ones lost

For my ancestors

For the future

Thank you, Karhu for the Arrows.

Thanks, Mom, for giving me the love of reading.

Thank you, Mrs. Howard, for showing me my power.

Wind Witch

Instructions for using QR Codes

The **QR Codes** are attached to a **YouTube Video with a mini-language lesson.**

Use your **phone camera** to take a **picture** of the QR Code. You will be directed to the **right connected language video**. You will be able to **hear** and **practice** the word or grouping of words.

This mode gives you the flexibility to learn a few words in Anishinaabemowin.

4

Wind Witch

[TOC TO BE REMADE]

QR Codes [Prologue]

Scan to hear the language

#	Intro	Anishinaabemowin	English	QR Code
2	Intro	*Ge-ze-kah*	Quickly	
3	Intro	*Aambe Zhaadaa*	Let's get moving	
4	Intro	*Bekaayaan binoojiinh.*	Shush little one.	

6

5	Intro	*Gwetaani bizaanyaan*	Be very still.	
6	Intro	*Mahn-pee binoo-jiinh*	Here child.	
5a	Intro	*Negoden enji bgo-ne-yak.*	Crawl into this hole.	
8	Intro	*Moo-da neen bees-kuhwah-gun*	Climb into my jacket.	

IN THE BEGINNING

A group of men stood over a dining room table, staring at a map and talking amongst themselves. Smoke from their cigarettes drifted through the air and circled above their heads. Dark tones of conversation could easily be heard by the ladies who were visiting as they worked in the kitchen. Everyone was startled when Jamison ran into the room where the men were. They turned to focus on him as he took a moment to collect himself. Jamison, a tall, lanky man, started pacing back and forth as he sorted out his thoughts. Then, finally, the four men rounded upon him to see what news he brought.

"The girl has been taken. Last night," said Jamison

The four men peered at each other and quickly recovered from the shock of the news. They were going to move the child, but their resources were minimal. Nevertheless, the partnership between the Native Americans and the wizard's world was just in his infant stage. The protective placements of the Native children were being established, but only a handful of those wizards and witches were willing to participate in the partnership. The men shifted uneasily on their feet as they braced themselves for Jamison's news.

"The black robes found where we hid her," Jamison said with a shake of his head. "Jacques was severely hurt in the whole assault. He is being attended to, so we will have to wait and see his fate. The night hours will tell."

Joseph thought for a moment and turned to study the map closely and spoke, "Which group raided her family?"

Jamison sunk into a chair, took his boots off, and began to rub his feet. He replied, "The southerners got her. They have been focusing on her whereabouts for some time. I suspect they paid others to look for her as well. Once the lumbermen start drinking, they will tell you anything for a drink or a few dollars."

Lyra's green eyes narrowed and met Jamison's and Joseph's eyes as she entered the room. Her green eyes shifted to a dark

8

greenish-grey gaze that settled into the pits of the men's stomachs. With a sideways glance at each other, they quickly turned their gaze away from her and looked toward the map. She walked over to the table to stand next to them and said, "So, maybe next time you will listen when I see visions. This could have been avoided if you had listened." Then, with a sharp turn, she returned to her scrying bowl to see if she could find the little one.

Earlier, In the Lumber Jack Camp

Jacques, a very tall and large man with a square body and well-built lumberjack shoulders, rushed into the rudely hewed shed where the family sat eating. The echo of his voice filled the room and seemed to bounce off the walls as he said, "Ge-ze-kah[2]"Quickly, the men are coming. We must move."

Sarah watched her parents as they gathered up food and necessities they would need with tears in her eyes. The rush of activity and the anxiety lofting in the air brought Sarah to tears. Anxiety turned into fear as the gunshots ran through the trees. Sarah covered her ears to stop the screams of the others around them. Fear fastened Sarah's feet to the ground and she refused to move when her mother pulled at her arm.

"Ge-ze-kah!"[2] "Quickly!", Jacques yelled as he scooped Sarah up into his arms. Aambe Zhaadaa[3] "Let's get moving!"

Sarah's small little body was tucked up into Jacques's leathery jacket. With each footstep Jacques took, the leather of Jacques' coat bit slightly at Sarah's cheek. The smell of his sweaty leather and the earthier roughness of the skins he wore smelled and stung Sarah's nose. Sarah lifted her hand and placed it between her face and the roughened leather coat to stop it from rubbing her cheek raw. Sarah could hear twigs and leaves crunch beneath the large man's feet as they traveled across the wooded forest.

"This way. This is the best chance we have," said Jacques in a brisk and hurried tone.

Wind Witch

In the distant background, the thunder rumbled in the air, and a flash of lightning silhouetted the outlines of her parents running behind them. Jacques's breathing was heaving heavily in his chest as he stopped for a moment to look for another escape. At that moment, a group of women surrounded Sarah's Mother, and her screams echoed through the air. Sarah screamed as she watched her father turn to fight and save his wife. Sarah's widened eyes watched as the town's women gathered together to throw stones at her parents. She cried out in grief as their bodies fell to the ground. Then, with a roll of thunder ringing through the trees and with a flash of light, Sarah watched her parents disappear in the darkness of the night.

Sarah felt her body slip under Jamison's hold, and she clung on tightly to his jacket. Sarah felt Jacques' body shift in a new direction, and she held on tight. Cut trees were felled and were piled high, and debris littered the forest floors. Finally, Jacques spotted a hiding spot and rushed to it. A small area between the fallen trees was just big enough for him and her to crawl into.

Jacques stopped and quickly placed her on the ground, squared Sarah's shoulders, looked her straight into her eyes, and said, "Bekaayaan binoojiinh.[4] "Shush, little one. Negoden enji bgo-ne-yak[7] Climb into this hole. Gwetaani bizaanyaan[5] Be very still. Go, get in there quickly."

Both parties squeezed into the dark and narrow space. Rough edges of the tree's bark clung to their clothing as they crawled in. Sarah would pause, but Jacques would push her to go further until the space was too small for them to go any further. Finally, Jacques stopped, shifted his frame, and formed a barrier to the entrance.

Maan-Pee Binoo-jin[6] Here child, Moo-da neen bees-kuh-wah-gun[8], climb into my jacket. It will protect you from anything they do," he whispered into her ear.

Darkness surrounded the pair as they sat still and silent. In the distance, the men's voices grew, and their footsteps echoed through the forest floors. Each step they took would snap the dry twigs laying on the ground, echoing through the trees. Sarah's little

10

body jumped as she heard the first footsteps in the clearing. Her breathing quickened as the dreaded steps drew closer to their hiding space. The moon was bright, and at the end of the opening, she saw a man's shadow pass by. She moved in closer to Jacques, tucked herself up to his side, and tucked her face into Jacques's jacket, hiding in fear.

"Grab something long, men, and start searching all the holes! They have to be here somewhere, hiding in one of those spaces," said a man with a gruff voice.

Soon, every man had a long pole or branch in their hands, and they began prodding in every open space they could find. The squeaky-voiced man kept taunting Jacque, yelling his name in various taunting tones, calling for them to reveal themselves. Sarah and Jacques remained as still and silent as they could. The men scuffled from space to space, looking for the pair driving their poles into dark crevasses of the log piles.

Sarah heard footsteps near their hiding spot and lowered Jacques's jacket to see men standing outside their hole. She listened to their chatter and winched at the high, screeching laughter of one of the men. One man bent over to peer into the hole. For a brief moment, Sarah's eyes fixed on the sneering man's smile as he nodded that they were there. Sarah's eyes widened when she saw the knotted branch heading towards her and Jacques; she pulled her head back into the safety of his jacket.

Jacques gave Sarah a little hug and said, "This may hurt, but the jacket will keep you from being cut."

Sarah buried her head deeper into Jacques's chest, and the blows from the tree limbs began to pelt away at the pair inside. She could feel Jacques jump as he was struck. Sarah's leg screamed in pain, then her arm and chest. More and more thuds pelted Jacques's body, and soon, she felt his body go limp. His arms loosened around her and she fell by his side. Sarah felt a sudden burst of pain in her eye, and darkness began to set in. The last thing she remembered of that moment was the laughter of the men as they pulled at Jacques' limp body and felt a sudden pull of hers.

11

Wind Witch

Dreams and Nightmares

[Flash] "I told ya, I knew they couldn't go far. Look at the olf; he should be out for hours. With that head wound, he may be dead." said a man nearby.

[Flash] "Are you sure she is the right one?" squeaked Father Unis.

"Yes," grumbled the old bishop. Sarah felt his cold hands on her arm, "See, on her arm, the mark of the wind. She is the right one," he said as he ran his cold, sweaty hands over the curving birthmark on her arm. Sarah stirred and pulled away.

"Bishop, why is she so important?" Father Unis inquired.

"She is one of four in this world. The church needs to keep them apart." Said the Bishop.

"Why not kill her now?" said Father Unis.

"If we kill her now, the others will not come. They will be drawn together. We need all four of them. Once we have found them all, then we will have to destroy them." Said the Bishop.

[Flash] "No," said the Bishop, "We must take her far away. She would be easily found at the Indian school here."

The Father hissed, "As you wish, I will arrange for long-distance transport. Of course, it will be costly, but I am sure I can find someone to do the drive."

Sarah woke to find that she was riding in a cage-like bed in the back of an old, rickety truck. Sun shone in, but Sarah closed her eyes in pain, and she hoped to drift off to sleep. Darkness overtook her, and back into darkness, she fell. Sara woke occasionally when the truck hit a rut in the road or another child was added to the cage, but she would fall back to sleep. Each time she opened her eyes, someone new was near her.

[Flash] "I think she will be okay," said a man looking down at her. "She took quite a hit on the head. More than likely, she will be fine in two days." said a fat man with a black medicine bag.

Wind Witch

"Thank you, Doctor; we'll continue," said the driver of the truck.

With a sudden jolt of the truck, Sarah startled awake. The truck's wheel fell into a rough rut and jarred the passengers inside. A sharp pain ran through her head, but she did not feel the need to pass out. She slowly opened her eyes to see a streak of light shining in on other children taken from their families. She looked at them as their heads bobbed up and down as they traveled down the bumpy road.

Taking a deep breath, Sarah lurched herself up to a sitting position. Her nose stung with the smell of ammonia, and she pinched her nose closed and looked around at the other children. She could see that the girl across from her had wet herself at some point in the trip. The others in the cage were in the same condition. Sarah looked down at her own neglected appearance and willed herself to hold her bladder as long as she could. She knew the men would not stop, so she balled herself up into the corner and held her bladder.

The truck stopped, and Sarah watched three men wander off to a nearby house. Sarah heard yelling, and the crying screams of a woman echoed through the air. Sarah jumped when gunfire rang through the trees. The air stood still for a moment, and the muffled cry from the boy's mother could still be heard. They appeared, and Sarah could see that the men were dragging a young boy behind them. When they arrived at the truck, they threw him in with Sarah and the other children. The boy rose and clung to the side of the cage as he watched his home disappear in the distance as the truck drove on.

Sarah watched the children come and go over the weeks she spent in the truck. Some were sold to other families, and some went into boarding schools. Sarah waited for her turn to leave the truck, but it did not happen for many nights of sleep.

13

Wind Witch

QR Codes: Chapter 1

Scan to hear the language

#	Chapter	Anishinaabemowin	English	QR Code
9	Ch. 1	*Aanii*	Hello	

Wind Witch

Chapter I:
THE CAPTIVE

Six years later

The cold air bit at Sarah's nose as it peeked out from under the blankets. Already, the fall weather was in the morning air. Early rising was expected for all those residing at the boarding school, and Sarah woke before the morning bell rang. She smiled to herself, for she found the peace at this hour so enjoyable.

Sarah rose onto her elbow and focused her eyes on the other children lying asleep in their beds. Many had their tattered blankets pulled up around them as they slept. As the little ones sought to get a pleasant night's sleep, they collected tattered blankets and wrapped themselves tightly in little bundles that looked like little bundles of rags. With a shiver, Sarah flung her feet over the side of the bed, slipped on her shoes, and fastened the laces; then, with a tug, she pulled her blanket over her shoulders and sighed as the warmth sunk in and chased away the morning chill.

Outside the school, Sarah heard a familiar sound of a truck echoing through the schoolyard. The morning bell sounded and startled Sarah out of her thoughts. Sarah glanced out the window again to see a truck arriving and saw that more children were being delivered to the school. She looked at her bed and began to tidy it up as quickly as she could. She had to get right to work first thing this morning. The nuns had already entered the room and began nagging kids to move quickly to dress.

Children rose from their beds as the Nuns quickly bustled about, shaking kids and yelling out orders to get dressed and get ready for the day. A new little girl fell to the floor and tried to hide under her bed when Sister Mary entered the room. Sister Mary spotted her at once and narrowed in on the girl. The other students sat and watched the girl's fate as Sister Mary stormed to her. In a matter of seconds, Sister Mary grabbed the girl by her ankle and dragged her from under the bed. The other children flinched every time the sister's hand met the little one's face. The nun smiled a

15

sneering grin as she admired the reddened cheeks of the young girl sitting on the bed where the nun thrust her and left her crying.

"Get up, get dressed, and get downstairs!" ordered the narrow-faced nun. She turned with a smile and walked out of the dorm, leaving the frightened girls in her wake.

'Yes,' Sarah thought, 'This is how a usual school year starts. Sister Mary always picks on one girl to torture so she can make everyone scared of her.' Sarah paused and thought back to the day when she arrived. She closed her eyes and let herself visit that fateful day.

Memory of Sarah's Arrival

Darkness covered the inside of the cage where Sarah had spent weeks riding in. Where she was, she did not know. The moon above illuminated the dirt road just enough for Sarah to see the trunks of trees passing by. Days of sitting in her feces were sickening, but her captors would not open the door to let her take care of her needs. The truck stopped in front of a large building, and Sarah could see the outline of its stature.

"Get her out of there, you barbarians!" shouted Sister Jane.

"Right away, Sister, right away!" said the driver as he rattled through a loop of keys.

With a click of the lock, the door swung open, and Sister Jane looked in at Sarah. Quickly, she drew back and covered her nose, for the smell was unbelievable. Sister Mary stepped into the doorway, peering at Sarah. Sarah's eyes widened, and she slid herself back on the truck's bed until her back met the cage. Sister Mary lurched her body forward, grabbed her feet, and pulled her out, smearing more feces into Sarah's dirty, stinky clothes. Sarah fell to the ground with a thud. She rolled over onto her back only to see Sister Mary's face peering down at her.

"Burn the clothes," said Sister Mary to Sister Jane. "Marcus, take her to the washroom." The Gauntly Nun turned and spat on Sarah, "Filthy Savages, all of them. Marcus, wait a minute."

Sarah's skin was instantly covered with goosebumps from the empty darkness in the nun's eyes. The old nun leaned over and grabbed Sarah's hair, and hoisted her to her feet. Sarah lowered her eyes steadfastly to the ground as Sister Mary circled the little being in a contemplative manner. Sarah didn't look at the Nun; she just watched the nun's shabby boots and skirts pass by her. Sarah shivered at the darkened shadow of the old nun as she passed by.

The smirk on Sister Mary's face was a mixture of pleasure and hatred. She lifted her apron, pulled out her favorite knife, and walked toward Sarah. She laid her hand on Sarah's shoulder and turned the little girl around. Sister Mary lifted her long-matted braid, wrapped the locks around her hand, and began sawing it off, leaving behind Sarah's hair falling around her face. She stood back, smiling at Sarah as she flipped the braid in her hand.

"Marcus, now you can take her to the washroom," the sister turned and walked into the building, throwing the braid in the garbage can as she walked by.

Father Unis was standing in the washroom when Marcus and Sarah entered. He walked up to her and tore off her dress, leaving Sarah standing in an undershirt and undies. Absent mindlessly, he threw the clothes towards Marcus, who caught them in his arms. The father circled her as if he was a wolf in sheep's clothing. He laughed as he touched her hair.

"Ah, Sister Mary did some fine cutting here," he looked down at Sarah's mark and said, "Marcus, she does not join the others. Make sure she is properly confined in the basement. This little one is a special little trinket in my collection." The Father walked out the door, and Sarah's eyes followed him.

Marcus ran up to the door, peering through the crack. He watched as Sister Mary and Father Unis talked in the hallway. After a moment, they turned and walked down the hallway together and soon were out of sight. Marcus turned around, and his bangs

Wind Witch

flopped across his eyes. He swiped them aside as he looked at Sarah with concern. Her underclothes were covered with filth, so much more than most children coming to the school. He peeked once again through the crack and smiled when he saw the corridor was empty.

After a moment, he smiled and walked over to the stove, stoked it, threw in another shovel of coal inside, and shut the door. He walked over to the shelf, pulled down a large kettle, and filled it with water. After a moment, Sarah could see white streams of vapor lofting up into the air, and Marcus dipped his finger in to see if the wash water was ready. He smiled and turned and fixed his eyes on a door at the back of the room and walked towards it. Sarah's eyes followed Marcus as he walked to a door in the back of the room and knocked. Sound rustled behind the door, and soon it opened.

Miss Jade, a stalky square woman, walked into the room. Her hair was dark and was short. Her dark eyes fixed on Sarah, and her expression became sad as she assessed the child before her. She kneeled in front of her to greet her in a kind manner. She held out her hand, hoping the child would accept the gesture. Sarah only stared at the open hand and did nothing. Miss Jade sighed and hoped the child understood that she was a friend.

"Marcus, will you step outside the room and keep watch?" Jade said with her eyes fixed on Sarah.

Marcus exited the room, and Miss Jade began to undress Sarah. A tear rolled down Sarah's cheek as Miss Jade worked to fill the washtub. Miss Jade assisted Sarah to step into the water, and Sarah sat down to soak away the crust that clung to her legs. As Sarah soaked, Jade gathered up her clothes and threw them into the fire. She set the second set of wash water on top of the stove.

Jade grabbed a rag and began to clean Sarah, and she hummed as she worked. Sarah's golden-brown skin began to show its true brilliance as Jade continued to work. Miss Jade washed her arm, eyed her birthmark, and gasped in recognition of who the child in the wash bin was. After a second wash, Jade quickly dressed Sarah and walked to the door.

Wind Witch

"Marcus, watch the door. I must get the bowl out. Any shadow, footsteps, or distant voices, you let me know."

Jade walked to the cabinet, pulled out a large bowl, and placed it on the table. She pumped some water into a pitcher, carried it to the bowl, and poured it in. With her finger, she stirred the water as she mumbled some words that Sarah could not hear. Sarah's eyes widened as the bowl began to glow.

"Joseph, she is here. She is badly in need of care, but I cannot believe they brought her all the way here!" said Jade into the bowl.

A deep voice echoed through the room. Sarah searched all the corners for its source, and it said, "They brought her to you? Good god, she cannot be well. Of course, she is in bad shape; that was weeks' worth of traveling in the worst conditions ever."

"Joseph, the mark is clear, and I do not think it would be the time to cover it. Father Unis knows it is there. Father Unis told Marcus to place her in the basement for safekeeping," Jade cried, and she glanced over her shoulder to see if Marcus was still watching for people.

A scoff filled the room, "That is fine; just make sure it is done before she goes up to the schoolroom. Eventually, they will forget about the mark. Does that mean she will not be attending school?" said the voice.

"No, Joseph, they are kept down there for a long time." Jade sighed and shook her head.

"She needs an education, Jade. She must learn to read and write. It is important that she has those skills," said Joseph.

"I will see what I can do," said Jade.

"Miss Jade!" Marcus turned from the door to alert her that company was coming.

Marcus quickly ran to Miss Jade, grabbed the bowl, carried it to the bin of wash water and dumped it in. With the evidence gone, Miss Jade grabbed a brush and acted as if she was grooming

19

Sarah's hair. The door opened, and Father Unis came into the room. His brown robe hung on his thin frame. His gaunt body and angular unshavened face seemed to slither around the door as he entered.

"Hum," said the squeaky father, "Ah, she looks better. Marcus, take her to the basement. The darkroom should do."

With a tug, Marcus grabbed Sarah and pulled her out of the room. Father Unis followed the pair to ensure his instructions were followed. At the top of the stairs was a door of grand stature, and Marcus struggled to get the door unlatched and opened. Behind the door were stone steps leading to the basement. In the corners of the hallway, cobwebs, dust, and fingerprints left in blood from other students clung to the walls. Sarah's eyes looked from side to side, and fear welled up inside of her. Marcus noticed Sarah had paused, and he quickly tugged at her hand.

Father Unis followed behind the kids, and his keys clinked against each other as he walked down the stairs. At the landing, the Father stopped to catch his breath and let the kids descend before him. Marcus rounded the corner, continued down the corridor, and stopped in front of the darkroom door. Father Unis came around the corner, and a smile emerged as he caught up with the children.

Father Unis pushed Marcus aside, unlocked the door, grabbed Sarah, and threw her in, saying, "Get in there, you little heathen."

Sarah landed on the floor. Searing pain bit her knees and palms. The hard floor was cold, and there wasn't anything for her to cover herself to keep the cold away. Sarah turned and looked around the space, and she saw a small girl sitting in the corner of the room.

"Aanii! [9] Hello!" said a small voice in the corner.

"Aanii! [9] Hello!" replied Sarah in return.

The door flew open, and Father Unis stepped into the room. His form made a bee-line for the voice in the corner. The little girl curled up into a little ball as the father towered over her. Sarah could see his slender and bony fingers grab the girl by the scruff of

Wind Witch

her neck and hit her squarely across the cheek, not just once but many times, saying, "You only speak English here!"

[Memory faded]

With a shiver, Sarah threw her shawl over her shoulders and went to assist Miss Jade in the washroom. The "new students" had arrived, and they would need to be cleaned up. She walked slowly down the hallway, deep in thought. She always wondered what she had done to be thrown into the basement cell. She knew it was because of her birthmark, but that never made sense to her. She stopped in front of the washroom door and squared her shoulders.

"I will not let anyone be taken to the basement; not today, not on my watch," she said as she turned the doorknob and entered the room.

QR Codes: Chapter 2

Scan to hear the language

#	Chapter	Anishinabemowin	English	QR code
10	Ch. 2.	*Oboodashkwaanishi inh*	Dragonfly	
11	Ch. 2	*Nookomis-Dibik-Giizis*	Grandmoth er Moon,	
12	Ch. 2	*Muh-kuh-da mtig-wah-wi*	Black Arrow	
13	Ch 2	*Zaagasi Geezis*	Shining Sun	

Wind Witch

Nodin Me-koom-maa-senh

23

Wind Witch

Chapter II:
OBOODASHKWAANISHIINH' S (10)
DRAGNOGYL'S AGREEMENT

Oboodashkwaanishiinh[10] Dragonfly stooped low to the ground to avoid being seen. He tucked himself in between the cruck of two trees to watch and assess the scene. Oboodashkwaanishiinh[10]Dragonfly could barely be seen except his ears and eyes as he peeked out from behind the tree. His large eyes were light-sensitive, and he strained to look at the burning houses. His eyes scanned the landscape as he searched for his friend amidst the chaos. Men were setting fire to homes that were nothing more than wooden sheds. He watched many women grabbing buckets and running to the water from the nearby lake to save their homes. Houses were ablaze, children were crying, parents were yelling, and spouses were being arrested for fighting back. Oboodashkwaanishiinh[10]Dragonfly shook his head as he thought, 'Another Indian village burned.'

A scream sounded through the woods, and Oboodashkwaanishiinh[10]Dragonfly focused on the familiar voice of a woman. He narrowed his eyes to see past a burning house to see his friend's wife laying over his friend's fallen body. Her body heaved in sharp morning cries, trying to call his friend Steve back from the spirit world. Oboodashkwaanishiinh[10]Dragonfly laid his head on the cruck of the trees and thought, 'Another Medicine Man murdered for his magic.' Oboodashkwaanishiinh[10] Dragonfly turned his back to the tree, slowly slid down the tree trunk, and wept and thought, 'I was not on time.' He held his head in his hands and wept and repeated, 'I was not on time.'

A loud warrior yell sounded through the air. Men began to yell and fight a young boy down by the water. Oboodashkwaanishiinh[10] Dragonfly wiped his face and quickly turned to see what was happening. His dark, earthen eyes focused on a group of men down by the water. They were laughing at the youth's attempt to vindicate his father's death. Oboodashkwaanishiinh[10]Dragonfly could see one man holding Peter in a neck chokehold. The others were wiping their brows from the

24

sweat they had earned from their battle with the boy. They stood there, chuckling amongst each other as they glanced at him.

Oboodashkwaanishiinh[10]'s Dragonfly's eyes widened as he continued to watch the men and Peter. In anger, Peter struggled against the man holding him captive, trying to make his escape. The men laughed at the young boy and pushed him to the ground. Oboodashkwaanishiinh[10]Dragonfly watched as the men tied the boy's hands behind him and held his head down in the grass with their boots. They stood chatting with each other for a moment, boasting about their victory. Oboodashkwaanishiinh[10]Dragonfly watched as Peter struggled against the rope restraint to no avail and began to focus more on the men.

'Peter is in trouble,' thought the old creature as he focused his eyes on the men. Oboodashkwaanishiinh[10]'s Dragonfly's thoughts were whizzing in his head, 'The boy has Steve's blood running through his veins.' He stopped his thoughts to listen to the men. They began to laugh, and Oboodashkwaanishiinh[10]Dragonfly cleared his head and returned to watching them and the boy.

"You little Savage!" One man's boot struck the boy in the side.

A tall man strode up to the boy's body, "Dumb Indian," he said as he kicked the boy's leg.

"You little red skin, you think you could overtake us?" said a fat farmer-looking man as he kicked Peter's face.

Another leaned over the boy, looked Peter in his eyes, and said, "Grave fertilizer."

Oboodashkwaanishiinh[10]Dragonfly could see the manic look in the man's eyes. With a quick hop, he landed squarely on his feet and readily listened to the men. Oboodashkwaanishiinh[10] Dragonfly carefully watched the men and Peter from his hiding spot. A chill ran down his back as the air began cooling down, and people's breath could be seen in the glowing embers of the burning buildings. He looked over at the men standing around Peter and watched as the boy struggled. Oboodashkwaanishiinh[10] Dragonfly marveled as Peter's breathing became more difficult and heavier.

25

Wind Witch

Peter's breath lingered in a fog above his head, and the fog began to loft towards the men in a swirl. Oboodashkwaanishiinh[10]'s Dragonfly eyes began to twitch at the sight of Peter's magic. A few seconds passed, and he could see a woman's form develop; she was moving as if she were dancing. He knew in that instance that the boy must be saved. Oboodashkwaanishiinh[10] Dragonfly readied his bow and lifted his long grey fingers over his shoulder, and a black arrow jumped into his hand from his quiver. Slowly, he lowered the arrow to rest in the nook of the bow and firmly secured the nock onto the bowstring, and he waited.

One of the men nudged his partner and pointed to Peter. One after the other, they stood looking at the woman dancing in amazement. They turned and looked at each other with a smiling snare. One man reached into his pocket, pulled out a red handkerchief, and began to fold it. The fat farmer man lowered his large body onto the ground and laid his hands in front of Peter's face. A second later, the large man lowered his face to rest in Peters's face, shook the handkerchief, and smiled. Peter's eyes widened as he listened to the man's words.

"Well, boys, it looks like we get two medicine men in one trip. Let's string him!" said the fat farmer man.

The fat man's face disappeared, and the boot lessened its hold on Peter's head. A sudden pull on Peter's shirt left the boy sitting at the base of the tree, taking deep, painful breaths. The fat man hoisted himself to stand, walked over to Peter, and covered his eyes.

Oboodashkwaanishiinh[10] dragonfly watched as the man placed the handkerchief over Peter's eyes, raised his bow, and took account of his actions.

One of the men ran to their truck, retrieved a rope, and carried it back to the men smiling. He worked quickly to form a noose in his hands. He turned and flung the other end over the tree and secured it to the trunk of the tree. The man stacked some wooden boxes, hoisted the boy onto the top of them, slipped the noose over his head, and adjusted the length. The men stood back to admire their work, and Peter's mother wailed and reached in vain for her son.

The fat man stopped and turned to look at the mother and then back to the boy with a smile. He walked up to Peter and removed his mask. Peter's eyes focused on his mother, and he broke to see her in such pain. His eyes shifted, and he could see another man approaching behind her, unbeknown to her. The man smiled at Peter, walked over to his mother, and wrapped his hand around her mouth, "Stop this noise, or you'll be next."

Peter's mother's eyes were fixed on him. He could see her tears cleaning the soot off her cheek as they ran down her face. The man's thumb and forefinger slid across her cheek, smearing ashes as they passed over her skin. Peter watched his mother's eyes panicked as the man's fingers pinched her nose. Her eyes steadied on her boy, and she straightened up to face her death as a friend. She didn't struggle. She nodded at Peter and gazed past him into the dark field and Peter watched as the light grew dark from her eyes. The man threw her lifeless body aside, walked up to stand in front of Peter and smiled with a sneer.

Oboodashkwaanishiinh[10] Dragonfly watched closely at the chain of events as they unfolded. He knew he had to wait for the right time. The time of possible death, not a moment before that. He drew the bow up to shoulder height, knocked the arrow, and lowered it to rest at his side as Oboodashkwaanishiinh[10] Dragonfly waited. When he saw the boy being placed onto the boxes, his eyes fixed on his target, and he waited for the right moment.

With a sneer on their face, the man looked Peter in the eye and began to chant, 'Dead Injun, Dead Injun, Dead Injun.'

A crowd began to gather around the chanting men. Men held their grieving wives as they became witnesses to the heinous acts of the men. The first box was removed, and Peter's feet fell, but the distance was not enough to make an impact. The men stabilized the boy on the remaining boxes. Peter stood on tiptoe to relieve the tightness of the rope on his neck. Chanting filled Peter's ears as he struggled to balance.

27

Wind Witch

The fat farmer turned to his friends and chanted again, 'Dead Injun, Dead Injun, Dead Injun.' He smiled when his friends joined in with the chanting. He turned to Peter, walked up to the boxes, and leaned over to grab the last box. He smiled over his shoulder at his friends and pulled the box from under Peter. He looked up and saw the boy dangling from the rope and turned his back and coaxed his friends to keep chanting, 'Dead Injun, Dead Injun, Dead Injun' as the boys struggling body began to lessen.

Oboodashkwaanishiinh[10] Dragonfly drew the bowstring back, and his hand was nestled in the crook of a grayish cheekbone. His goblin-like ears were folded back over his hairless head. Oboodashkwaanishiinh[10]'s Dragonfly eyes focused on the rope that hung over the limb and narrowed in on his target. He lowered the tip of the arrow until it found its mark.

He said, "Nookomis-Dibik-Giizis[11] Grandmother Moon, I call thee now!"

The arrow began to glow a brilliant white light, and he released the arrow. Straight and true, the arrow flew and struck the rope suspended over the tree. A bright flash of light surged through the air and knocked all the spectators down as Peter's body fell to the ground.

Oboodashkwaanishiinh[10] Dragonfly appeared next to Peter's body, and he grabbed him and disappeared instantly. With a loud crack, he and Peter landed in Joseph's yard. Oboodashkwaanishiinh[10] Dragonfly grabbed and loosened the noose, and the boy gasped for fresh air. Once he saw Peter was breathing, he took off for a dead run for Joseph's door.

Joseph heard the company's arrival and walked to the door to see who was coming. His step quickened when he heard his old friend yelling for help from a distance. Oboodashkwaanishiinh[10] Dragonfly met the wizard at the door and pointed to Peter's body lying on the ground. Joseph's eyes focused on Peter's limp body, then down to his friend, and took off to the injured boy.

"He was hung. He is still alive but barely," said Oboodashkwaanishiinh[10] Dragonfly as he ran alongside Joseph.

28

Joseph called for Jamison and Jacque to come and help. The men rushed to Peter's side, hoisted an arm over their shoulders, and carried him into the cabin. Lyra and Verna were talking with each other next to the fire when the men rounded the doorway with Peter in between them. The two men had no trouble lifting the boy to the cushions to rest. Verna set her teacup down on the table, rushed to the boy, and began to assess his wounds.

Jamison looked over to Oboodashkwaanishiinh[10] Dragonfly and said, "Oboodashkwaanishiinh[10], why did you save him? He wasn't your watch."

Oboodashkwaanishiinh[10] Dragonfly narrowed his eyes and peered at the half-breed, and said, "He's magic, I tell you. He used the smoke to make an image of a woman. Seeing that he's a direct descendant of Steve, who is now dead, I chose to save him for my friend's sake." Oboodashkwaanishiinh[10] Dragonfly turned away from Jamison and made a horrible hiss as he found a place to sit in the room to wallow in grief.

"See Joseph; they are hunting medicine men," said Jamison as he stared at the boy. "They wouldn't have touched him if he didn't show magic."

Verna began to attend to the boy's neck as Lyra summoned the elders. Verna could see that a burn was ringing his neck. She knew that burn was more than what a rope could make. She rushed off to her room, returned with a brown bottle, and began applying the ointment to the burn. She wrapped his neck in a cloth and sat next to the boy.

"Why did he get burned like this?" she asked the creature sitting in the corner.

"I used a Muh-kuh-da mtig-wah-wi[12] black arrow. The arrow's hit is as strong as a lightning strike. I guess it burned him when it hit the mark.", said the creature with a shrug. "I'm glad he's alive."

Peter stirred and opened his eyes for a moment. He quickly looked around the room and focused on Verna's warm smile. He shifted his hand, touched his neck, and struggled to speak. Verna grabbed his hand and placed it back to his side.

"Oboodashkwaanishiinh[10] Dragonfly brought you here for safekeeping," she said to the frightened and weak boy. "It's time for you to rest."

Oboodashkwaanishiinh[10] Dragonfly jumped on top of the couch and walked along the top until he came into Peter's view. Peter gave the creature a small smile of 'thanks' as he fell into sleep. The creature sat for a moment, considering the boy with great thought. He rose to his feet, began pacing along the ridge, and glanced back down at the boy once in a while as he paced.

Four loud cracks sounded from outside, and Joseph said, "Ah, our guests are arriving. Thank you, Lyra, for summoning them."

Lyra opened the door to allow the elders into the house. She led the four ladies to the couch where the boy lay. For a moment, they considered the boy and began to whisper amongst them. The ladies walked to the table and sat down in confusion. They took a deep breath and shook their head as they listened to Oboodashkwaanishiinh[10]'s Dragonfly tale. When Oboodashkwaanishiinh[10] Dragonfly got to the part where Peter's magic could be seen, their eyes widened, and they leaned and looked over to the boy lying on the couch in unison. Oboodashkwaanishiinh[10] Dragonfly continued his story, and when it was time for his part, he reached over his shoulder and laid the Muh-kuh-da mtig-wah-wi[12]black arrow in front of him on the table. The ladies looked at the arrow in disbelief as the story continued. When the story ended, Lyra placed a cup of tea in front of the ladies.

"Where do we go from here?" said Zaagasi Geezis[13]Shining Sun.

Oboodashkwaanishiinh[10] Dragonfly looked down at the arrow in front of him, picked it up, and looked at the ladies, "I was Steve's protector. If I am allowed, I would like to be Peter's."

30

Wind Witch

The ladies stared at the creature and his arrow, deep in thought. They looked from side to side, nodded, huddled together, and took in council regarding Oboodashkwaanishiinh[(10)]'s Dragonfly request. One elder looked over her shoulder at the creature and then returned to the conversation of the others. One by one, they deliberated until they returned to the waiting wizards and Native men waiting for their input.

Zaagasi Geezis[(13)]Shining Sun. stood, "We agree that my young cousin will need protection, Oboodashkwaanishiinh[(10)] Dragonfly. I must ask why you couldn't save Steve?"

Oboodashkwaanishiinh[(10)]Dragonfly lowered his eyes, "My mate passed, and I was by her side until they placed her into the ground. So much loss, so much loss." The creature's eyes lowered to the ground, "I was on my way back to Steve to find him already passed. I have failed him, but I would be honored to watch over Peter."

Zaagasi Geezis'[(13)]Shining Sun's. brow creased, "Can you tell us the history of this arrow and your compact to protect."

Oboodashkwaanishiinh[(10)] Dragonfly sat on the table, crossed his legs, placed the arrow across his lap, and said, "It is told by my ancestors that there is another in this world somewhere. Where is it? I do not know, but my people were given this arrow to keep safe to protect Peter's ancestors. We made an agreement to protect the medicine men and their families. Generation after generation, we have done so. In the past century, I have kept watch of many, and I only failed this one time. I promise I will do my best not to become distracted from my duties. I will do everything I can to protect Peter. I owe this to Steve."

Zaagasi Geezis[(13)] Shining Sun looked at the creature and back at the ladies, "I am sorry for your loss. Thank you for saving Peter without an agreement. I will sorely miss my cousin. Steve was such a talented man." She turned to the ladies, "Are we in agreement to grant Peter Oboodashkwaanishiinh[(10)]'s Dragonfly protection?"

The ladies' eyes showed great compassion for the creature. Each   elder   nodded   in   agreement   and   granted

31

Wind Witch

Oboodashkwaanishiinh[10] Dragonfly permission to take on his new role as Peter's protector. Oboodashkwaanishiinh[10] Dragonfly bowed to the elders, placed his arrow back into his quiver, jumped to the floor, and sat on the couch ridge next to Peter. Zaagasi Geezis[13]Shining Sun turned her head for a glance into the room and smiled and thought, "Another young pup for him to watch and raise." She smiled at the proud creature sitting in a watch and returned to her ladies and her hot cup of tea.

Jacques' snoring rattled through the living room space when Oboodashkwaanishiinh[10] Dragonfly entered. He had pushed through the night to get to Joseph's home. Another loud snore erupted from the chair; he startled himself awake, thrust himself from the chair, and stood to fight. His eyes were wide as he looked around the room. Slowly, a smile emerged, and a low chuckle began as he laughed at himself. He walked out to the kitchen to join the others in a foggy gaze.

Lyra turned and smiled at Jacques and whispered, "You're just in time. They are going to talk about Sarah."

The elders sat with their eyes fixed on Jacques. He felt their stare and turned his good side to them. The elders turned to each other and whispered among them. Zaagasi Geezis[13]Shining Sun rose, walked over to the large man, tugged at his hand, and motioned for him to take a knee. Jacques's large frame lowered to the floor, and Zaagasi Geezis[13] Shining Sun shifted her body to stand in front of him.

"My kind man," she reached up and touched his scar. "You have suffered greatly over the years.," she said as she fixed her eyes on Jacques. In her hand was a bundle of (A)Sema[15] tobacco, and she held it out in front of her, "Will you please rescue Sarah from that damn school?" Slowly, in her other hand rose a pipe. "If you need time to consult the pipe, we understand."

Jacques's smile showed as he looked around the room. He looked back at Zaagasi Geezis[13] Shining Sun and then down at the (A)Sema[15] tobacco she held and a sly smile at the pipe.

"Dear pipe, you have sent me the answer many times in my dreams. Rest this time," said Jacques as he lifted the pouch from her hand; he tried to speak but nodded his yes to his beloved friend instead. The agreement had been made, and Zaagasi Geezis[13] Shining Sun smiled at the man who had proven to be an excellent protector. Everyone began to clap, and Jacques blushed at their merriment.

Joseph cleared his throat, and everyone settled down while he began to speak, "We were going to send Sarah to stay with Seth and Lori. We have Peter now. What are we going to do with him?"

Verna cleared her throat, and everyone turned to look at her and waited for her to speak, "I have two friends in Wisconsin. They have wanted children for years. Their cabin is in the middle of the woods, and the children would have lots of space to learn. To be honest, Marshal shows signs of Native Magic. He can do things most of us can't. I can see if Marshal and Mary could take the two of them."

Verna watched as pensive thoughts began to cloud the eyes of those in the room. Thoughts were running through their minds of a safe secluded place out in the middle of nowhere. Little smiles emerged, and sideway nods showed that they all thought that this would be a good thing. Nods began to occur around the room, and Joseph got out a map and had Verna show where the cabin was. The men pondered the map and discussed the drive that Jacques and Lyra would have to make with Sarah in the car. A matter of minutes passed, and the men agreed to the placement and then, in turn, consulted the elders of their escape plans.

The elders had formed a small group to the side and deliberated amongst themselves. Soon, Zaagasi Geezis[13]Shining Sun approached the table. Everyone turned and waited for her to speak.

"We agree with this placement as long as I am to be sent to teach the two our magic," she insisted.

Joseph and Robert looked at Zaagasi Geezis[13], Shining Sun, in a stunned manner. Zaagasi Geezis[13] Shining Sun could not determine if her request was too much or if they didn't approve. Silence hung in the air for a moment as the two men considered the request.

33

Wind Witch

"Good gravy, I didn't even think about schooling when it came time for placement. I think this is a good idea, Joseph," said Robert as he stared at the floor in thought.

"Out in the middle of the woods, there wouldn't be a school," mumbled Joseph. "I will have to get council's approval before we go and get Sarah, but I think that is a good idea, Zaagasi Geezis[13] Shining Sun. Council approval should be easy to get."

Lyra jumped to her feet and exited the room. When she returned, she held her scrying bowl to Verna and, with a sly smile, said, "Shall we see if Marshal and Mary could take the kids?"

Everyone watched as Lyra filled her bowl with water. She leaned over the bowl and stirred the water with her finger as she whispered a low chant towards the water. The light from the bowl began to glow, and Lyra's face lit brightly. Since there was no response from the other side, she once again swirled the water with her finger and chanted.

"Lyra, is Verna okay?" came a startled voice through the water.

"She is very okay. She needs to ask you and Marshal a question," Lyra said excitedly.

Lyra stepped aside, and Verna took her place. Verna leaned over the bowl and smiled at her friend on the other side with a sheepish grin. When she saw Mary and Marshal's image in the water, her smile was that of excitement with a touch of mischief in it.

"My friends, I have the biggest favor to ask of you. There are two Native children who need a place to live. I had mentioned that you might take them. I think your cabin would be a perfect place for the children to live," she shared.

Silence fell. The room was so still. Verna stood staring in the bowl at her friends, whose image appeared to be of bewilderment. Verna watched as the couple stared at each other. Marshal's eyes became wide, and he nodded at his wife. She smiled in return and then back to Verna.

34

Wind Witch

"I would love that! Marshal and I would love that! When will they arrive?" queried Mary.

"Sarah will be there in two weeks. Peter, well, in a few days. He is too weak right now to travel. I will come and stay there and help with his wounds," Verna said, smiling at her friends.

"It is done then!" announced Robert from across the room.

Smiles and happy nudges were exchanged between the elders. The ladies bid the couple a goodnight and disposed of the bowl. In preparation for the trip to Wisconsin, the men gathered around the map. They knew the next two weeks would be busy, but the kids were worth the work. They had a plan in place and only a little bit of time to get it all together. Everyone left Joseph's house with their part to fill. Sarah's rescue had to come without a glitch.

Chapter 3:
The Mark of Chavo

Chapter III:
THE MARK OF CHAVO

A stream of light beamed through a small window of the washroom. The sun's rays showed a stark difference between the light and darkness on the cement wall. Sarah stood in the sunlight for a moment to feel the warmth on her face. She took a deep breath and turned around to look upon all the scared little faces waiting to be cleaned.

After six years of living here, Sarah knew that this would be the beginning of each of their nightmares. This washroom is the beginning of the deconstruction of the Native child. An innocent child of light enters here after their hair has been cut and life experience; a child of betrayal and brokenness will exit. Sarah hated this truth, but who was she to shine a light on the atrocities that happened at the school? She was only a kid living in an adult world. She was and felt so powerless over this truth.

Sarah shook off the goosebumps that crept up on her skin. She had shivers running up her spine as she began her chore. Her eyes kept a close watch on everyone in the room. The Nuns of the institution were unpredictable, as well as those who fed the building with new children. As the water heated, Sarah watched the five children with curiosity. They all stood in a line, staring at their feet as they tried to keep themselves composed. Sarah's heart hurt for them as she watched their tears roll down their cheeks.

'Be Strong' was the phrase most parents said as they left their home. The children were taken from their mother's loving arms and brought to the coldest place on earth. The uncaring establishment wouldn't even let her go and hug the scared kids or talk to them to soothe them. Sarah could see that many of them were doing their best to find their strength at that moment. She readied the three boys and two girls for bathing. She led them to stand next to a bin as she began to pour the water into them. Sarah sighed as she placed shoes, shirts, and pants next to the bin.

"Sarah! There you are!" said Jade as she burst into the room. "Come and help. I can see the basins are almost ready."

Wind Witch

Sarah nodded and proceeded to place the buckets near a woodstove. She grabbed a few more buckets and began filling them and placing them back on top to heat. Sarah took a deep breath and turned to collect the clothes lying on the floor. Each item was checked for quality to be sold, and the damaged ones would be burned.

Jade walked up behind Sarah and whispered in her ear, "There is a rumor that one of the boys may be marked. Make sure to use the special soap to cover the mark. Understood? Oh, and remember you must say the spell: Cloak of darkness conceal this mark, for this mark is one of truth."

Sarah nodded and looked over at the shelf where the bar of soap was hidden. She nodded, walked towards the shelf, took down two bars of soap, and slipped the black one into her pocket. She looked over her shoulder at the boys and chose one to start on. Chavo was standing there downtrodden, and his eye was blackened. This was not an uncommon sight when the boys arrived. She walked up to Chavo and handed him a bar of soap; then, she poured a bucket of water into the wash bin.

Chavo watched Sarah fill his tub with warm water. She avoided his eyes. She didn't want to see the pain and fear that filled his being at that moment. Jade watched closely as Chavo lowered himself to the water. Sarah told him to wash and clean himself. She watched his hands move over his skin as she looked for any evidence of a mark. He washed his arms and legs, and Sarah didn't see a mark.

Sarah felt eyes looking at them, and she looked up to meet Father Unis' eyes and quickly looked back at the chore at hand. The weight of the Father's glare bore down on Sarah. She could feel the desire to acquire another trinket for his collection. The father's eyes followed every stroke of the soap as it revealed the boy's true color. Arms, legs, and belly were washed, and no mark could be seen. The Father shook his head as he watched the boy wash, and he knew there wasn't a mark. In a frustrated grunt, he stomped out of the room. When he slammed the door shut, Sarah sighed with relief.

Chavo wore a long braid as dark as night. Beautiful locks of dark strains of hair were gathered and woven around each other in a thick, tight braid. Sarah sighed, knowing that in a few moments, that beautiful braid would decorate the floor of the nun's room. Chavo shifted in the water, and Sarah saw the water pull down the waistband of his underpants, and a speck of blue skin peeked out of its hiding place.

Sarah quickly lowered her hand on Chavo's shoulder and said, "Sit and be still."

Startled, Chavo shifted and splashed water onto the floor. Jade was busy with her child, and she jumped when she heard Chavo splashing in the water. Jade leveled her eyes at Sarah, and Sarah moved her hand and grabbed her arm to alert Jade that Chavo was indeed marked. With a nod, she pretended not to watch Chavo and Sarah.

Jade was a sturdy woman. She was very square in stature and nowhere near graceful. She rose from her wash bin, instantly tripped over a doll laying on the floor, and landed straight on Sister Jane's robe. She quickly rose to her feet, reached down to pick up the doll, walked to the stove, and tossed it in. Jade returned to Sister Jane and began to apologize for her clumsy mistake.

Sarah knew this was her chance to hand Chavo the soap. Quickly she reached into her pocket and drew the black soap out of her pocket. She carefully slipped the soap into the water. Chavo looked up at her with a confused look.

Sarah leaned in close to him and whispered, "Can you speak their tongue? Just nod, don't speak."

Chavo glared at Sarah with a look that could have shown his hatred for this experience. He pursed his lips together, narrowed his eyes, and nodded a 'yes.' Sarah smiled and sighed with relief. She leaned in closer to him and continued to talk to him in a whisper.

"You have a mark on your butt cheek that needs to be covered so the nuns won't see it. I put a black bar of soap in your water. You must wash the spot where your birthmark is with it.

39

Understand that you must wash the entire spot with black soap. Do you understand?" Sarah said with a whisper in his ear.

Chavo searched the wash bin for the bar of soap. After a moment or two, Sarah saw that he was beginning to wash the area, and she softly whispered, "Cloak of darkness conceal the mark, for this mark is one of truth."

Sarah watched as Chavo scrubbed the spot where his birthmark was hiding. She watched the blue spot fade, and the skin began to match the surrounding skin. Sarah smiled a small smile as she laid her hand on his shoulder. He looked at her, and she nodded that it was okay to stop. Sarah reached into his bath water, and Chavo knew to give Sarah the bar of soap. She slid the soap back into her pocket, stood, and nodded in Jade's direction.

Sister Jane heard Sarah talking to Chavo and glanced over Jade's shoulder. Her eyes fixed on the pair for a moment or two and saw nothing unusual. With a sigh, Jade began to speak to the Nun again, and they continued their conversation. Jade had exceptional skills at distracting others. Sarah returned to Chavo and handed him a towel and a set of clean clothes.

Sister Jane scanned Chavo's body with her eyes. She was convinced that he wasn't marked and bid Jade goodbye and left to go to the next room to help cut hair. Jade returned to the two children with a smile.

"That was close! I thought for sure we were going to get caught. I am sorry to say it is time to go to the next room where Sister Mary is working on cutting hair," said Jade.

Chavo had an older brother who attended the boarding school. Once his brother returned home, he told his siblings of the horrible stories of the dealings within. Chavo knew that Sister Mary would be the one who would cut off his braided hair. He really did not look forward to the ridicule she would make him endure. His eyes widened as he remembered his brother's stories of how she would become demonic while she cut everyone's hair. Chavo looked up at Jade with fear in his eyes.

Jade wrapped her arm around his shoulder, said, "Be Strong," and led him from the room.

41

Chapter 4:
The Meeting

QR Codes: Chapter 4

Scan to hear the language

#	Chapter	Annishinabemowin	English	QR Code
14	Ch. 4	Mshkwodewashk	Sage	
15	Ch. 4	(A)Sema	Tobacco	
16	Ch. 4	Aki mnidookaazo	Earth magic	
17	Ch. 4	Shkode mnidookaazo	Fire magic	

Wind Witch

18	Ch. 4	De-bwa-min-aa-gwa-se	Reveal	

Wind Witch

Chapter IV:
THE MEETING

The next day, Joseph's home was flooded with guests who came to examine the child, who was still sleeping on the couch. The night's event had made him an orphan, and he was close to the age of placement. Verna took a seat at the table in a spot where she could keep a very close eye on the boy as he lay tossing and turning in troubled dreams. Jacques sat in the chair near the fire, close to the boy, just in case he woke up in a fight. Lyra busied herself in the kitchen for a moment, preparing a plate of snacks because it appeared that the day would drag on for a while.

As soon as Lyra completed her task, she carried a plate of cakes and cookies back into the dining room. She paused for a moment at the doorway and admired the congregation of people at the table. The wizarding folk, the council of elders, and the medicine man were all gathered together in one place. 'Such an unusual sight,' she thought. As she walked past the living room door, she glanced over to the couch and then saw Oboodashkwaanishiinh[10] Dragonfly resting on the upper edge of the couch, and she could hear Jacques's snoring coming from the chair. Lyra smiled, placed the cookies in front of Jack, and laid her hand on his shoulder.

As Lyra took a seat next to Joseph, she said, "I believe we are ready to begin."

Robert looked over to his friend and said, "It is time, my friend, to prepare a smudge."

Jack picked up his bag, drew out his Mshkwodewashk[14]sage, (A)Semaa[15]tobacco, and a little metal skillet, and placed them on the table. He rolled a ball of Mshkwodewashk[14]sage in between his hands and placed the ball in the center of the pan. He drew out a long, thin stick, walked to the fireplace, and lit the stick in the flames. He slowly made his way to the other room, and as he did so, he guarded the fire against blowing out. He seemed to talk to the fire as he walked, but no one could hear what he was saying. Everyone watched as he lowered

45

the flame to the Mshkwodewashk[14]sage and lit it. Everyone watched as the dance between the fire and medicine began.

Smoke lofted into the air in swirls and spread out into the air. The smell of Mshkwodewashk[14]sage burning seemed to soften and lighten the atmosphere as everyone took deep breaths, followed by silence, and a moment of peace set in. As they watched Jack work, they all took a moment to rest their minds. Jack was busy cleaning himself and his feather with the smoking Mshkwodewashk[14] sage. Once he was done, he carried the burning Mshkwodewashk[14]sage to the others around the table. He began to move from person to person to clean their souls and to rid them of ill intent so the discussion would be peaceful and all would be willing to work together.

Jack had finished smudging the people in the dining room and continued into the living room. To not disturb his large friend, he smudged him as he slept. Jack smiled as Jacques' snoring lessened, and his breathing became rhythmic and peaceful. A shuffling sound came from the blankets as Peter's arms pushed and pulled at them. Jack turned to see that the boy was participating in the nightmarish dream. With a half-smile, Jack lowered the Mshkwodewashk[14]sage over the boy's body and began to cover his being from head to foot with smoke. Peter's troubled dreams seemed to lessen as the smoke lofted over him, and he rolled over and snuggled into a comfortable sleeping position. Jack's lips parted a little in a smile as he watched the boy drift into a restful sleep. Oboodashkwaanishiinh[10] Dragonfly smiled up at Jack, smudged himself in the smoke, and settled back to rest alongside his new charge. In a slow manner, Jack walked back to the dining room and sat next to Robert.

Robert, a business-like man, leaned on the table and gathered his thoughts. He rubbed his hair in deep thought. Everyone waited for him to speak out of respect for his people. He leaned back in his chair, looked around at his friends, and smiled.

"Isn't it amazing how one night can change our plans?" Robert asked as he looked around the table. "This is something we didn't expect. The burning of the village, the death of a medicine

46

man, the hanging of a child, the rescue by an ancient one, the gathering of the elders and now, we need to assess the child."

Joseph looked across the table at Robert, "So true, my friend. Peter still had another year at the school before placement would occur."

"This is an issue, my friend; his mark is covered. How are we going to see what has been covered?" asked Robert, looking across the room at the elders.

Zaagasi Geezis's[13] Shining Sun's smile widened, "Oboodashkwaanishiinh[10] Dragonfly can show us with the arrow."

The gathering stopped and peered a moment at Zaagasi Geezis[13]Shining Sun. She shifted in her chair while shaking her head and said with a sigh, "The black arrow's light will show us any of the covered marks we have hidden over the years. Oboodashkwaanishiinh's[10] Dragonfly arrow will give us the answer."

Robert walked over to the sleeping boy on the couch, "Oboodashkwaanishiinh[10] Dragonfly, would you reveal his mark so we know what magic he wields?"

Oboodashkwaanishiinh[10] Dragonfly slipped off his perch on the couch and stationed himself in front of Peter. Verna came to assist the creature in lifting the boy's shirt and lowering his waistband. Peter began to stir and started to struggle. She reached into her pocket, pulled out a vile filled with lavender oil, and held it under his nose. Once he snuggled back into sleep, Oboodashkwaanishiinh[10] Dragonfly continued to work.

Oboodashkwaanishiinh[10] Dragonfly drew the arrow out of its quiver, brought it close to Peter's skin, and said, "De-bwa-min-aa-gwa-se [18] Reveal."

Oboodashkwaanishiinh[10] Dragonfly pursed his lips in concentration, then they parted into a smile, and a hiss drew through his lips as the black arrow began to glow. A warm white light could be seen by those watching. They closed their eyes as a warm breeze filled the room and swirled around them. They opened their eyes when they heard Oboodashkwaanishiinh[10] Dragonfly hissed.

Wind Witch

They began to gather around the couch, watching and waiting for the results. The arrow's light grew, and Peter's mark slowly appeared. A small blue mark appeared in the shape of a birch leaf. An audible gasp could be heard through the room as the evidence of the mark became clearer. Oboodashkwaanishiinh[10] Dragonfly quieted the arrow and placed it back into his quiver.

"Birch leaf," said Zaagasi Geezis[13]Shining Sun. "Aki Mnidookaazo[16] Earth magic. His father was Shkode Mnidookaazo[17], fire magic. He wouldn't have been able to train him appropriately."

The clock began to chime on the wall, noting the hour. Ten clangs rang through the air as the ladies and gentlemen walked back into the dining room. Joseph walked to the cabinet, removed a stack of paper, and placed it on the table. He sat down, pulled two pieces of paper from the pile, and sat them in front of him. One had the name Sarah Shingwak, and the other Peter Shimonwak. He took a moment to make a note on Peter's paper and wrote, 'Earth Magic.' He yawned and placed the papers in the middle of the table.

Oboodashkwaanishiinh[10] Dragonfly stumbled his way to the table and tugged on Joseph's cuff, and said, "Even though Peter is earth magic, what I saw at the burning was Shkode mnidookaazo[17] fire magic."

Zaagasi Geezis[13]Shining Sun nodded and began to speak, "It is not uncommon for children to show multiple talents. One will be stronger than the other. I will have to watch his skills."

"The council asked about their education. Can you teach them to read and write?" inquired Joseph as he walked up to Zaagasi Geezis[13] Shining Sun.

"I can. Turtle clan people are teachers. I studied to be a teacher for my people. With the men taking the kids all the time, I couldn't teach. No white school would have me. That is okay; I am here for these two now," shared Zaagasi Geezis[13]Shining Sun.

Robert looked at Joseph and asked, "Can we get her the proper supplies?"

Joseph nodded and, in pensive thought, mumbled, "I don't think that will be an issue. I am sure I can get some books and supplies. Now that the council knows you can teach, I believe they will approve your tutelage for the kids."

Joseph rubbed his eyes and picked up a pen to scribe a note. Everyone waited as he scratched a note to the council. Carefully, he folded the paper and placed it into the envelope. He grabbed his stick of blue wax and a candle and held the pair over the paper. Joseph held the blue wax to the candle to melt. His eyes watched as the blue wax began to hang from the tip. Soon, a bead of blue liquid fell onto the paper. He looked at the hot wax, blew a few puffs of air onto the wax, and smiled. His hands quickly picked up his metal stamp and pressed it into the molten wax. He lifted the stamp, and the embossed emblem showed a deep blue imprint of an owl sitting on a limb. As he walked to the window, he stretched and yawned, then handed the envelope to the bird."Zaagasi Geezis[13] Shining Sun, If the council has approved for a cabin to be built for the school and your living space. What adaptions will you need in your cabin?" inquired Joseph.

"Could I ask for an apothecary?" ventured Zaagasi Geezis[13], Shining Sun, in a humble manner.

Joseph's eyes began to smile and shimmer as he looked at the old crone and nodded. Zaagasi Geezis[13] Shining Sun ran up to the old man and gave him a jumping and shaking hug. She was so short that she barely came up to his chest and almost picked him up when she jumped up and down. Joseph began to chuckle as he worked hard to keep his balance during her excited hug. He drew back and smiled appreciatively as he was impressed by the old lady's fortitude in her later years. She chuckled with delight and returned to the other elders in the room.

A few hours passed, and the ladies kept busy. They tended to Peter's wounds, made more medicine, and prepared a noon meal. The time was silent as everyone sat eating in uncertain thoughts. The ladies gathered the dishes and began to clean up. Joseph lounged in his chair near the window, resting as he waited for his owl to return. When he saw the great grey owl land on the sill, he glanced over to Lyra who retrieved the envelope from the bird.

49

Joseph rose from his chair, retrieved the envelope from his friend, and settled down at the table to read the contents.

He broke the seal and read the contents out loud, "Joseph, the Council agrees to employ Zaagasi Geezis[13]Shining Sun as the teacher for the children. Please plan for the construction of appropriate housing."

Verna smiled and sweetly said, "Oh, Marshal is a master of the forest. I am sure he can help you with that. Just get a hold of him and get plans together."

Joseph sat down in a chair and slid down in a lounging slouch. His eyes were heavy with weariness, and he nodded. Lyra sent a cup of coffee to rest in front of him. Joseph stared out the window as he took long slurps. Occasionally, he paused and sighed as he sipped at the black liquid. In a shaky manner, he placed the cup in the saucer. Robert and Jack watched the old man in concern as he seemed to struggle more from age.

"I am so glad we have approval. This will make things go quicker," mumbled Joseph.

"Joseph, Jack, and I can make sure the cabin gets built. We'll head to Marshal and Mary's place and help them prepare for everyone's arrival," said Robert.

Joseph rose to his feet, stretched, and yawned, then said, "I would appreciate that. These past few days have been very busy. I need to rest."

Robert looked at Jack and said, "I believe we have reached an agreement. Please light the pipe, my friend. We must get busy. The days will pass quickly."

Jack drew out a bundle from his backpack and unrolled it. He carefully prepared the pipe and continued his task with others looking on. Jack walked from person to person so each person could take a draw on the pipe, sealing the agreement. Once completed, Jack put away the pipe, bid the group good night, and left Joseph's house.

50

Chapter 5:
Leaving

Chapter V:
LEAVING

Fall closed in on the boarding school. Leaves had fallen from the trees, and the day was cold and rainy. The Hunter's full moon would soon happen, and Sarah sat on the porch pouting. Jade was stressed from taking care of Father Unis. He was ill and needed her attention most of the time. His fever was high, and he shook from chills as he slept. Sarah tried to help, but Jade ushered her out of the room. Sarah sat on the ground and thought about Jade's mood.

"Little one, you do not need to see this. I want you and Marcus to go and attend to other chores," commanded Jade as she grabbed the scruff of Sarah's coat and escorted her out of Father Unis' room.

Sarah stumbled out into the hallway and straightened herself up as she went to sit on the porch. Bewilderment filled her mind because she had never seen Jade like that before. Usually, she is one of the kindest people in the room. The look on her face was of emotional turmoil, and Sarah did not understand her. The level of Jade's frustration was high, and she was easily angered by the littlest thing. Sarah was always in her way, and Jade's eyes often peered at her as an intrusion rather than being a helper. Then, to throw her out of the room was unexpected. Stunned, she sat there as the rain began to trickle. Sarah was in such deep thought she didn't hear Marcus's approach.

"What are you doing?" Marcus approached Sarah cautiously.

Sarah's puzzled face stopped Marcus in his tracks. "I do not understand what is happening today. Jade has been awful to me all day."

"All the nuns have been extra mean. With Father Unis ill, they are all concerned he will not survive," said Marcus with a shrug.

52

"They are whispering and talking amongst themselves. Jade is worn thin. I don't think she has slept in a few days, and if she has, it must have been a few minutes at a time," said Sarah with a shake of her head.

"I hope he does die; he's a horrible person. A father is supposed to be a shepherd who takes care of his flock. He is not even close to that. I have witnessed horrible things, and other kids have told of his horrible deeds done to them. I will be happy to see him go. Come on, let's go," said Marcus as he pulled Sarah into the building and down the hall, "I have something to show you."

The children trotted down the hallway to a door well-known by all the children. A simple door made of wood enclosed the office of Father Unis. Sarah looked around the room at the belt hanging on a nail in the corner. She thought, 'his favorite'. Dusty books sat on the shelf, and the room was so dark and gloomy. Sarah watched Marcus as he walked toward the Father's desk, and picked up a piece of paper.

"I was cleaning today, and I saw something I think you need to see." Marcus briefly looked over the paper and handed it to Sarah.

Sarah took the letter and began to read:

Dear Father Unis,

I am writing in response to your advertisement in the paper. I am interested in purchasing an Indian child to help around my farm. We have many children and need some assistance with childcare. I am expecting a child around the age of eleven. We feel a girl would be a perfect choice.

My wife and I will be in your area the last week of October. I will stop by and pick a child of my choice. Please have a few children to choose from and ready to go. My wife and I hope to arrive on Tuesday due to our scheduled trip. I have attached ten dollars in advance payment. Thank you for attending to this task.

Sincerely,

Wind Witch

Mr. & Mrs. Pauly

Sarah's eyes devoured the words as she read, and excitement dared to enter her being. She pursed her lips together, thinking about caring for many children. She thought, 'What's the difference? I help take care of many here.' She nodded as if she was okay taking care of the kids. Sarah looked at the calendar, noting that today was indeed the last week of October. 'Tuesday? Today is Tuesday!' she thought as she quickly glanced up at the calendar and then, with wide eyes, looked at Marcus.

"You're 11, aren't you?" Marcus' eyes were wide and inquiring.

Sarah laid the letter on the desk, "I just turned 11 the other day."

"Then, you could go, right?" Marcus looked at Sarah with an optimistic expression. A smile stretched across his crooked teeth. "I believe, if we plan it right, we can get you out of here."

Sarah grabbed the letter, "I wonder how many children they have. It could be worse."

Sarah's eyes scanned the paper for any clues. The handwriting was so eloquent, and Sarah thought, 'This may be my only hope to get out of here.' As she reread the letter, she wondered what life was like outside the school. She had been there since she was five. In some ways, the letter brought her hope, but fear crept into her thoughts.

"Come on, we have chores to do," said Marcus.

Marcus and Sarah walked down the hallway together. Nuns passed by them with linens and wash bins. Sarah turned and walked backward to watch them as they entered the Father's room. Jade held the door open for the nuns, and she peeked down the hallway at the two children. Her eyes flew wide and made a signal to do dishes. Sarah nodded and picked up speed, and Marcus followed suit. Around the corner and through the halls, the kids flew. They brushed past a group of girls and made their way to the kitchen. Carefully, they opened the door and tried to sneak in.

Wind Witch

"It's about time the two of you showed up," Sister Mary said with a snarl, "We already have enough to do with a sick father and a supper to get on the tables."

Sister Mary grabbed a towel and rolled it in her hands. As Sarah felt a pain in her leg, a piercing crack reverberated through the air. She tripped against Marcus as she leaped. Sarah was knocked to the ground by a powerful blow. Everyone gasped as they watched the Sister kick her squarely in her back. Pain in her thigh, pain in her back, and scraping pain at her knees and hands bit at Sarah as she climbed to her feet. Sarah felt the heat of her skinned knees, and soon, blood began to appear. The tall nun approached Sarah and scoffed at the little scrapes on her knees. She shook her head, and she chuckled as she exited the room.

"She really doesn't like you," said Marcus as he helped Sarah to her feet and turned to wash the dishes.

Sarah grabbed a rag, tied it around her knee, and said, "She never has. I don't think any of us have found her favor. She even hates Jade, and Jade does so much for them," mumbled Sarah as she hobbled to the wash bin to help Marcus with the chore.

In a flurry, Jade and two other nuns rushed into the kitchen. The two children stepped back against the stone wall and watched the ladies grab some supplies. Sarah could see that Jade was beside herself. Her hair was all ruffled with the day's struggle. The two other nuns kept stopping and taking deep breaths as if they were overwhelmed.

"The old loon is out of control. His fever is driving him mad. He keeps flaring his arms around and grabbing at people. I swear, one more tug at my hair, and I will lose a chunk out of my scalp. Find anything to tie him down," said Jade.

A young nun ran to the scrap bin and pulled out long strips of fabric. "Will this do?" she spoke.

Jade nodded, and the two ladies rushed out of the room. The whispers of the nuns began to increase, and fear set into their eyes. Sarah and Marcus knew not to talk, so they returned to their chores. Every time someone came in, the two children heard the

55

developing story of Father Unis' death. Once the dishes were done, the children exited the kitchen without notice.

"Why is there so much fear around Father Unis' death?" said Marcus.

"I wish I knew. I have never seen the nuns so scared," Sarah said thoughtfully.

"Come with me. I have an idea." Marcus took off on a dead run and led Sarah toward Father Unis's room. "In the closet, there is a peek hole; if we can get into that room, we might be able to see what is happening," he said in strained pants.

In the distance, a familiar sound of tires crunched on the gravel as the truck approached the building. Sarah stopped and looked out the window to see a blue Chevy truck pulling up in front of the school. A lady with a flower dress slowly emerged from the truck. A large man strode up to stand next to her. Sarah stopped for a moment to look at the couple, but Marcus kept running, so she had to catch up.

The two children came to a halt at the corner and slowly peered around the edge of the wall to see the vacant corridor. A moment later, a nun came out of the room with a wash bin and walked away. The two children began to move toward the closet as quickly as possible. Sister Mary opened the door to find the two kids in the hallway. She rushed up to them, and they stumbled backward. Sister Mary grabbed Sarah and shoved her until she was pinned between the nun and a table. Sarah screamed in pain as the nun pushed her ribs into the table's solid frame.

"What are you doing here?" Sarah could smell the rot of the Nun's breath as she spoke to her.

"We need to get the ladder from the closet," said Sarah as she turned her head to avoid the rotten stench coming from her mouth. "It is in that closet over there."

"You need the ladder, do you? Okay, let's go and get the ladder."

Sister Mary grabbed Sarah by the arm and pulled her over to the door. With a turn of the nob, she thrust open the door and pushed Sarah inside the closet. Behind her, the door slammed, and a latch clicked. The light above and below the door was the only light Sarah could see.

Sister Mary turned and fixed onto Marcus and said, "I believe you have chores to do. Get out of here and get busy."

Sister Mary grabbed Marcus' collar and pulled him down the hallway to escort him on his way. Once she was certain he was gone, she turned and went back into the room where Father Unis lay dying. Sarah tried to open the closet door but found that she was trapped. Around her, she could see brooms, bed linen, and towels but no ladder. However, she was right where she wanted to be. She began to hear the sisters gathering in the next room chanting. "Hail Mary full of grace..." The father's last rights began.

'There is a peek hole,' thought Sarah. 'I have got to find the peek hole.' Her hand searched the wall that separated her from the chanting nuns. 'Marcus said it was here.' Her finger jabbed into a nob, and she drew back her finger and rubbed the pain away. Carefully, she found the nob again and found it to move. She smiled and tested the little door for noise. The noise it made was minimal if she slowly moved it. She could see the hole emerge as her little fingers strained to reach and slide the knob. A little ray of light streamed through the hole. 'A couple more pushes,' she said to herself and coaxed herself on.

With a little strained nudge, a light from the hole cascaded across the closet space and landed on an old crate. 'Yes, just right,' she accepted with a nod. She lifted the brooms out of the crate and leaned them against the wall. Sarah's body leaned onto the side of the box, and she pushed it squarely onto its side on the floor. She only had to move it ten inches, but the wooden crate was hard to move. As quickly as she could, she moved the crate into place and hoisted herself up to stand up on the top. After a slight wiggle, she steadied herself on top of the crate and adjusted her feet to gain balance. Securely stationed on the box, Sarah turned to see the hole was within reach. She thought, 'If I stand on my tip toes, I might be

57

able to reach it.' With determination, Sarah found a handhold and stood on her toes to peer through the hole.

Sarah peered through the peephole to see the nuns kneeling by the bedside of Father Unis' bed. Prayers and chanting of his last rights continued in unison. The feverish chanting seemed to strengthen as the father dwindled. With a last rasping breath, the father's body arched, and a blackness rose from the body. Sarah watched as the nuns screamed and ran from the room, leaving the blackened being forming and rising from the father's body behind.

Sarah watched as the black monster with horns and claws began to move. It took a deep breath as it stretched its limbs out and began to move its bony fingers. It reached up high, stretched its trunk, and swayed back and forth to loosen its muscles. The beast slid off the table and steadied himself on his feet, and with one last stretch, he stood to its full stature. Sarah's eyes grew wide with fear as she watched the beast.

The beast began to sniff the air in the room. Sarah watched as the drool began to drip from its fangs. A few deep breaths from the beast, and it focused its yellow eyes in Sarah's direction. Sarah froze as she watched the monster sniff its way towards her. The horrid beast narrowed in on the hole and shifted one eye to meet Sarah's. A dark, hollow feeling hit Sarah's gut. She quickly closed the peek hole, jumped off the crate, and crawled into the far corner of the closet in total fear.

The monster's roar rang high and sharp. Sarah covered her ears, for the screeching was deafening. She sat in the corner of the closet and listened to the thing scraping and clawing at the door, trying to escape the bedroom. The beast's scrapping nails on the wooden door sounded. Sarah could tell that the cracking boards wouldn't last long. Sarah sat in the darkened closet and hoped it couldn't get through. A moment later, a loud crash alerted Sarah to its escape. Sarah Jumped and pulled her legs to her as she waited.

Sarah's eyes fixed on the lower ledge of the door. She could see flickers of shadows pass by the opened space. The growling stopped, and Sarah watched as the blackened shadow grew to conceal the light at the bottom of the door. Sarah drew everything back and tucked her skirt around her so the beast couldn't grab it and pull her to it. Her eyes widened as drops of drool began to collect in grey stains on the cement floor.

Sarah watched as the beast's shadowy arm reached easily under the door. Long and thin appendages of dammed fingers stretch across to touch Sarah's feet. The coldness of death crept in to feast on her. The sickening chill of its touch caused Sarah to recoil. Then, the hand retreated suddenly.

Flashes of light protruded into the closet from the top and bottom of the door. Sarah covered her ears from the screams of the beast and lowered her head to her knees to cover her eyes from the bright flash. Screams of pain came from the beast as a bright light cascaded from the bottom of the door. Sarah jumped when she heard the glass shatter from the window in the background. Sarah covered her ears and left them there until the sound of the beast faded. Sarah heard the door unlatch and was quickly flung back, and Jade rushed in. She fell to her knees in exhaustion in front of Sarah.

"Are you okay?" Jade inquired as she gathered the scared child into her arms.

"My side is hurting, my knees are scuffed, but I'm okay. What was that? What did he become?" said Sarah in a shaky voice.

"That was a wendigo. The Father became a wendigo. He's gone now, and you are safe," said Jade inspecting Sarah. "Sarah, the people are here to take you away. They are people you know and will be happy to see, but you must not show you know them. There are others to choose from, but you are the one they will choose. Just look at your feet the whole time. Just look at your feet. Don't mess this up; it's your only hope for a long time."

The church parlor wasn't much to look at, but the chairs were inviting and comfortable. Mr. and Mrs. Pauly sat in wait for the girls to be brought down for the choosing. Minutes passed by, and they began to pace. They would hear footsteps and hoped it was time to see Sarah for the first time in many years. After an hour, Jacques and Lyra began to ask questions to the passing nuns.

"Why the delay?" barked Jacques at them. "We told you to be ready for us."

The nuns ignored them and strolled on by with no answer. In the washroom, two other young ladies were bathing when Sarah arrived. Quickly, she undressed and began washing herself to get ready to go. Fresh clothing was given to her, and she quickly dressed. Sarah took deep breaths as she progressed down the hallway with the other anxious girls. She gave them sideway glances with sadness. She knew in a few moments that their excitement was for not. Sister Jane walked the three girls down to the room and paused for a moment to adjust their appearance. She looked down at them and smiled as she proceeded towards the waiting couple.

Sarah's heart was pounding with excitement. She knew she had to escape this place. Her feet moved quickly to keep up with Sister Jane. Her breathing increased, and her thoughts kept racing through her head, and she struggled to remain calm. Her mind raced with the thoughts of the people she might know. 'Who would she know outside the boarding school? Delivery truck men or local gardeners, perhaps?' Sarah's nerves began to rise, and she calmed herself by chanting, 'Keep your eyes lowered. Keep your eyes lowered, and don't act out.' Sister Jane stopped quickly, and Sarah ran into her.

"Pay attention, girl," said the nun as they entered the room.

Sister Mary was in the room when the girls arrived. "Ah, there they are. These three are of age and are hardworking, and WHAT is Sarah doing here?" hissed the nun.

Sister Jane stepped up to stand behind Sarah and said, "Now that Father Unis has passed, I thought you might like to get rid of her." She nodded at the nun wide-eyed and encouraging.

"Perhaps you're right." Sister Mary walked over to Sarah and lifted her sleeve, "No mark, she can go. That is if they will take her."

Jacques' eyes landed on Sarah for a moment, and he turned his back to the girls. He quickly turned and looked out the window until he collected himself. He felt the sudden urge to run up to Sarah, grab her and make a beeline for the door. Lyra laid a hand on her supposed husband's shoulder and smiled in understanding. She nudged him to get back to the chore at hand. Jacques and Lyra inspected all the girls one by one. When they came to Sarah, the couple stopped and stood in front of her. Jacques's big feet came into Sarah's view. Large shoes blended in with long pants that met a stout body. She began to see a thick, full beard and lowered her eyes before seeing who it was. 'No, Sarah, just look at the floor. Don't blow this,' she thought.

A large hand reached down and turned her hand over, and his deep voice said, "This one is a hard worker. Look at these callused hands," said Jacques.

Sarah's eyes widened, and she thought, 'That voice, I know that voice.' She told to herself, 'Don't look up, Sarah. Don't you dare look up!'

"A hardworking one? Let me see." Lyra's voice made Sarah jump in recognition.

Sarah thought, 'I know that voice too! Don't mess this up, Sarah. Eyes down.' Sarah took a deep breath and withdrew her hand from Jacques's large hand. The torment of the excitement began to well inside of her. She just wanted to look up and run into Lyra's arms. She knew she had to stay strong this time, just in a different way. Somehow, the conversation in the room blurred. She had to maintain no expression and display a bit of apathy. Sarah thought, 'Bite your lip; you won't think about it.' The effort was excruciating as the minutes passed by, but it worked. Sarah thought, 'A little pain now is worth the chance to leave.'

The couple walked away from the girls to discuss who to choose. As they talked, Sarah heard everything they said. She heard them say that one of them was ugly, another too short, and the other wouldn't look at you, but her hands showed that she was a good worker. After a brief negotiation, the couple chose Sarah. All three girls were escorted from the room so the adults could complete the purchase. Sarah sighed with excitement as she knew she would be leaving the school once and for all.

Wind Witch

In the hallway, the other girls stood with their eyes lowered in disappointment. Sarah took a moment to imagine how they must be feeling. She watched as Sister Jane walked up to them. Her eyes crunched in pain looking at the girls' disappointment. She kneeled, unfolded her arms and held them open to the girls. Their feet slowly scuffled their way toward her, and she pulled them into her and gave them her strong, warm, long-lasting hugs. She held them tight for a moment and pulled back to wipe a tear or two away. She looked over to Sarah, smiled and nodded. Sister Jane was among the kindest people in the school, and many liked her. Sarah and the girls could count on a hug without fail. She stood and laid an arm around their shoulders and began to lead them back to the school. About midway down the hall, Sarah saw her wave a good by-wave. Sarah smiled and looked at the door to the sitting room, and began to wait.

As Sarah waited, she thought, 'This is scary and exciting all at the same time. What if this couple was mean, too? What if life is worse with them? Then what?' Sarah paused and thought, 'Wait, that is silly. Jade said they are my friends, and I swear that was Lyra's voice.' She heard the couple enter the hallway. 'Just look at your feet,' she said to herself. 'Don't mess this up.'

Sarah heard the couple come out of the parlor and bid the sister goodbye. They turned to Sarah and beckoned her to come with them. Step by step, Sarah exited the building with a new chance at life, climbed in the truck, and never looked back. She didn't even wave goodbye to Jade, who stood watching out the window with a smile.

"Be still, little one. We are not clear from school yet. Sit still a little longer." Sarah sighed a sigh of relief when she knew it was for sure Lyra. She was the only person who called her little one in the scrying bowl.

Sarah slid her hand over to Lyra's hand, slipped her fingers in between hers, and held on tightly. She leaned in closer to her friend's side and just took a moment to breathe a sigh of relief. With a sideways glance, Sarah peered to her left to take a glance at the driver.

62

"Be still," said Lyra with a slight hiss. "Don't mess this up."

The wendigo crouched in the thickets across the road from the school. Its black form rose above the withered brownfield grass. When it saw Sarah leaving the school, it rose in anger and yowled a loud scream. The whole school shivered as the screeching Wendigo yelled out. Little faces began to appear at the windows, and many of the nuns and children saw the black figure. The nuns began to cry as they watched Father Unis disappear into the fields.

Chapter 6: United

QR Codes: Chapter 6

The Meeting

Scan to hear the language

#	Chapter	Anishinaabemowin	English	QR Code
6	Ch. 6	Mahn-pee binoo-jiinh	Here child.	

Chapter VI:
UNITED

The wind outside was whipping the leaves off the branches of the trees, and they ran past the truck's windshield in a fury. The cold, damp air made Sarah shiver, and she pulled her jacket around her. Flashes of lightning were crackling in the skies as the rain hit hard on the windshield. Sarah's hand held Lyra's firmly; her breathing quickened as she kept her eyes lowered. With each gust of wind, Lyra could feel the intensity increase. Lyra looked down at Sarah and noticed that with every big breath the child took, the truck responded to a gust of wind. She came to realize that Sarah was causing the sudden rush of wind.

"Sarah, you must calm yourself," Lyra whispered into Sarah's ear. "Take deep breaths and calm yourself. You're making it storm."

Sarah fought with all her might to steady herself. She thought, 'Just relax, and soon you will be safe.' She started taking deep breaths, trying to calm herself with positive thoughts. 'Lyra is a good person, and Jade trusts her.' Another deep breath was taken. 'You are not being kidnapped. You are being rescued.' She took in many deep breaths as she kept repeating this thought.

Sarah noticed that Jacques's large body didn't nudge into her as much. The wind was calming down, and the rain slowed. Sarah seemed to retreat into her head and kept breathing to bring her into a good breathing rhythm. 'Slow and steady,' Sarah thought, 'slow and steady.' The rain still came down hard, but the wind seemed quieter.

With a sigh of relief at the wind subsiding, Lyra peered off into the distance of the trees. She noticed the dark form that followed near the tree line. Her eyes squinted as the lightning flashed, and a sudden fear encased her when she saw a pair of yellow eyes flash in its flair. For a moment, it reeled back and screamed as lightning struck it. The screeching yowl of the beast ran through the air, sending shivers of fear over the party. Lyra lifted her arm around the child and held her close. She didn't know

Wind Witch

what the beast was nor why it was chasing them. Lyra fixed her eyes on Jacques' driving and observed the monster as it traveled alongside them. She squeezed Sarah slightly as she lifted her wand from her inside pocket. She smiled sweetly at the child and turned to watch for the beast.

Lights flashed, and screeching continued, and Jacques sped up. Sarah placed her hands over her ears and said, "That cry. I heard that when Father Unis turned into the monster." Sarah leaned toward the truck's window to see if it was Father Unis.

"Put that pretty head down, young lady," Jacques said firmly.

Sarah frowned, nodded, and did what she was told. As she sat there, she thought, 'That voice. I know that voice.' In submission, she tucked her face into Lyra's chest.

Outside the window, Lyra could see men and ladies in the woods throwing spells at the shadow that lurked. Lyra looked over at Jacques. His face was filled with growing concern as his eyes were fixed on the road in front of them. The battle outside was entirely of light. Screams of men could be heard on the wefts of the wind. Lyra clinched her wand tightly as if to say, 'Not today, you are not getting her today.' She fixed her eyes on the wooden battle and held tight to the little one in protection.

A man on a broom swished down over the truck to fly directly in front of them. The man waved his arm to indicate to Jacques that he should follow him. The man continued to fly in front of them, and two more broom riders took a side to escort the truck to safety. When they noticed that witches and wizards surrounded them, Lyra and Jacques realized that the party was in trouble. A moment later, the wizard in the lead pointed to a dirt road.

"Hold on, Lyra, this is going to be a bumpy ride," growled Jacques as he made a sharp turn down a farmer's two-track.

Instantly, the riders in the truck were thrown back and forth as each wheel hit holes in the unkept driveway. The broom rider headed towards the barn and landed outside the door of the barn.

Wind Witch

He ran, grabbed the barn handle, and slid open the large wooden door. Jacques drove the truck inside and pulled in until it was clear of the door. The wizard closed the big barn door and fastened it shut with a heavy board.

"Thank you, Jamison! What in the world is happening?" Said Jacques as he climbed out of the truck. The two men's brows frowned as they shook hands. "There has been lightning and rain since we've started."

"Thank you, my friend. There is a monster hunting you three. We can't kill it, but we are keeping it at bay. What is for certain, it wants Sarah," said Jamison as he walked around the side of the truck, opened Lyra's door, and helped the two ladies out of the truck.

Jamison looked down at Sarah's dark hair and lowered himself to his knees so he could look up into her face. He smiled and held out his hand for Sarah to take. Sarah's eyes widened as she saw for a moment her dad smiling at her. Her breath quickened, and then she slowed her breathing when she realized that it wasn't her father but Jamison. Her eyes lowered and considered his offering a moment then grabbed it. Jamison smiled.

"Young lady," Jamison said with a smile, "We have a surprise for you. Close your eyes and keep them closed until you are told to open them."

Sarah closed her eyes tightly. She scrunched her eyes so tight that wrinkles formed across the rim of her nose. The thunder outside muffled the sound of the heavy boots advancing toward her. She could hear the big boots of the driver shuffle hay as he rounded the back of the truck. She felt warm yet shaking hands wrapped around her fingers, roughened skin, and yet kind and non-threatening to Sarah. She could hear a sniffle, and the man cleared his throat.

"Don't open your eyes yet, little one. You see, the night I lost you and your parents, I received a frightful scar. Many people fear me now. I hope you won't be. When you are ready to see your

Wind Witch

old friend, go ahead and open your eyes," muttered Jacques in a choked voice.

Sarah thought a moment of his words, "The night I lost you." Her forehead creased when she realized who she was about to see. She lifted her hands to her face as her broken, grieving heart heaved in waves of memory of that night. Nightmarish images flashed across her mind, and for the first time in years, she cried for her parents.

After a moment, Sarah's grief lessened. Silence took hold, and Sarah steadied herself to look at the man in front of her. Sarah stood tall, took a deep breath, and opened her eyes. The darkness faded into the dim light, and soon, she could see a man on his knees with his eyes lowered. His brown flannel shirt blended into his hair, and Sarah stood and studied him. She lifted her small hand to his chin and lifted Jacques's face until their eyes met. A sideways smile emerged from under his mustache. Jacque slowly opened his arms to offer her a hug, Mahn-pee binoo-jiinh[6] Here child as if he was begging for her acceptance. A child-like excitement stirred inside of her. Sarah threw her arms around Jacques's neck and held on to him and wept, for she thought he was dead too.

Sarah pulled back to look at her friend. With puffy eyes from crying, Sarah took a good, long, hard look at her friend's scar. The scar was deep purple, and it bunched together like a rope was stapled to the side of his face. Sarah met his gaze as she lifted her hand to touch it. Jacques's hand met her in midair to stop her. Sarah smiled and shook her head "no" to the large man and pushed his hand away. Her little fingers met the roughened skin and followed its path along its length. She reached inside her jacket pocket, pulled out a little glass bottle, and unscrewed the top.

Sarah's midnight-dark eyes studied the man's face for a moment, and she dipped her finger into the ointment. With a deep breath, she closed her eyes and concentrated for a moment on her task. A warm breeze entered through a crack in the barn wall and wrapped itself around Sarah and Jacques. Sarah opened her eyes and applied the bear grease and herbs to Jacques's scar. Sarah smiled when Jacques sighed at the warmth of the heated ointment. Sarah's soft touch seemed to soothe the rough tissue away each time

69

Wind Witch

she ran over various areas on the scar. Sarah leaned in close and blew a warm stream of air over the bear grease to keep it warm and make the scar pliable. Sarah's little hands pulled the tissue one way and the other the next moment. Soon, the tissue relaxed, and Jacques's scar was nothing more than a red line that ran where the scar lay.

Lyra watched the reunion of the two friends with such warmth. Even more, as she watched Sarah's work with amazement. Sarah's hand moved gracefully over the scar, and the more she worked, the more the scar faded. Lyra watched as Sarah's magic unfolded in front of her. She wondered how this could be. No wands were used in performing the magic. The child just willed it to happen. It was all just her and her magic. When Sarah was done, she turned to Lyra with a smile.

"See, He's as handsome as the day I remember him!" exclaimed Sarah. Sarah smiled up at Jacques, "By the way, you're not as big as I remember you! Not to mention a lot older." She toyed at her friend's graying beard.

Sarah threw her arms around his neck and gave him a big hug. Jacques scooped her up in his arms and stood holding her and crying. His arms held her close, not out of fear or protection, but in love for the little one. There was no better hug than that of love, and Sarah sunk into its warmth.

Jamison stood in amazement. Every child has different abilities in the Native Culture, but he had not seen this kind of magic displayed yet. The children are growing and changing in strength as the years have passed. Sarah was marked to be a Nodin Me-koom-maa-senh(1) Wind Witch; this was very clear. However, many medicine men and women did not make it through the scourging of the government and the church. The amount of medicine men left to train children was becoming alarmingly low. After all he had witnessed, he knew that Sarah was too amazing not to protect. Jamison took a deep breath and sat down to consider the next steps that were needed.

70

Wind Witch

The storm raged outside as the four of them remained safe inside. Lightning flashed, but thunder did not follow. 'Unusual,' thought Sarah, 'no thunder, just a lot of light.'

Yelling began to rise in the fields. Sarah clung to Jacques and held tight to him. 'Don't let go.' she thought to herself as the yelling grew louder and neared the barn.

The parties' eyes darted left and right, looking in all directions for any clue of what was happening outside. Jamison and Jacques stood at the ready, and their wands were held out in front of them. The lights flashed, men yelled orders, and some screamed in pain. A sudden silence fell, and all was quiet. After a moment, they lowered their wands. Sarah could see the adults were all concerned, but she felt safe for the first time in many years.

Jacques tucked the young girl into his arms and held her close. The warmth of his body and the security of his arms felt safe and secure. The day just seemed to melt away as he held her close. The sounds outside subsided, and the lightning drew dark, and Sarah began to nod off in Jacques' arms.

Lyra could see that Sarah's eyes began to droop, so she made her bed on the front seat of the truck. Wrapped in Jacques's jacket, Sarah fell fast asleep, safe and secure. Lyra closed the truck door to see a bag in the back of the truck wiggle. She took a few steps, but Lyra stopped when she thought the bag had moved again. She went to take a step, and it shifted once again. Lyra signaled Jacques and Jamison to come over and assist her with the bag in the back of the truck.

Wind Witch

Chapter 7:
An Old Friend

Chapter VII:
AN OLD FRIEND

The wind whipped through the trees, causing them to bend with each gust that was thrown at them. Snowflakes clung to the needles of the tree, decorating them with white frosting. The pine tree outside Peter's room knocked rhythmically against the cabin's wall as if it were a gentle wake-up call. The window stopped the full gust of wind, but a slight separation between the window frame allowed the cold breeze to brush across Peter's face. He listened for a moment, all nestled in bed, enjoying the peace of the wind's whisper as he drifted in and out of sleep.

The smell of bread baking in the oven filled every corner of the cabin. Peter's nose alerted his stomach that it was time to eat. Peter gave a broad smile when he heard his stomach growling louder than the screaming wind outside. Peter shifted once again and opened his eyes to see a streak of light through the window. He lifted his form to stretch and look out at the weather. The skies were so grey, and he could see the snow all blustery, and the frost on the window was proof of the cold. A wisp of cold air kissed his skin, and a cold shiver ran all over his body as he slid out of the bed and stood. To chase the chill away, he pulled a blanket over his shoulders and steadied himself. His stomach rumbled again, and he slowly strode his way out of his room.

The smell of bread led Peter to a little rustic kitchen, and there was a side room, a living space with a fireplace to help warm the cabin. A lady with dark hair was tending to some plants on the countertop. He silently watched her as she worked on her task. He could hear her speaking softly and lovingly as she worked harvesting leaves off a bundle of dried plants. He watched as she placed each leaf in a bowl with great intentions. Her whisper was musical, and her hand flowed in circular patterns over the bowl before she placed the leaf into the bowl. He watched her repeat the ritual and wondered what she was doing. He smiled when he spied a pan of freshly baked dinner rolls sitting on the countertop.

Peter made a soft cough, and the startled woman jumped and turned. Her startled gaze came to focus on Peter, and her eyes

73

widened then a smile stretched over her white teeth to greet Peter. The first thing he noticed was a white streak of hair twisted and turned with black hair to frame her face perfectly. Her smile was soft and sweet as she waved her hand, and the mortar and pestle went to work on their own grinding the leaves. She peeked in the bowl and nodded and turned to focus on Peter.

"Good afternoon. My name is Mary. I suppose your nose woke you up." Mary smiled at Peter and gestured for him to sit down at the table.

Mary sat down across the table and looked at the boy with a concerned look. Her gaze was very motherly and kind. Peter smiled and nodded. With a flick of her wand, a bowl emerged from the cabinet, flew over to the kettle on the stove, and hovered in midair as if it were waiting for something. The pot's lid raised on its own, and the smell of chicken soup lofted from the pan. A nearby ladle went to work and filled the waiting bowl with soup. Peter's eyes widened as the bowl traveled across the room and settled itself in front of him. He looked up at the woman sitting at the table and saw her sweet smile.

"I know you have never seen magic in this form. Don't worry. You are not crazy. As I am to understand, you have your own magic." Mary stopped and looked at Peter's expression as he processed his thoughts. "Oboodashkwaanishiinh[10] Dragonfly told us about your abilities. You were wielding magic, he said; he told us of the mark that you have. He showed us your mark the night he brought you here." She got up from the table, walked to the oven, and lowered the door to see the progress of the cooking bread.

"I assure you, the soup turned out well. Eat slowly. You were hurt badly when the men hung you. I think you should be okay to eat, though," warned Mary.

Mary leaned over and pulled out a fresh batch of rolls from the oven and placed them on the top of the stove. With a wave of her hand, the icebox opened, and a bowl lofted through the air and landed next to her. She worked diligently to cover the golden-brown crowns with unhealthy amounts of butter from the bowl. She glanced over her shoulder and smiled.

74

"Think fast!" Mary yelled as she tossed the roll in the boy's direction, sitting at the table.

Peter went to catch the roll, but the sudden movement made him cringe, and he grabbed his arm instead of the roll. He closed his eyes in anguish for a brief minute and squinched his nose, waiting for the roll to smack him dead in the face. When no impact happened, he opened his eyes to find the roll was floating in front of him in mid-air. He stared at the roll for a few minutes; then, he glanced at Mary before grabbing it. He looked down at his hands and smiled as he felt the hot, squishy, buttered roll waiting for him. He remembered being spooned broth in faded dreams, and his stomach demanded more. His eyes were fixed on his treat, and it just begged him to eat it. Without hesitation, he bit into the warm treat. The soreness of his jaw did not hinder him from enjoying a fine, warm dinner roll and slurps of hot chicken soup.

Marshal opened the door, walked into the room and Peter chuckled as he watched the man's glasses fog up in the cabin's warmth. Marshal shook his head, removed his glasses, gave them an annoyed look, and set them on the table to clear. The man stood with his back toward them, and Peter could hear his oversized leather jacket unzip. With a quick shift of his shoulders, he threw off his jacket. Skillfully catching its weight as it fell to the floor. With a flick of his hand, the jacket left his hand and flew to its nail that was stationed next to a burning fireplace.

Marshal shuffled to the chair and sat down. The wooden chair grumbled and squeaked and groaned with every shift the man's body made. Left boot, then right, they landed with a thud on the floor. Peter's eyes surmised the large man for a moment as he watched him slip on a pair of old leather slippers. The man leaned back in the chair and smiled at his feet. He sighed as he shifted his toes and rolled his feet to fit just right in their familiar, comfortable space. The large man pulled his feet to a standing position and hoisted his large frame up. With a loud yawning stretch, Marshal glanced over to the table and placed his glasses back on his nose.

Peter smiled when Marshal noticed his glasses were still fogged. The man huffed, untucked his shirt, and used it to clean each lens as he walked to the table. Peter watched as the man

75

approached, and something caught his eye. A movement near the fire. Peter adjusted his line of site to see that the jacket seemed to lean itself closer to the fire, then sway and shift and present a new section to warm and dry. The arms of the jacket seem to alternate back and forth, warming each sleeve and then the other. Peter watched the wetness of the snow begin to fade from the limbs quicker than normal. Marshal eyed the boy closely as he sat down at the table and studied the boy a little while before speaking.

"I am so glad to see you up and moving about. My name is Marshal. I see that Mary has already begun to spoil you." He smiled at the roll in Peter's hand.

With a childish grin, Mary sent a hot roll floating over to her husband. Marshal smiled and reached for the roll but missed. Mary giggled as she was playing. Her mischievous eyes watched her husband closely and kept moving the roll the moment he grabbed it. Marshal straightened his shoulders and narrowed his eyes toward his wife. He reached once again for his tasty treat, and once again, it slid sideways. Marshal missed his mark, and Mary giggled.

"Mary, please. I am so hungry." Marshal held his hands out sideways in a begging manner.

With a wide smile, Mary let Marshal catch his dinner roll, and she turned to prepare his meal. A blue and white soup bowl lofted from the shelf with a wave of a wand and traveled to the stove. Ladles of noodles, veggies, and chicken filled the bowl and settled themselves in front of Marshal. A warm stream lofted up and covered Marshal's glasses as he took a deep breath over his bowl. He raised his head to look at his wife, but all he saw were frosted glasses and stifled a laugh. Marshal cleaned his glasses and dug into the warm broth. Mary smiled as she watched the two men enjoy their meal.

Peter sat in the chair, watching the strange couple as he ate. He kept glancing at the bowls, the jacket, the mortar, and two adults in the room. Even though he was eating, his stomach grumbled loudly, and everyone turned to look at him with a smile.

76

"You better eat before your stomach eats you!" noted Marshal.

After half a bowl of soup, Peter could see the door open slowly behind Marshal. He went to speak and tell the others about the door, but nothing came out. He raised his hands to his throat and tried to speak again. Nothing came out, and the door was opening more and more. Suddenly, he stood quickly and pointed to the door. The two adults turned quickly towards the door. A flash of light filled the room, and Peter dropped to the floor and crawled under the table for protection.

"Marshal and Mary! What kind of welcome is that?" exclaimed Oboodashkwaanishiinh[10] Dragonfly. "It's a good thing that spell doesn't work on me!"

"I'm sorry, Oboodashkwaanishiinh[10] Dragonfly, we are so jumpy as of late. We know that Peter will be hunted, so we have been trying to be on alert. I guess we are too alert," shared Mary as she crouched down to coax Peter from under the table.

Oboodashkwaanishiinh[10] Dragonfly strolled over to Mary's side and peered over her shoulder. Peter looked at the creature's ears and oddly shaped face. For a moment, Peter stared at Oboodashkwaanishiinh[10] Dragonfly as if he saw a ghost. A smile stretched over his teeth, and he crawled over to Oboodashkwaanishiinh[10] Dragonfly and hugged him tightly. Peter thought, "I remember." Oboodashkwaanishiinh[10] Dragonfly hugged him back and sighed in relief, for each other was here safe and sound.

Peter pulled back with tears in his eyes. His eyes darted back and forth, searching his memory of the past few days. With a confused look, Peter went to speak to Oboodashkwaanishiinh[10] Dragonfly, and once again, nothing came out. The room went silent as everyone realized that Peter couldn't speak. Peter kept trying to speak and asked questions, but no one could understand what he wanted. Soon, his frustration drove him to surrender to the non-verbal life he might live. With a frown, he plopped down into the chair with a scowl.

"He was in a boarding school for a few years. Perhaps he can read and write?" Mary walked to a dresser, pulled out a pencil and paper, and placed it in front of Peter. "Can you write what you need to say?"

With a sigh, Peter picked up the pencil and began to write. "Where am I?

"You are in a small town in Wisconsin," said Mary.

Peter shook his head from side to side and wrote, "Why am I here?"

Oboodashkwaanishiinh[10] Dragonfly walked over to the boy. "I saw what happened to your dad and what the villagers did to you and your family. I saw your magic, and so did the villagers, so they hung you. My friend Joseph asked Mary and Marshal to take care of you for a while. So, we brought you here."

Peter looked around the cabin and wrote, "Am I dreaming? Is all this stuff happening, or am I losing my mind?"

Marshal's laughter filled the room, "Oh well, this is magic, my boy. Mary and I are magic folks."

Oboodashkwaanishiinh[10]'s Dragonfly head tilted sideways as he struggled to smile at the boy. "Do you remember the days when we went fishing? Do you remember how the fish would jump out of the stream and land right in our hands?" He waited for the boy to nod. "Magic is something that's in a person—energy of sorts. Mary and Marshal use wands to focus their magic, but for Natives, their magic is from deep inside and very spiritual and earthly. Most of the Native's magic is unseen but powerful once one learns to use it correctly. Some use objects such as feathers, pipes, drums, shakers, dancing, and many other means to wield their magic. Someday, you may discover a tool you can use to focus your magic. However, inside you are earth and fire magic. You will not know which will rule until you learn your skills."

Peter was still looking at his hands as if the fish was still lying there. He shifted the pencil in his hand once again and wrote, "So, why am I here?

78

Oboodashkwaanishiinh[10] Dragonfly sat down on the floor with the boy. "Your dad was a medicine man. You know he had his magic. You saw the men kill him for his magical skills. When you had passed out after fighting the men, your magic showed itself. That's when the men decided to hang you so you wouldn't learn how to use your magic. Your mother, I am sorry to say, was a victim of men's will. Once the men hung you, I rescued you and took you to my friends. Joseph thought you should be here with Marshal and Mary. You need time to heal and learn some magic of your own."

Peter looked down at his hands again. He dropped the pencil on the floor, and it bounced and rolled. He went to speak once again, and once again, nothing came out. In a frustrating moment, he stomped his foot and began to walk towards the pencil.

Oboodashkwaanishiinh[10] Dragonfly reached up, grabbed Peter's hand, and stopped him. He looked up at the boy and the pencil and said, "Will it to come!"

Peter looked up to Marshal and Mary with unease. He looked at the pencil and back to Oboodashkwaanishiinh[10] Dragonfly and nodded. His dark eyes narrowed as he focused on the pencil. He looked at the pencil and back at his hand. He focused on the pencil and thought, 'Here!' The pencil jumped an inch and rolled a bit. With an astonishing smile, he looked down at his friend.

Oboodashkwaanishiinh[10] Dragonfly tucked his ears down and looked at the pencil. Immediately, the pencil flew through the air and landed in his hand. "Just practice, my friend, and you will get better." His sideways smile was almost kid-like as he looked proudly at the boy.

Peter nodded and grabbed the pencil that Oboodashkwaanishiinh[10] Dragonfly held up to him. He turned back to the table and wrote, "Will you show me what happened to my family? I want to see the whole thing."

Oboodashkwaanishiinh[10]'s Dragonfly's head bowed, and the air in the room became cold. Marshal and Mary drew their arms close to their body, for the air was quite chilled. The air was so cold that

79

Wind Witch

they began to shiver. Oboodashkwaanishiinh[10]'s Dragonfly's face rose as he looked toward the ceiling; he drew their frozen breaths together to form shapes of the people of the village. Peter watched them run from men with guns. Then he saw his father fall from gunfire. His eyes widened as he watched his mother surrender to death. He lowered his head after he watched his hanging. Oboodashkwaanishiinh[10] Dragonfly looked over to the boy with compassion.

Oboodashkwaanishiinh[10] Dragonfly reached up and grabbed the boy's hand. "Yes, Peter, your family is on their long walk. No one survived except your sister, Amelia."

In a silent yell, Peter rose and ran to the door. With a turn of the knob, the boy was on a dead run, and Oboodashkwaanishiinh[10] Dragonfly was in pursuit. Peter's body screamed in pain, but he didn't care. He ran out of anger, he ran out of fear, he ran just to run and leave the ugly truth behind him. Oboodashkwaanishiinh[10] Dragonfly followed closely behind the injured boy. Peter collapsed in the sandy, snowy, and needle-covered ground. He pounded his fist on the ground in a moment of anger. If one could hear his words, he would have said, "I was too late. I was too late. Daddy, I was too late." The boy stopped beating the ground and sat there panting in exhaustion.

As Oboodashkwaanishiinh[10] Dragonfly watched the boy's anguish, he knew every word the boy didn't say, and he felt the ache of the boy's loss. Oboodashkwaanishiinh[10] Dragonfly went and wrapped the boy in his skeleton-like arms and held the boy tight. He whispered, "I will always run to you. Please stay here and stay safe for a spell. You will know when it is time to leave." Peter nodded, and the pair walked back to the cabin.

Mary and Marshal watched the two friends the whole time. As they waited for their approach, they thought about Peter's magic. They whispered to each other about what they had seen and what they would tell Joseph and Robert. They were told that every child would have different kinds of magic, and they had never seen Peter's kind of magic before. They pondered how the boy made the image of the woman dancing, but it was clear he was magical. What was clear is that Peter and Oboodashkwaanishiinh[10] Dragonfly were friends and both had magic that was unlike any they had known.

For a moment, Peter stopped and looked at his friend and then the odd couple standing at the door. Oboodashkwaanishiinh[10] Dragonfly tugged his hand a little and prodded Peter to keep moving. Peter walked towards a place of uncertainty but trusted his little friend, which gave him strength. He didn't understand everything that was happening, but he knew this cabin in the woods was where he needed to stay.

Marshal and Mary watched the two friends walk toward them and then into their home. Three different types of magic beings would come together to make sure the Natives would not lose their magic—a very different home of magic in the middle of a pine forest.

Wind Witch

Chapter 8:
Chavo's Message

QR Codes: Chapter 8

Scan to hear the language

#	Chapter	Anishinaabemowin	English	QR Code
18	Ch.8	De-bwa-min-aa-gwa-se	Reveal	
19	Ch. 8	Enh	Yes	

Chapter VIII:
CHAVO'S MESSAGE

Peter took a deep breath, pulled his sore arm over his chest, and hoisted himself into a seated position. He cupped his head into his hands and began to rub his eyes to clear his vision. His left arm throbbed, and his hand ached. With a wiggle of his toes and a shift of his rib cage, he found the stiffness and soreness were manageable. He grabbed his left arm and rose to his feet to stand. The room began to spin, and he sat back down on his bed until it stopped.

Peter sat and gained control of the spinning room. He sat back down and listened to the voices outside his room momentarily. Some of the voices were known, and some he did not know. Once again, he hoisted himself to stand, and the room did not spin. He looked down at his feet and saw the bruises from being kicked by the men and noticed they had faded greatly as he listened to the others in the other room as he assessed his bruised body. Every limb seemed to ache with trauma. A slight itch began to twinge, and he lifted his hand to scratch it. He jumped a bit when his fingernails hit the stitches over his right eye. After a small cringe, he sighed and continued to listen.

"The boy is more than welcome here, Joseph." ruffled Marshal. "Mary has already attended to his neck and other wounds. He has already come out for food. He even has come to accept to stay here. Oboodashkwaanishiinh[10] Dragonfly feels certain he will stay."

Oboodashkwaanishiinh[10] Dragonfly wandered over to the table and stood on a chair, and in his hiss-like voice, "There is a place nearby where I can stay for the winter. A cave where I can morn my Delphi. I will be near."

"One child safe and secure is a blessing. We have so many things to worry about in the next few days. It warms my heart to know that he is in Mary's and Verna's care." said Joseph. "I will let you know of any updates. Bye for now."

84

Marshal slid the bowl aside and sat down in his chair. He closed his eyes, took a deep breath, held it for a few moments, and let it go. He felt the table jiggle and opened his eyes to see what was happening. Oboodashkwaanishiinh[10] Dragonfly was sitting on the table in front of him. Marshal drew back in surprise. In a matter of seconds, his expression changed from surprise to concern as he watched the creature's old and bony fingers search in his pouch for something.

Marshal's eyes fixed on the creature's bag, and he listened to the ancient one mumble to himself. The creature smiled, shuffled the bag, and smiled up at Marshal as he held up the coin. Marshal's eyes fixed on the black coin as Oboodashkwaanishiinh[10] Dragonfly placed it on the table. Oboodashkwaanishiinh[10] Dragonfly slid the coin across the table to Marshal. Marshal peered at the coin. On it was a stamp of a white spider. Marcus noticed how nicely the white filled in the lines on the black ore. On the reverse side was a spider web design as brilliantly crafted as the front. He glanced up at Oboodashkwaanishiinh[10] Dragonfly in confusion.

"The boy should carry that all the time," he said, nodding toward the medallion. "When trouble strikes, or evil is in its energy field, I will feel it, and I will come to his aide."

Marshal looked at the coin and nodded in understanding. He tucked the coin into his pocket, walked Oboodashkwaanishiinh[10] Dragonfly to the door, and watched the creature move quickly and agilely across the snow. Marshal turned and sat down at the table and took a deep breath. He began to wait in silence like everyone else anxiously.

Marshal rose from his chair at the table and tended to the fire. He glanced over his shoulder at Mary and smiled. He thought, 'all these years waiting.' He poked thoughtlessly at the glowing embers of the fire, 'and just like that, we will have a son and a daughter.' He ran his hands through his hair and began pacing back and forth in front of the fireplace.

Mary and Verna worked in the kitchen preparing meals for those in the cabin. Unexpected hours passed, and everyone was on edge. Robert took out a cigarette and lit it. Smoke lofted in the air and filled the ceiling with a white haze. Marshal settled lazily in his chair as sleep threatened to take him. With a sudden jolt, he startled awake when a loud crack echoed in the valley. Everyone rose and rushed to the valley because they were not expecting company. Instead, Joseph advanced at a near run."

"The wizards called for backup. I don't know what is happening there, but we must be ready," he said as he pushed past those standing on the porch.

On the table sat a large bowl filled with water. Everyone gathered near it and watched the clock click by. As Joseph paced the floor, he would glance over to the bowl, and, in frustration, he would rub his beard in thought. Silence fell, and the men and women sat in their queasy thoughts as they waited.

Everyone in the room jumped when they saw the bowl begin to emit light. Yellowish pulsating light filled the space above it, and everyone in the room gathered around the bowl. Joseph leaned over to the bowl and peered into the water. A small picture of Lyra appeared in its shimmering waters.

"Joseph, we are stuck in a barn. Wizards are fighting a creature outside that followed us from the school when we picked up Sarah." Informed Lyra.

Joseph hesitated, "A monster followed you from the school? What kind of monster?"

Lyra shook her head, "I do not know. All I could ever see from the truck was a black deerlike form in the distance. Joseph, that's not all." Lyra stepped out of view and came back into view in the bowl, "We had an unexpected guest traveling with us after picking Sarah up."

Lyra stepped aside and drew Chavo close to the bowl so everyone could see him. An audible sigh came from the direction of the bowl. The three men stood up quickly and looked at each other in surprise. Joseph snapped out of Lyra's view and looked at those in the cabin. Lyra heard the men's voices rising as they talked to each other.

"Chavo, he is ten moons only." insisted Robert. "He has one more year before his placement should occur."

"Yes, Robert, but the boy is out of there now, and I can't send Jacques and Lyra back there to return the boy." snapped Joseph.

Lyra could hear Jack's voice in the distance, "Those at the school will be hunting him too, just like Peter's dad. He can't go back now."

Robert's voice echoed loudly, "Hopefully, they won't notice he is gone until we can get you four clear and Sarah to the cabin. But what will we do with the boy?"

Mary sat down at the table, considering her husband for a moment, and announced, "We will take Chavo as well."

Joseph turned back to the water, "Are you sure? We have no idea what all this means. This seems to be more serious than we thought. Okay, let me speak to Chavo." The boy's image reappeared, "Chavo, you need to understand that you can't return to that school. Now, you will be hunted, and the only way to be safe is to be placed with a family. Marshal and Mary are good people and agreed to allow you to stay with Sarah and Peter. This is not punishment, so please don't run. That would make our job so much harder."

Chavo glanced up from the water as if he had seen a ghost. He glanced around the room at the adults watching the exchange. His eyes were wide, and his brow was crunched in confusion. He looked back to the water.

"First, I have a message for Robert," exclaimed Chavo, staring into the water.

Joseph stepped aside, and Robert's image appeared to Chavo, "What's the message?"

"Jade said the Father turned into a Wendigo. He escaped the school when she fought the beast off Sarah. The beast wasn't seriously harmed by any spell she threw!" Chavo's eyes widened as he heard the familiar cry of the wendigo sounding through the air and he looked up then back down to the bowl. "Jade threw me into the back of the truck so I could get the message to you."

"Joseph! We must get them out of there. Quickly!" The urgency in Robert's voice sent a shiver over everyone's body.

Joseph's face quickly turned back to the bowl and firmly growled, "Lyra, Activate the bowl."

Lyra tapped the bowl four times with her wand, and an orange glow began to emit and pulsate. She lifted the bowl, wrapped it in her arms, and closed her eyes. The light in the bowl surrounded her in an orange haze. Everyone watched as the stress signal began. Lyra stood as a beacon of light surging and pulsating in rhythmic beats: short beam, short beam, short beam, long, long, long, then back to repeat the short beam, short beam, short, and the pattern continued. They knew it would only be a matter of seconds, and Joseph would be there.

A loud crack shook the shabby barn, and Joseph yelled, "Get Sarah. Let's get everyone out of here!"

Jacques ran to the truck and scooped up the startled child from the front seat. Jacques struggled as he lifted her nearly grown body from the truck and wrapped Sarah in his arms. He quickly hurried over to the group, who were huddled close together as they prepared to leave.

The voices outside rose, and lightning flashed through the cracks in the barn door. A loud ramming blow hit the door. The doors concaved in, startling those trapped inside. Lights flashed again, and everyone saw the Wendigo on the other side of the door. Its yellow eye peered through the crack in the door and screamed as it looked at those within. He turned and stepped away a few yards, and with a running start, the wendigo burst through the door as the group of people vanished in mid-air. The beast screamed at the top of his lungs and slashed into the air in a fit of rage.

Chapter 9:
Unexpected Arrival

Chapter IX:
UNEXPECTED ARRIVAL

The sounds of the forest encased Peter as he lay in his room resting. In the distance, the wolves were howling in the moonlit night. Their singing was eerily comforting to Peter. The animal songs of the night were in full force and echoed through the trees. Yet, the wind rested, and the snow drifts around the cabin were touching the eves of the window. Peter, tucked into a nice warm bed, felt safe and accepted that this was a good time of rest and peace.

Mary and Marshal sat at the table, waiting for some kind of news about the rescue mission. The urgency of Joseph's disappearance littered their thoughts with anxiety. Robert glanced at his watch and paced back and forth in front of the fire. Verna busied herself in the kitchen. She knew there would be a lot of people to feed in a few minutes. Marshal rose from the table, threw some logs on the fire, and stoked the embers.

The tea kettle began singing, and the steam was lofting out of the spout. "Screeee," it sang. Mary rose to attend to the kettle. She reached up and grabbed a jar filled with her special brew of tea from the shelf and carefully measured it into the teapot. She chanted a small spell and added hot water to the pot. As it steeped, she set four cups on the countertop and added a touch of honey to each cup. In each saucer, Mary added a little cookie to the saucer to go with the tea. She poured the tea, gave Marshal his, and scuttled down the hall to give Peter his.

"Marshal is going to town tomorrow to buy you some clothes. Do you know what size you wear?" inquired Mary.

Peter wrote, "I don't know. I just wore whatever they gave me."

Marshal yelled down the hallway, "Mary, the bowl is glowing."

A familiar crack rang through the air. Mary turned and listened for a moment and then ran out of Peter's room. As she ran

90

down the hallway, she quickly pulled out her wand. She could see Marshal in the dining area, prepared to strike whatever made it through the door. Oboodashkwaanishiinh[(10)] Dragonfly popped into the cabin just outside Peter's room and readied his bow. Marshal looked down the darken hallway and saw that Peter's protector had taken a stand at the door of Peter's room. Witches and Wizard levied their wands at the door.

"Marshal and Mary! Open up!" Jack yelled through the door. "I am here. Take down the seal!"

With a sigh of relief, Mary flicked her wand, and a green light began to grow brightly around the door frame. With another small gesture, the light faded, and the lock clicked open. Mary opened the door to her trusted friend with a smile. Jack appeared through the open doorway and entered the cabin.

The older man looked at Mary and stepped uncertainly through the door. The air smelled heavy, and he said to his friends, "Once again, I have been called here." His eyes searched the faces of his friends. "In the middle of a wonderful dream, the ancestors picked me up and placed me here. What in the name for? "

Robert raised his hand, gave a hello nod to his friend and said, 'Sarah's rescue came with a glitch. Joseph went to rescue them, and they will arrive with her shortly."

Just as Robert was beginning to explain the night's events, the loud cracking noise announced that the others had arrived. Jack sat back, observing the events closely. The ancestors wanted him there, and he wanted to know why. He squinched his eyes as he watched the party walk by him. Joseph's eyes fixed on his old friend as he passed by, and he patted him on the shoulder as he passed. Lyra, Jamison, Jacques, Sarah, and a boy walking towards and by him. Jack stood with a confused look on his face as Marshal and Mary welcomed their friends into their home.

Even though Jacques was a very large man, Sarah's weight bit at his arms, and he was so thankful to place the young girl on Marshal's and Mary's Porch. He smiled down to Sarah, lifted his coat from her shoulders, and walked inside together. When the two of them entered, everyone stopped for a moment and stared at them. The mission was complete. Jacque brought Sarah safely home.

Merriment and handshakes occurred, and hugs lit the room in joy. Sarah's eyes scanned the room; she thought, 'so odd to be the reason for celebration and yet not be a part of its joy.' This sudden change in her world at this moment overwhelmed her. Her eyes searched the room and knew only a few. She slowly backed into Jacques' body and pushed tighter into him. He laid his arm across her and cupped his hand to lay on her shoulder. He maintained a firm hold on her until he felt her relax in his safety. Together, they stood as the others advanced toward them in excitement.

"Sarah, come and meet Mary and Marshal." Said Lyra.

Sarah stood still for a moment and looked up at Jacques. Jacques nodded, and he smiled at her. He poked his nose and slightly pursed his lips in the direction of Lyra. Sarah smiled and looked over to the ladies, then back up to Jacques. Lyra reached a hand to her and began to lead her away when there came an audible gasp through the room. Time stood still as everyone stood there staring at Jacques. Sarah's eyes searched their faces and saw shock and wonderment. Sarah smiled as she looked upon her friend with a warm smile. Jacques' eyes welled with tears as he took in their amazement at his new look.

"Ah, just this quick, I forgot that Sarah had fixed my face," Jacques replied shyly. He shuffled his feet as he peered down lovingly at Sarah.

Verna walked over to Jacques to examine his scar. The scar was no longer thick and bubbling on his skin. He was no longer marred, and he smiled at his friend.

Verna turned to Sarah with a smile. "You did this, child? You can heal injuries like this?"

Sarah looked at her feet and whispered, "I found out I could do that about three years ago. There was a young girl who was beaten and hurt badly. She was brought into my cell, and I helped her tend to the strap marks. Mom used to blow on my wounds to make them feel better, so I thought I would try it on her. I blew slow and steady breaths and watched them heal more each time I tended to them. Jade gave me bear grease to use on her. I would rub in the grease, and her marks would lessen. If I touched and blew on them, I could see that the welts disappeared." She looked up at her friend, "I thought I would give it a try on Jacques, and it worked!"

Jack walked over to the child and kneeled in front of her. "Oboodashkwaanishiinh[10] Dragonfly, please show us her mark."

Oboodashkwaanishiinh[10] Dragonfly rose off the floor and bounded over the table to stand in front of the child. Sarah's eyes widened, and she slowly walked backward until she leaned on Jacques's body. She had never seen Oboodashkwaanishiinh[10]'s Dragonfly's kind. Oboodashkwaanishiinh[10] Dragonfly tried to smile to comfort the child, but that only made her turn and hide her face in Jacques's stomach.

"Here, here, child, he will not harm you. We must see what can't be seen." Jacques softly said to the child with a nudge, "Oboodashkwaanishiinh[10] Dragonfly can show us. He will not harm you." said Jacques as he gave Sarah's shoulder a little squeeze and turned her around to look at Oboodashkwaanishiinh[10] Dragonfly.

"My mark is covered. No one can see it now," said Sarah.

Oboodashkwaanishiinh[10] Dragonfly reached his hand over his quiver where the black arrow slumbered. Oboodashkwaanishiinh[10] Dragonfly snapped his fingers, and the arrow jumped into his hand. His dark eyes never left Sarah's eyes, and with a smile, he stepped closer to her. His wide half, toothless grin scared her a bit. His midnight dark eyes spoke of death, yet she knew, somehow, that she was safe. Sarah's eyes widened as the tip of Oboodashkwaanishiinh[10]'s arrow was lowered to her face.

"So, child, where do we look for your mark?" hissed Oboodashkwaanishiinh[10] Dragonfly.

With a shiver, Sarah lifted her sleeve to reveal her arm. Nothing but the skin could be seen. The creature thumped a few steps, touched the arrow onto Sarah's arm, and said, "De-bwa-min-

93

aa-gwa-se [18]" "Reveal." The white light from the arrow began to glow, and as it worked, it grew warmer. Soon, the outline of Sarah's mark began to appear. First, a slight red swaying line began to appear. The arrow's heat increased, and the mark became clearer to those watching. The warmth of the arrow started to fill Sarah with comfort as she watched the brown birthmark appear on her arm.

"Whoa! Look at that!" Sarah turned to see Chavo standing behind Joseph.

"Chavo. What are you doing here?" snapped Sarah.

Chavo stopped when he realized that Sarah didn't know he stowed away in the truck. He mindlessly kicked at a chair leg as he thought about what to say. The day had been unexplainable so far. He looked at Sarah, shrugged his shoulders, and looked at her like he hadn't a clue.

"Well, you see, Jade put me in the truck so that I could get a message to Robert. Then, Joseph had to come and rescue us from the Wendigo. Somehow, we ended up here." Chavo looked around the cabin and the guests therein.

"Well, I guess I better make more tea so we can hear this whole story," murmured Mary, and Verna rose from her seat to assist in the kitchen.

Joseph sat down, closed his eyes, and said, "I believe we are in a pickle here." He steadied his eyes on Chavo. "We had two things happen today that we had never anticipated."

Chavo lowered his eyes, for he felt ashamed to be a part of the problem. However, he knew that his part was minor, but how did he tell them about the monster? He wondered, 'What was a wendigo? Why was he brought here? Where was here?' He began to shake from fear and exhaustion as all eyes were leveled upon him. He felt all his nerves at the edge, for he never had to speak in front of so many people.

"Jack, run a smudge for us, please, before we have the boy tell his tale," said Robert.

"Enh[19] Yes, but first, I must go and talk to Peter.

Everyone turned as he emerged from the darkened and out-of-the-way corner. He smiled and as he straightened his clothes, began sauntering towards Verna. With a half-smirked smile, he gestured for her to show him the boy. Verna giggled and took the lead, bounding down the hallway to Peter's room. Jack stopped to watch as she bustled down the hallway steps ahead of him. Everyone watched as their forms disappeared into the darkness.

95

Chapter 10:
Jack and Peter

Chapter X:
JACK AND PETER

Confused by the conversation in the other room, Peter sat on his bed. He didn't know what was happening, so he thought it would be wise if he stayed in his room. He heard many voices speaking and became concerned when one of the voices mentioned a wendigo. He heard the elders and his father tell stories about such a creature. He became fearful and crawled under the covers. Yet, his ears were ready to listen to every word they said.

Scurrying feet filled the cabin as more people entered. Peter could hear people hustling and bustling around the room, talking amongst themselves. They spoke the word Wendigo so loudly that Peter's eyes grew large and fearful. His heart raced, and he pulled the covers over his head as he continued to listen. Soon, he could hear some lighter steps coming to his door. He balled himself up in a little lump in the bed, hoping not to be seen. Sweat began to form on his forehead as he heard the advancing footsteps advancing on his door.

The door began to creak, and Peter's skin crawled with fear. Pictures in his head were forming from the tales he was told. Images flashed through his mind of a beast with no soul. Nothing but darkness and hate buds from the blackened soul of the damned being inside. He balled up smaller to conceal himself in a little bundle of fear as he listened to the footsteps enter his room. He drew his blankets tight about him as he worried that the advancing footsteps were that of the wendigo. His body began to shake in fear as pictures ran wildly in his head. The door creaked open, and Peter knew, just knew, that the beast was entering his room. He knew he would be swept away from the cabin to never be heard from again.

The door cracked open wider, and Verna appeared around the ledge and smiled. She could clearly see that Peter was trying to hide. Verna chuckled and pulled at the blankets. The blankets came alive and wiggled and shifted as the boy tried to escape danger. The tug of war began. Verna tugged and chuckled, and Peter pulled back. Verna's giggle filled the room, and all of a sudden, the war was over. Peter began to chuckle once he realized he wasn't battling a wendigo but Verna. His giggle erupted from under the covers, and Verna peeked around the end of the bedsheet and grinned at the boy. All sweaty with fear, Peter felt foolish but giggled up at his caretaker with a wide smile. With a shake of her head, Verna lifted the blankets up to allow Peter to hurry back into his resting place as Jack knocked before entering.

Jack walked into the room, pulled up chairs next to the bed, and Verna and he sat down. Jack's eyes searched the boy's face with great concern, and he sat silent. Confused with the visit, Peter's eyes searched the pair uneasily. Verna nudged Jack and cleared her throat. She threw a 'Come on' glance at him, then back at Peter. Jack nodded, took a deep breath, and sat back in his chair with his arms crossed over his chest.

"Well, my boy, Oboodashkwaanishiinh[10] Dragonfly has told us you have a talent of vision." The old medicine man smiled at Peter. "A group of unexpected visitors are here and have brought some friends with them. I sure could use your help. If you would." He lifted a pouch of tobacco to the boy and waited for him to accept or reject the request.

Peter's brow frowned for a moment. He sat up in his bed and held his head to steady his thoughts. His hands slid down to his throat and cupped it in his hands. He shifted to ease his screaming muscles and threw his legs over the side of the bed. After he steadied himself, he stood to face his old friend. He lowered his eyes to the pouch of tobacco and nodded in agreement and, lifted the bag and placed it in a robe pocket that Verna placed around his shoulders.

"Ah, there you go. Take your time; they are still in a furry over the events that happened tonight." Jack went on, "Oboodashkwaanishiinh[10] Dragonfly saw that you could make images from your memories. There are two frightened and scared Native kids just like yourself out there. Each one has a part of the story tucked away in their memory. Tonight, I want you to try and show us what happened to them. I know you're tired, but we need to see everything that happened so we can understand what we are dealing with. Are you willing to try?"

98

Wind Witch

Peter lowered his eyes and thought about Jack's request. He knew he could show his visions, but how would he show theirs? With a tilt of his head, he thought for a moment.

"If you are confused on how," whispered Jack, "All you must do is hold their hands and concentrate on them and let yourself see what they saw. I think the ancestors will show the rest of us if we offer enough Mshkwodewashk[14]sage."

Peter's face searched his friend's face for a moment. He thought, 'feel them, and let them tell their story.' He considered those words for a moment. Then, with a slow, pensive nod, he agreed and walked toward the door. Verna and Jack exited the room, and Peter followed behind them into the kitchen.

Everyone stood talking amongst themselves as Chavo and Sarah sat silently and watched the adults. Peter snickered to himself as he watched Chavo take deep breaths and hold them. He could see he was trying to soothe himself. He studied him for a moment and couldn't decide if he was overly excited or overly scared. One thing he knew, if he was close to the door, he would make a run for it. Sarah seemed to be shut down. She just stood staring off in thought. Her body just hung and had no more to give. Peter thought, 'One submits to fear, and the other is ready to fight. The destruction of their soul was deep, he thought.' People took notice upon their arrival and stopped talking so they could get back to business.

Peter walked up to Chavo and Sarah and smiled. He knew they were tired, scared, and greatly overwhelmed with the day's events. He waved hello and stood beside them and waited. Chavo gave Peter a side look as he wondered who this kid was. Sarah stood there in a haze-like state and seemed to be numb. She didn't respond or even notice Peter standing beside her. With a shrug, Peter focused on the group and listened and watched.

Verna and Mary began to busy themselves in the kitchen. They were not even close to ready for so many people to visit. Water was set on the stove, and the teapot grew larger to accommodate the amount of tea they would need. Cookies landed on plates, and the plate lofted itself to the table without the children noticing. The men were gathered outside for a moment as they

99

puffed away on their cigarettes, and the children just waited patiently like they had been taught in the boarding school. They were to be seen and not heard, and they learned that lesson well and displayed as much at this moment. They just stood there waiting: the reason for the celebration but not a part of it.

Chapter 11:
Chavo's and Sarah's Story

QR Codes: Chapter 11

Scan to hear the language

#	Chapter	Annishinaabemow in	English	QR Code
20	Ch. 11	Ngashi (z)	Mother	
22	Ch. 11	Enh, Ngwis, Ndaa'aa Maampii.	Yes, my son. I am here.	
23	Ch. 11	Jack miinawaa giin Kiidamtaam…	Jack and you have been busy, I see.	
24	Ch. 11	Enh, ngiidamtaami	Yes, we have	
24 a		Jiish-da-gan	Broom	

Wind Witch

| 25 | Ch. 11 | G'Zaaginim giin Miinawaa G'Dawenmaa | I love you and your brother. | |

Chapter XI:
CHAVO'S AND SARAH'S STORY

The older medicine man began the chore of preparing the smudge. His leather backpack was placed on the table, where he extracted the Mshkwodewashk[14]sage and his little iron pan. Everyone watched in silence as Jack prepared the Mshkwodewashk[14]sage for smudging. Before lighting the Mshkwodewashk[14]sage, Jack pulled out a long red-covered card-like case from the bag, pulled out his feather, and placed it on the table.

As Jack worked, the children inched closer to the table to watch the man. They watched every move he made and how intent in his work he was. For the first time in years, they were with their people in the traditional way. When Jack took out a stick as he walked to the fire, they watched him walk slowly so the flame on the end of the stick was not extinguished. They watched the flaming stick ignite the Mshkwodewashk[14]sage afire. After a moment, they could smell the smoke filling their noses with a familiar smell. Sarah closed her eyes, drew in the scent, and marveled that she had forgotten its comforting smell. When she opened her eyes, she focused on Jack who worked to smudge everyone, and Sarah waited for her turn.

Six years had passed since Sarah had been with her people. She watched everyone clean their being in the smoke. Jack stepped in front of her, and his eyes focused on the young girl. And placed the burning Mshkwodewashk[14]sage in front of her. Sarah drew in a deep breath and held it for a moment. It burned her lungs slightly then she exhaled a sigh of relief. She washed her hands and arms in the smoke and brushed the smoke over her hair. Jack circled Sarah and washed all the parts of her body with the smudge and fan. Sarah felt lighter, and her mind was clearer as Jack moved on to the next person.

"Now that everyone has been cleaned," Robert turned to Chavo. "It is time to tell your tale."

Wind Witch

"Let's get comfortable first." countered Mary as she waved her wand.

Chavo watched chairs pop up out of nowhere. No one, including Robert and Jack, seemed to think that this was an odd thing to happen. He watched people situate their chairs around the table, which seemed to grow. The table grew so big that it nearly filled the room. However, everyone seemed to have their own comfortable space, and they quickly settled into their spots. This was crazy; even the Medicine Man accepted the odd events as normal with an agreeable grunt. Once everyone was seated, he watched cups of tea floating in the air as a teapot filled them. Chavo just sat there feeling overwhelmed at the odd events and glanced at a smiling Peter.

Peter walked up to Chavo and handed him a note that said, "No, you are not going crazy; they are magic folk. I'll explain more later." He smiled at Chavo and walked away and sat down in his seat.

Slurps of tea were heard as a plate of cookies floated from person to person. The children watched in awe as the plate moved on its own in front of them. Three pop bottles settled in front of the children, and they smiled at the treat. The bottles hissed as tops were pried off, and soon, the kids were sipping the sweetness of the liquid within. Their eyes widened when bowls of chips settled near them. Everyone watched them as they were biting into their first taste of salty chips. When the plate of cookies came to them, they carefully lifted a cookie off the plate and watched it drift to the next person. They said nothing, but their heads began to swell in the confusion of the illusion. Their eyes searched for any real reason why a plate would float in the air and move on its own. The children glanced at each other, and Peter's smile filled his whole face. If he could have laughed, he would have as he watched the others figure out how the plates could float like that.

Marshal rose, walked to the fire, and set a few more logs in the flames. The fire began to spit and sputter as it began to consume the new pieces of wood. The crackling noise soothed the exhausted people sitting at the table. Jack leaned forward and tended to the smudge. The smoke from the Mshkwodewashk[14]sage

105

continued to loft, and everyone watched the smoke as it drifted up into the air. It was clear to Jack that the medicine was working, and he noticed Peter was in deep contemplation.

Peter's eyes focused on the pan and thought about his father. He was a medicine man, just like Jack. He watched Jack lean forward and place another ball of Mshkwodewashk[14]sage into the pan. Jack leaned in closer to the ball and blew on the smoldering ashes. Peter watched as the small ball ignited. He sat, lost in thought, watching the leaves catch on fire, cascading a line of red embers as it ate. Peter settled his thoughts and drifted back to the moments when he watched his father do the same thing. Jack leaned back in his chair and smiled at Peter.

"Well, boy," He looked at Chavo and stated, "You have a story to tell." Jack crossed his arms and concentrated his attention on the boy for a moment.

"I really don't know where to begin because I do not understand everything that happened. I will tell you what I know." Chavo's thoughts trailed off in a moment of contemplation.

Chavo drew himself up to the table and leaned his elbows on top. He cupped his head into his hands, rubbed his face in exhaustion, and gathered in his thoughts before he began. Everyone could see the distress of the day weighed heavily on him, and they allowed him the time he needed. After a moment, he looked up to the others in the room and began to tell his tale.

"The day was very odd. The nuns and Jade were in a panic all day. The Father was deathly ill, and everyone seemed to be focused on his care. Sister Mary was brutal, and I went to the washroom to do my chores. Jade came running in, grabbed me, and told me the message to give to Robert. I had no idea what had happened in the Father's room, but she quickly took me to the truck and covered me under the blanket. She told me to stay low and not move. I had never seen Jade so flustered in my life. I didn't have any idea that I would be put into this situation." His thoughts trailed off momentarily, and he continued, "I knew Sarah was getting ready to leave because Marcus told me of the letter in the Father's office. He and I talked about it when Jade interrupted us and pulled

106

me to the truck." Chavo stopped and looked up at the expressionless faces around the table.

Sarah listened to Chavo but said nothing. She was in such a state of uncertainty that she couldn't speak. When Chavo finished his part, everyone looked at Sarah. Peter could see that Sarah wasn't able to respond on her own. She seemed so weak and tired. He took a deep breath, stood, walked over to Jack, and nodded. Jack responded with a nod, placed more Mshkwodewashk(14)sage onto the smoldering embers, and blew a slow, steady stream of air on the ball. Smoke lifted up in the air with greater vigor than a usual smudge.

Peter walked to Sarah and smiled and offered his hand to her. She looked up into his eyes as she took it. He offered his hand to Chavo, who in turn took his hand. The three stood side by side, and Peter looked over his shoulder and saw Jack readying his drum by smudging it in the smoke. Jack nodded and began to beat rhythmically on the drum. Peter closed his eyes and allowed the sound to mesmerize him into a trance. The two children stood with him, trusting in Peter's offer of friendship.

Everyone sat and watched the smoke pull itself to the children. The smoke lifted and swirled around them and lofted up into the air. Everyone's faces were turned upward as images began to appear in the smoke above their heads. The wizards and witches watched the day's events unfold in front of them. A gasp of disgust escaped from their lips as they watched the Father's soul leave its body and transform into the wendigo. They watched how the beast's arm reached under the door for Sarah. They watched flashes of light cascade from under the door. They heard the beast escape from the broken window. They watched Jade's rescue. Everyone watched as Sarah bathed. Many smiled as they watched as Jacques and Lyra chose Sarah. They sighed with relief when Sarah was safely out of the school. They watched the storm rage as Jacques drove. They looked at Sarah as she learned to calm herself, and the wind and rain calmed themselves, too. They all nodded at the discovery of Chavo, and the fear in Chavo's eyes showed as they watched the wendigo break through the barn door. Many sat there stunned as the story was completed.

Wind Witch

The drumming stopped, and Peter opened his eyes and smiled at Sarah and Chavo. The two children stood staring at the now empty space above the table and back to Peter. Their eyes were wide and overwhelmed as they looked back at the strange boy. Peter smiled, and he stood tall and proud. He looked over his shoulder and smiled at Jack. Jack sat in his chair contemplating the events he had seen in smoke and marveled at Peter's talents, too. Everyone waited for the other to speak, for the events were overwhelming to everyone.

Jack cleared his throat and spoke, "I must be clear; we are in trouble. A wendigo on the loose is a dangerous thing."

Mary's eyes focused on Jack and asked, "Why did he become such a creature?"

Jack hesitated, "One must eat the flesh of men. It is a betrayal of nature." Jack met the gaze of the gathered members, "He can't be killed."

The men and women sat there stunned. They looked from side to side, hoping that the others would have an idea of how to conquer the beast. Yet, no one spoke. This beast was from the dark side of magic, and they did not know how it could be destroyed.

Joseph turned to Robert and said, "Robert, I think it is good that the three of them should stay together. Oboodashkwaanishiinh[10] Dragonfly is nearby to protect Peter. His arrow may be of help if the wendigo makes it here."

Robert peered at Marshal and Mary and asked, "Are you two sure that you are willing to keep these three here? This could be very dangerous."

Mary walked over to Peter, pulled him close to her, and turned to her husband, "Marshal, let's try. Perhaps we can be of some good for them?"

Marshal tilted his head and smiled at his wife, saying, "Yes, dear, we can support them for a time. Will you remain and assist Mary to acclimatize to caring for them, Verna?" When Verna nodded in agreement, he grinned.

Robert sighed, "We need to locate that Wendigo and see what it is up to. I believe this is far enough away for all of them to be safe here for the time being."

As the men began discussing the children's lives, Mary and Verna took them from the room and placed them into bed. The day was overwhelming, and they needed rest. Once the children were tucked into their beds, the ladies returned to the waiting men at the table.

"Jack, my friend," yawned Robert. "Will you please consult the ancestors on this event? There must be a reason why this is happening at this time."

Jack rose, grabbed his drum, walked to the fireplace, and closed his eyes. Those in the room lowered their eyes, pulled back, and gave him space. Jack drew in the hot air lofting from the flames and reveled in how he felt in its warm welcome. Through his closed eyes, he could sense the fire's glow on a red picturesque screen. He waited for the flames to dance on his mental screen to their rhythmic dance. Soon, the fire began to rise and fall to the beat of the drum. A moment later, Jack noticed the flame's rhythm changing, and in response, Jack started to match the fire's given rhythm. He opened his being to willingly sync his drum with the fire's dance. Jack could never tell the exact moment when he and his spirit would join the ancestors, but he could feel it was approaching, and he took one long inhale of warm, hot air and became the messenger.

Everyone watched Jack as he began to drum. The fire began to flame, and faces pushed through the flames and then retreated into the spirit world. At last, a woman appeared in the fire, steadied her gaze on Jamison, and smiled.

"Ngashi (z)[20] Mother." He whispered.

"Enh, ngwis, ndaa'aa maampi.[21] Yes, my son. I am here. Jack miinawaa giin Kiidamtaam[22], Jack and you have been busy I see." she smiled.

"Enh, ngidamtaami [23] Yes, we have been busy. We need to know what is happening with Sarah and these special children?" inquired Jamison.

Wind Witch

The smile faded from her face, and she gave a dead stare at her son, "The church is hunting anyone who they think possesses magic. The children, rising now, have source magic coming to light, and the church is determined to destroy them. Many children are joining us here, and we are upset about this. Our culture is dying with each child's passing."

"Mom, the government pays for those establishments. Why would the government care?" asked Jamison.

"Well, son, they don't have to pay for the dead now, do they?" she said in a mournful manner.

Jamison rubbed his long braid as he said, "Why are the churches seeking out our children?"

"Son, everyone has their own skills; call it magic, if you will. The church cannot control that aspect of the human. They do not understand it, so they have sought to destroy the magic folk. Your father spoke of how his village was destroyed and, all the drums were burnt, and he was white. Witch hunters are real, and your father ran to protect his magic. Witches and wizards, too, were hunted." she turned her head and smiled at the witches and wizards standing in the room and nodded.

Many of the onlookers lowered their eyes, for this truth was one they all knew to some extent. They nodded in agreement, knowing that this was the truth. Many of their ancestors came to the United States because they were running to protect their magic. Jamison watched as the onlookers acknowledged this truth with a nod and a smile. He returned to view his mother's beautiful face in the glow of the firelight as the wizard's and witches' eyes were turned for a moment to wipe a tear or two away.

"Son, you need to know Sarah's mark is that of the 'Nodin Me-koom-maa-senh(1) Wind Witch. She can wield all aspects of all the winds. Each time one returns, they have their own purpose. We do not know her purpose. As she grows, it will become clear. Make sure she learns to control herself." Warned his mother.

Wind Witch

Jamison hesitated for a moment, "She seems to favor the northern wind. She had caused storms already when she was upset. She knocked me off my broom by the gust of wind she caused."

Jamison smiled as he heard his mother's laughter fill the room; she turned her ghostly head to view his broom sitting in the corner, nodded her nose, and pursed her lips slightly towards the broom; then she teased, "You and that stick are amazing. It must have been very windy for you to fall off that Jiish-da-gan[24] broom."

"It is time to go. G'Zaaginim Giin Miinawaa G'Dawenmaa.[25] I love you and your brother," she said as her image faded into the flames.

Jack stopped drumming and he came back to focus on the people around him. His expression and theirs was of disgust. He looked around the room and saw the reality of the situation plastered on the faces of those who listened. They looked at one another, just stunned. After a moment, the company noticed the late hour and began withdrawing from the cabin in their thoughts.

Wind Witch

Chapter 12:
Witches Winter

Chapter XII:
WITCHES WINTER

The three ladies prepared an excellent breakfast the following day, and the children ate with vigor. Eggs, bacon, potatoes, and toast fortified the youth. Lyra, Mary, and Verna watched the children eat so fervently that they feared there wouldn't be enough for Marshal's breakfast.

The morning shone brightly outside, and the storm that had raged all night was no longer a concern. Marshal finished his morning tasks in the barn and stepped outside to see the fresh white snow. An owl flew towards him, which drew his attention. He watched as it flew right to him, dropped a note in his hands, and then flew away to rest in the barn. Marshal unfolded the letter to read it, then folded it up and paused for a while to collect his thoughts.

As he walked towards the house, he paused and watched the children through the window. He thought, 'Those three need our help. I can't imagine being hunted as a child. One thing that was clear, there was a reason why the church so hated them. Their magic must have been a threat to them.' He walked on, and with a deep breath, he opened the door. A stream of bright sunlight rushed through the door as he stepped inside and closed the door.

After removing his leather jacket, he pulled the letter from his pocket, "I was going to run into town today. The fresh snow on the ground would have been a nice ride. The sun just sparkles off it. Beautiful, simply beautiful. However, you three have caused a big stir, and I must go to the wizard's council today instead. Oh, Lyra, would you accompany me? Mary doesn't like to go there, and I feel you should be there just in case they need clarification of events in the barn."

Marshal sat down at the table and began to serve himself some breakfast. After his plate was loaded with potatoes and eggs, he shoved a piece of toast into his mouth. A cup of deep-roasted coffee landed before him, and he nodded a thank you to his wife.

113

Wind Witch

"When do we have to be there?' inquired Lyra.

"Two hours." He said through a half-chewed piece of potato.

Lyra walked over to the table and topped off his cup of coffee, "I guess I better get ready then. Oh, by the way, I received news that the cabin has been shielded, and other wizards are keeping guard around its border. Verna, Mary, and the kids will be well protected while we are gone."

Marshal stopped chewing for a moment, "What? The wizard council upped up our protection. Oh my, I guess there will be something we need to know then. I wonder what it is. Peter, will you come here a moment?"

Peter walked over to the table and sat down. Marshal reached into his pocket and pulled out the coin Oboodashkwaanishiinh[10] Dragonfly gave to him. He placed the coin on the table and slid it over to Peter. Peter picked it up, and with a surprised look on his face, he glanced up at Marshal.

"Oboodashkwaanishiinh[10] Dragonfly gave this to me the night you arrived. He had pledged to protect you. You know, his kind has its magic. Apparently, he will feel when danger is near you. If danger is close, he will come to your help. I must warn you, though, he will not help unless you are about to be killed. His kind usually does not work well with humans." Marshal took another bite of his toast and chewed slowly as he watched Peter turn the coin over and over in his hand.

So, Peter picked up his pencil, "My dad had one of these in his pocket."

"Well, I am not surprised; the way that Oboodashkwaanishiinh[10] Dragonfly was so insistent that you receive this one shows how important it is. Please always keep it in your pocket. This is not a toy." With a side glance, Marshal watched Peter tuck the coin into his pocket.

Wind Witch

Peter sat there for a moment, lost in thought. The room grew cold, and Marshal looked up at the boy who began to write, then passed the note. "Marshal, he didn't rescue my dad."

Marshal lowered his glasses, set them on the table, studied the boy, and began, "Let me make this clear, my boy. After burying his wife, he started back to your father as quickly as he could. He arrived at the moment when the gun was released. Witnesses said the men came in and ruined the village and left quickly. It all happened so quickly. They had planned the attack. Oboodashkwaanishiinh[10] Dragonfly had said there was no hope. However, he was there for you, and he saved you. Even without an agreement, he chose to save you."

Peter pondered Marshals' word for a moment, and his anger subsided. The warmth of the fireplace began to radiate through the room, instantly chasing the chill out of the air. The dirty dishes rising from the table broke his train of thought. He watched as the dishes floated to the sink. Verna waved her wand, and the faucet turned on. Chavo and Sarah got up from the couch and walked over to the sink as a bottle of dish soap rose and added cleaning solution to the water.

"I wish we knew how to do this when we were at the school. We would have had dishes done in no time. Day after day, I stood at that sink scrubbing dishes." Sarah said in amazement as she watched the food being scrubbed away on the plates.

Lyra and Marshal excused themselves from the table and got ready for the meeting. Peter stood for a moment, took the coin from his pocket, thought about his father's last moments, and felt so sorry for Oboodashkwaanishiinh's [10] Dragonfly loss. He wandered back to the couch, followed by Sarah and Chavo.

The children gathered themselves together and looked at the coin in Peter's hand. Their eyes searched each side in a confused expression. Peter gave the coin to Sarah, and she could feel something different about it. She couldn't figure out what she was feeling. She quickly passed the coin to Chavo.

"Can you feel it? Can you feel it vibrate?" exclaimed Sarah!

Chavo studied the coin for a moment or two. His eyes widened as he passed the coin back to Peter. Peter closed his eyes for a brief moment and let the coin sit in the center of his palm. A small vibration could be felt, and Peter could feel the energy travel through his hand. His eyes opened wide, and he quickly scribbled, "It feels like it is alive!"

Outside, on top of the nearby hill, rested Jack's friend, Ralph. Ralph, the captain of the Yetis, rested until morning, and the sun woke him. Ralph spent most of the night traveling to the cabin, so he welcomed what little rest he could get before sunrise.

In the early morning hours, he arrived at the top of the ravine overlooking the cabin. Snow and ice cycles gathered on the limbs of the trees and glistened in the moonlight. He noticed a group of pine trees slightly off the clearing and found the underbrush of the trees welcoming and safe from the blowing wind. He rested on the darkened floor of the nearby pine tree nook. Close but concealed from anyone who may be wondering.

The morning sun woke the beast from his slumber, and he made his way into the sunlight and shuffled his way across the snow. He yawned, stretched, and settled into his spot on the top of the hill. He surveyed the ravine and found a space where he could keep a close watch on the cabin. His large feet crunched through the snow until he came to a place where he could watch all the activities below.

In the valley below sat the cabin where the children were kept. Oddly, he noticed four wizards were keeping watch as well. He thought this was odd because Jack hadn't told him any extra people were keeping guard. He shrugged and began to pull burrs out of his fur as he watched people come and go.

The morning turned noon, and Marshal and Lyra exited the cabin and vanished into mid-air. Ralph wondered where Marshal would be going, knowing that the kids needed protection. He watched as Mary and Verna ushered the children back inside and closed the door. He watched as the glow of greenlight appeared around the door frame, sealing those inside from danger. He yawned and stretched again and took a deep cleansing breath. He closed his eyes, lifted his snout-like nose to the air, and took a deep breath. He didn't smell any danger in the air, so he decided to take a break. After a small snack to tidy his stomach, he settled in for a long-deserved rest.

Ralph leaned back on a rock and thought about Jack's visit the night before. Jack was an unusual person. He was a friend of man and wolf. To be honest, there wasn't any creature Jack didn't know. To the yeti, he was a friend and a confidant, and Ralph was willing to help him whenever he asked. Knowing that Jack was so persistent about seeking his help, he knew it was urgent to watch the cabin, so he rushed to the spot on top of the hill. Ralph settled in and blended so well into the snow that no one noticed.

Ralph yawned and stretched and smiled at the men keeping watch below. He thought, 'eh, even if they did see me, the wizards would erase their memory after they saw me. Except for Jack, they leave him alone with his memories intact.' He shook his head and yawned. He sniffed at the air a moment later and felt no discourse in the area. He closed his eyes for a catnap.

Chapter 13:
Wizard's Council

QR Codes: Chapter 13

Scan to hear the language

#	Chapter	Annishinaabemowin	English	QR Code
26	Ch. 13	Mistress Gaagaapshiinh	Mistress Raven	

Wind Witch

Chapter XIII:
WIZARD'S COUNCIL

Marshal and Lyra met Jamison and Joseph in the hallway of the council chamber. They arrived early, so they settled down in the hallway to discuss the night's events. Seeing that the council summoned them, they ensured their stories were in sync. Accuracy was important in conveying the night's events.

The large door opened to the chamber, and a short man opened the door and invited them in. There was only a small group of wizards and witches seated at the table in the middle of the room. Joseph greeted each person, and the four of them sat down at the table in ornate chairs.

"We have called you here to inform you that the wendigo is on the move to Marshal's cabin," informed Mistress Gaagaapshiinh [26] Raven. The beast is about 90 days travel, so you will have to move the children soon."

"I was afraid of that." hissed Joseph.

Mistress Gaagaapshiinh [26] Raven straightened her robe as she said, "Most of the wendigos travel to their birthplace. Most priests come from European regions because of migration. However, Father Unis was from southern Michigan. At first, he started to head home; then, he made a course change to head in your direction.

Jamison unfolded a map and laid it in front of him on the table. "Where was the last sighting of the beast?"

Mistress Gaagaapshiinh [26] Raven lowered her spectacles and leaned over the map. "Here, just at the Ohio border. He is heading towards Indiana." She gave Joseph a stern side look and met Joseph's gaze, "That horrid creature ate two of ours last night." She sat back down in her seat and waved her wand, and a bowl settled on the table in front of the guest. They leaned over the bowl to view the memory of one of the men who followed the beast.

Wind Witch

The water began to churn the bowl. Swirling colors began to show the boarding school at the moment when the beast broke through the window. The creature crouched low behind a bush growing next to the wooded area. As soon as the truck began to move, the beast ran just outside the view of the travelers. It ran on all fours like an ape and just as limber, swinging from tree to tree. The growing distance between the trucks increased, and so did his speed. They gasped as they watched the limber movement of the beast swing through the trees. The water began to shift to show another image.

The image of the truck appeared, and they watched the storm drift quickly toward the truck. The storm was raging, and the wizards had difficulties staying on the brooms as they flew guard over the truck. Rain, wind, and, at one point, hail battered the broom riders, and some were forced to land. The riders' drenched forms ran to the barn's safety and stood undercover of a lean-to. With wands at the ready, they stood guard.

Lyra watched the truck pull into safety, and the wizards took guard around the barn. The storm drummed the rain against the side of the building. Thunder sounded, and lightning crackled in the distance. Yet, the men stood on guard despite the rain. In the darkness of the woods, Lyra could hear the familiar cry of the wendigo and shiver with the memory of the moment.

The group gathered so they could look over her shoulder. Their expressions changed at the moment when one man screamed as he was pulled into the woods. Lyra listened to the man's screams, and everyone could hear the bones cracking. They mourned the poor man's demise. A moment later, a wizard began throwing spells at the beast as it advanced upon him. With a swipe of its large claws, it struck down the man and jumped upon him, tearing at his neck. The animal seemed to revel in the moment's feast. In horror, the chamber inhabitants stood there and watched the scene.

As the bowl darkened, Lyra and the team looked up from the bowl. They all sat down and looked around the table. The stoic expression of the room showed the magnitude of the beast's ability. With a gentle push of the bowl, Lyra sat back warily in the chair.

Wind Witch

"Joseph, I think we are in trouble." Lyra surrendered in an exasperated tone.

"Jack has told us about these beasts, but we the wizards haven't paid much attention to them because they are just spirit beings. Most just give guidance. Where there is light there is darkness. This is the second Father from that school that developed the dark version of the beast." Said Jamison.

Jamison was a half-breed between a witch and a Native man. He was taught some of the lore of his people by his half-brother Jack. He sat back in his chair, considering the connection between the children's magic and the church. Now, there is a Wendigo hunting Sarah. His mind drifted off to Jack's travels to the yeti's encampment. He was thankful that Jack was gathering protection outside of the wizarding world.

"Jack told us last night that these dark things can't be destroyed. Jade herself fought the beast and found no effective spell to use against it. Just like other ghosts, they are not affected by our magic." Jamison stated.

Joseph cleared his throat, "When I got to the barn, the beast was ready to break through the barn door. We got out just as the beast burst through. Seeing that we had an escapee, we took everyone to the cabin where Peter had been placed. Once there, Peter was able to show us what had happened. Peter has the gift of vision. He was able to combine Sarah's and Chavo's memory of the event. It is clear; this beast is something we cannot battle."

"There is more," said Jamison. "Jack called upon the ancestors after the children went to bed. We found out that the church is hunting the children who are showing magic. The government supported the destruction of Native children and was willing to pay the church to do so. They are stopping us from growing in numbers. Their treaties cost them a lot of money to keep those schools active. If they kill us off, they will not have to uphold the treaties. The schools struggle to feed the kids. We can see that Father Unis ate human flesh, or he wouldn't have turned into the dark wendigo. I wonder how that came to be."

Wind Witch

The council looked at each other with the clarity given by the group. Mistress Gaagaapshiinh[26]Raven stopped the chattering around the council room by hitting a mallet on the tabletop. Everyone settled down and shifted their focus back to business.

"What about the children? We know they are in the cabin. What are the plans moving forward?" Countered Mistress Gaagaapshiinh [26] Raven.

Joseph coughed and slumped in his chair, weary from lack of rest, and he offered, "Mary and Marshal have agreed to keep the children. Oboodashkwaanishiinh[10] Dragonfly is stationed nearby, and he will protect Peter and may be an asset to the protection of all of them."

"Supplies will be short," said Marshal. "We were not prepared to take on additional children. We ask for food and clothes for them."

Lyra swirled the water in the bowl. Forms of the children appeared, and everyone could view the condition of the children. Mistress Raven peered into the bowl and shook her head. She could see that they had overly worn shoes. Sarah's dress was presentable but not a dress of warmth. Chavo's pants showed wear and tear in the knees, and his shirt was grossly oversized. Peter's clothes were torn in spots from limbs and bushes during his escape.

Jamison cleared his throat. "Sarah's mark is not like the others. Her mark is the birthmark of the wind. The ancestors called her Nodin Me-koom-maa-senh[1] Wind Witch'. Apparently, she can wield all types of wind. There hasn't been a Nodin Me-koom-maa-senh[1] Wind Witch' for many years. They couldn't guide us in this matter, but it is clear she needs to be protected until she comes to full power."

Silence fell once again as the council reviewed this information with each other. No one had any answers for the meaning of this news. This was new territory in their experience. Native magic works with the earth and all elements around them. They never considered the magic that existed in these realms.

123

Wind Witch

"I suggest we support the care of these children. We do not know the meaning of these events, but I am sure they will affect our world. We ask for food, clothing, protection, and training of these children." Joseph pleaded. "Whatever assistance you can give would be greatly appreciated."

The council left the room to deliberate Joseph's request. After a two-hour deliberation, the council approved assistance for the care of the children. Mistress Gaagaapshiinh[26] Raven approved of the clothes aid and financial support for supplies. The crew was discharged, and they returned to the cabin, where they told Mary and Verna the entire story.

124

Wind Witch

Chapter 14:
Winter's Work

CHAPTER XIV:
WINTER'S WORK

The cabin became very busy with people coming to bring supplies. It was clear to Sarah that the group of them were bedding down for the winter. Supplies lined shelves, and the children sat in awe at that abundance in front of them. They would be safe and secure in the cabin and the wizarding folk proved to be an asset.

A tailor popped into the main room, followed by a few young girls. With a giggle, the girls got out their supplies and placed them on the table. Scissors and thread followed and lined up on the table next to the measuring tape in proper order. The girls measured each child, and the tailor flicked his wand and bolts of material appeared from a bag that was way too small to carry such cargo. The children watched in amazement as the colorful fabric was laid before them. The children chose their fabric, and they stood back to watch the tailor work.

The kitchen was busy constructing new clothes for the children. The children watched the scissors cut out their new shirts and pants. The young girls set up machines that whirred and stitched the pieces together. Stitch by stitch Sarah's dress took shape, and the young girls began to thread a needle and set to sew on buttons, and another made some cute flowers on the collar of Sarah's dress.

After the children had three changes of clothes, the tailor and his helpers gathered up their supplies and left the cabin. Marshal followed them outside, thanked them for their help, and bid them goodbye. He turned to gather more wood for the cabin and placed a load of wood in a nearby cart. He worked diligently, for he knew that Mary and Verna were getting ready for lunch. The kids would be off bathing and changing and would be all ready to show off their new clothes. Marshal worked quickly and returned his attention to tossing pieces of wood on the pull sled.

Inside the cabin, the children quickly bathed and slipped on their new clothes. Sarah felt as if she was a princess in her new dress. The boys emerged from their room in their new clothes and

126

smiled bashfully at Sarah. They stood posing for each other. They never had such fine clothes. With a smile at the children, Mary set them down for a nice lunch of salty ham, potatoes, and corn. They began to eat, and Mary settled down in a chair at the table and smiled at her family. After a moment, she sat up straight and looked at each one.

"We need to talk about school," stated Mary. "It is obvious that you cannot go to public school. The council has agreed to send a teacher to assist you in developing your skills."

The children stopped mid-chew and shifted uneasily in their seats at the thought of school. Education has not been a good experience for them. They looked at each other and saw the distress in each other's eyes. Chavo folded his arms over his chest to express his unwillingness to have the conversation. Sarah stared at Mary with a half-chewed mouthful of food. Mary could see that this conversation wasn't sitting well with the children.

Peter began to write a note to Mary fervently. "Why should we do that? I mean, seriously, why should we continue to go to school?"

The letters were heavy with anger on the paper. Peter's direct stare at Mary was blackened with the undertone of anger. The flames in the fireplace began to sputter, and flames threw an orange glow across the living room. Chavo and Sarah sat back in their chairs, watching Peter's mood change with apprehension.

"First of all, young man, close your eyes and calm yourself before you set us on fire," demanded Mary.

Peter folded his arms over his chest and glanced over to the fire. Another engorged orange flame spurted up the fire flue and out of the chimney. The fire rumbled through the pipes, and vibrations caused everyone to cringe. With a smile, Peter leveled his eyes on Mary defiantly. She walked up to him, laid her hand on his shoulder and squeezed a warning grip on him.

"Peter, I am serious. Please calm yourself. I like our little home." commanded Mary.

127

Peter looked up at Mary with a scowl. For a moment, she thought he was going to send another shot of fire from the flue. Her eyes met his, and for a moment, their eyes locked. Peter looked down at his feet and then over to the fireplace. Peter closed his eyes and began to calm the inner demon that came with the thoughts of school. The orange glow from the fire began to fade, and Sarah and Chavo began to breathe easier. Peter's eyes opened, and he sheepishly looked at his friends.

"I can see that you do not wish to keep learning. However, it would be best if you did so. In this world, words drive one's understanding. There are many secrets held in books, and those books are gold. Not to mention spells and teachings from other countries are very helpful. Seeing that medicine men are being hunted, soon their knowledge will have to be found from other sources. If you want to learn how to wield magic, you need to understand how the earth works, for your magic is driven from the earth. Imagine becoming so powerful that you outshine us. Your magic is so impressive. Imagine growing a greater skill than frying us in the house." Mary steadied her gaze onto Peter.

Peter got up from his chair and walked to the fire. He closed his eyes and took a deep breath. The flames danced as Peter caused them to increase and decrease in size. Mary watched him and noticed that Peter's breathing was the fuel for the inflation and deflation in the flames. He smiled as he played with the flames in a more controlled manner. A second later another shot of fire flew out of the flue. He turned and leveled his eyes at the kids and smiled with a wink.

Marshal ran into the house with wide eyes and heavy out of breath words, "Good gravy! Why, in heaven's sake?" He paused for a moment tossing his hands out in front of him in an asking manner. "Why did I see flames shooting out of the chimney?" He gaped around the room at everyone looking at Peter. His demeanor shifting to an impressed young schoolboy, "They flew at least five feet high. It was an epic sight, but what in heaven's sake happened?"

Mary leaned her head toward Peter, "Someone doesn't want to go to school. He threw a fit, a bit," Mary smiled over to Peter, "He just had a moment of anger to deal with."

Marshal rolled his eyes and walked over to Peter, "Son, there is so much you can do in life if you continue to learn. Learning is something one should never stop doing. No matter what stage in life you are in. There is always something to learn. Mary loves to grow plants and use them for medicine. She must read to give others medicine safely. I learn how to take care of the woods by finding ways to heal the trees recovering from fires and illness. Different trees have different benefits for man, and I study that too. Scientists study nature all the time. As I understand it, your ways deal with how they all work together. As you read the new stuff available, the more you can grow your skill."

The children at the table considered Marshals' words. Silence filled the room, and they shifted uncomfortably in their chairs. Images danced in their heads of their classrooms. The desk was lined up, and children sat in their desk dodging blows from nuns who were unhappy with them. Sarah's hand covered her eyes, and she began to cry.

Marshal rose from Peter's side and walked over to Sarah. He picked her up and held her close. He sat down at the table and began to rock her gently, "My goodness, little one, I don't know what you have experienced, but I can see that school doesn't bring good memories to you." He sat there rocking Sarah until her tears subsided.

Chavo sat at the table with a furrowed brow and his arms tightly bound to his chest. His eyes fixed themselves on the floor. He closed his eyes, and his breathing became heavier with each breath he took. The air hung still for a moment, and everyone paused. The room began a low rumble. The ground started shaking. Dishes on the shelf began to rattle against each other, and a bowl fell from the shelf. Mary and Marshal looked around at the shaking pots and pans with wide eyes. Chavo stood and tightened his crossed arms over his chest. The vibrations increased as his expression turned dark. Mary quickly moved to Chavo and lowered to meet his eyes.

129

Wind Witch

"Chavo!" she said as she watched a container of flour fall off the shelf spreading a white mess all over the counter and floor. "Chavo. Oh, my goodness. Please stop!" She laid her hand on the boy's shoulder and drew her eyes to his. "Please breathe with me. Close your eyes and breathe with me."

Mary wrapped Chavo in her arms and said, "Breathe in, hold it for a few moments, okay, let it go and breathe out." She felt the boy's frame loosen. "Good, let's do it again. Breathe in and hold it. Okay, let it go." They repeated this saying until the house stopped vibrating.

The wide eyes of terror were seen around the cabin. Chavo had not shown any magic until that point. Verna had made her way out of her bedroom and to the kitchen to see what was happening. She hung onto the walls of the hallway to steady herself as she scanned the destruction of the kitchen. Her eyes settled on Mary and Chavo in the middle of the kitchen.

"Oh, my goodness. What in the world happened here?" she said in an exasperated tone.

"Well, apparently, Chavo doesn't want to go to school. We knew he was earth magic, but blimey! I had no idea he could cause the earth to shake. Mary is calming him, and he seems to be calming down now." whispered Marshal as he gawked at the boy wrapped in Mary's arm.

Chavo pulled slightly away from Mary and smiled. He looked around the room and saw the disaster he had caused. He lowered his head in shame. Mary looked at the boy and pulled him close. The boy burst into tears and covered her shoulder in tears. Mary held him until his internal storm subsided.

Verna watched the pair with love. She could see that Marshal and Mary truly cared for them. With a wave of her wand, the dishes straightened themselves on the shelves. Sarah watched the bag of flour gather itself back into the bag and settle in its place. The pots and pans no longer shook, and the broom began to work to clean the floor of spilled supplies. Verna sat down at the table and smiled at the loving couple. She thought, 'I knew they would be good for the children.'

Back on the hilltop, snowflakes were drifting through the air, and Ralph sat in his spot watching the wind play with the flakes. The chickadees were jumping around the limbs of the great white pine tree without care. Ralph smiled a toothlike grin. Large teeth and long fangs were shown while he smiled. His snout-like nose gathered ridges together like rolling hills of flesh. His eyes showed bright with delight as he watched the birds play and dance in the tree. Their little chirps rang through the air, and Ralph relished the moment.

He leaned back on the tree and settled in with his thoughts. A moment later, he saw the flames shooting up into the sky from the chimney. His eyes widened as he watched intently at the cabin's chimney flue as it was shooting fire into the air. The fire licked at the air as puffs of smoke drew a dark purge of chimney soot from the top. Ralph wasn't concerned about the cabin itself. The flames didn't go close to the roof at all. He watched Marshal turn drop a load of wood, as he marveled at the flames shooting out of the chimney. Marshal stood there and awe for a few moments before collecting himself, and his awe turned into fear. Ralph laughed as Marshal sprinted towards the house.

The flames from the chimney died down, and soon, the fire was no longer a concern. Ralph began to laugh a hard laugh. He was impressed with the burst of fire, and he rolled laughing on the ground. He gained control of himself and smiled, knowing that one of the kids' magic ran amuck. The image made him chuckle many times during the day.

Ralph settled back down in his spot and began to drift off in a daydream. A moment later, the ground began to shake. The trees quivered, and their snow-covered branches released snow to fall all over Ralph. He looked around and didn't see any danger, but he did notice the earth's quaking stopped. With a confused expression, he focused on the cabin. He shook his head in confusion and kept an eye on the homestead below.

131

Wind Witch

A loud crack rang from the valley below, and Ralph's attention once again focused on the cabin. Jack and Jamison appeared and approached the cabin. Another cracking noise sounded; the second group of people began to pop into the valley. Marshal exited the cabin and greeted his friends at the door. After a moment, they all walked down a path to a clearing that Marshal had for them.

Logs were lying along the side of the trail, and the limbs were cut up and placed in piles for kindling or burning. Jamison began to act. Ralph watched the logs split into wooden beams, and long pieces of timber were cut to be used in the building. The open space was filled with construction material, and Marshal, Jamison and Jack worked together to erect a cabin in the clearing.

Ralph watched from the top of the hill as the building took shape. The men worked together with the assistance of their magic skills. In no time, the frame was set, and the sideboards were fastened to the sides. By sunset, the building was done, and the extra wood was stacked for drying.

Jamison and Marshal walked into the house. Jack, however, stood in the clearing, scanning the landscape. Ralph rose to his feet and stood in front of a large pine tree. Jack's eyes caught his movement, and he smiled and waved up to his furry friend, keeping guard on top of the hill. Jack then turned and went to finish the day inside the cabin with his friends.

Chapter 15:
The Crone

QR Codes: Chapter 15

Scan to hear the language

#	Chapter	Anishinabemowin	English	QR Code
27	Ch. 15	Giizhkaandok	Cedar	
28	Ch. 15	Wiingashk	Sweetgrass	
29	Ch. 15	Gizhemanidoo	Creator, please guide this lesson.	
30	Ch. 15	Miigwech	Thank you	
31	Ch. 15	Zaagasi Geezis ndonooziwin	My name is Shining Sun.	

134

32	Ch. 15	Mshiikenh ndodem	I am from the turtle clan.	
33	Ch. 15	Niijaanis	My child.	
34	Ch. 15	Maptoo waawaashkeshii	Running Deer	
35	Ch. 15	Babagwaashkini ezibikenh	Jumping spider	
36	Ch. 15	oo-si-min (father)	Dad	
37	Ch. 15	Nguhsh A-ki, gashi-aki shkakimikwe.	Mother Earth, she is waiting for you to join her.	

135

38	Ch. 15	Boontaan Sarah	Stop Sarah	
39	Ch. 15	An-wah-tin Maan-duh nchee-wat	Calm the storm.	
40	Ch. 15	Bi-Zahah Gaa-chin Benoojiinh.	Come little one.	
41	Ch. 15	Bizhaan maampi.	Come to me.	

Chapter XV:
THE CRONE

The next morning, a dark cloud-covered sky blanketed the valley. As Sarah woke, she lay in her bed watching the clouds swirl around each other. Chavo knocked on the door and peeked inside at Sarah. He noticed how comfortable she looked curled up with the doll that Verna had made for her.

"Breakfast is almost ready. Mary said to get dressed because we will be starting school today." Chavo closed the door and left Sarah to her thoughts as she dressed.

In the pit of her stomach, Sarah felt dread at the thought of going to school. What she knew of school left Sarah's stomach sour and churning. The hunger she first felt had turned against her and into acid, eating her from the inside out. She sat at the side of her bed and looked at the new clothes, sitting on the chair and began to dress. She didn't want to eat. Her stomach was not agreeable this morning.

With an exhausted shuffle, Sarah made her way to the dining room table and flopped down in the chair to find a bowl of cornmeal. Her stomach was hurting, but she thought cornmeal might help settle it. She prepared the warm bowl of cornmeal mush by adding sugar, a bit of butter, and a drizzle of milk to the bowl and mixing them. She smiled as she dipped the buttered toast into the hot mush and blew on it until it was cool enough to eat. Sarah closed her eyes as the medley of flavors danced in her mouth.

"Your teacher arrived this morning. Lessons will begin today," said Marshal. "Mind yourselves today, for she has come a long way to work with you three." He pulled on his boots one at a time. "I warn you three, she is a bit different, but Jamison said she will be a good teacher for you."

In the distance, low drumming began to sound through the trees, and the children jumped out of their chairs and ran to the window. The drumming came from the direction of the cabin, and the children could see a woman standing on the porch. The

137

woman's long brown jacket covered much of her skirted frame. Her fur hat covered her crown, and her long, grey, wavy hair continued down the middle of her back. She placed the drum in a red slouch bag and continued to work, and smoke lifted in the air from an earthen bowl. The children watched her with curiosity. After a moment, the lady turned and walked back into the school.

"Your breakfast is getting cold. If you don't eat it soon, it will be all lumpy," said Mary.

The children drew themselves away from the window and, made their way back to the table and quickly ate their mush. A crow landed on the windowsill and tapped its beak on the glass. The kids watched the crow tilt his head from side to side, peering one eye in to look at the children. The three kids smiled as they watched the black and white bird hop around excitedly as it watched them put on their winter gear. In coats and boots, the children exited the cabin and followed the crow as it jumped and flapped its wings. He would speed ahead of them, then turn and squawk at them until they caught up. It didn't take long for them to reach the schoolhouse.

Mary stood outside the door watching the children sounding happy going to their first day of school. Marshal exited the barn, walked over to his wife and wrapped his arms around her. They watched the children laugh happily as they followed the speckled crow to school. Both Mary and Marshal smiled at each other, then turned and yelled goodbye to them. They were apprehensive, but they knew the children would be safe. Besides, they weren't too far away; they were just outside their door.

Smoke rose from the chimney of the cabin. On the porch was a rocking chair and, in that chair, sat a lady puffing on a curved pipe. The smell of clove-laden pipe tobacco drifted through the air and tickled the noses of the anxious children. The crow took flight and landed on the woman's shoulder. With a caw, it noticed its breakfast laying on the windowsill and flew to its feast. The woman's pipe left thick white plumes of smoke that hung in the air. The smoke was so thick in the winter's air that it covered her face so the children couldn't see her. Soon, she stood and began walking towards the children.

Wind Witch

As the children approached, her outline became clearer. The children stopped as they watched her walk through the smoke and to the top of the steps to greet the children. She lowered her pipe and poked at its contents to loosen debris. With a twist of her wrist, she emptied her pipe on the ground by tapping it on the porch's railing. The contents lofted down to the ground and settled itself in the snow. The children looked up and saw the sweetest smile. Dark black eyes were crinkled, and the crow's feet appeared next to her eyes when she smiled. Her wrinkled hands waved hello at the leery children.

"Hello, everyone. Come on in! We will do a proper introduction inside as our first lesson." She turned and walked into the cabin, and the children followed behind her.

The wooden frame of the cabin walls was covered with plants drying. Bunches of plants were hung on nails, and other unusual firs stretched out on frames. Jars were stacked on shelves. Some held dried plants, and other jars held liquids. A fire burned in a wood stove, and the cabin was warm. The lady's back was turned to them as she hung her jacket near the fire to warm and dry. The children could see hooks for their jackets, and they slipped theirs off and hung them with hers. The children turned and marveled at how different this space looked from the school they had known.

The children looked around the cabin to see no chairs, chalkboards, or desks; only four leather pelts were laid on the floor in a circular pattern. In the center was a bowl filled with Mskwodewashk[14] sage, Giizhkaandok[27] cedar, Wiingashk[28] sweetgrass, and (A)Sema[15] tobacco. The children could see that she had a metal pan like Jack's cast iron pan. They turned when they heard the stove door open, and they watched the lady scoop out a few red-hot coals and place them in the pan. Her face glowed red as she carried them to the circle and placed them on a hot block near the bowl. Her smiling eyes rose and focused on the children who stood near the jackets waiting for instructions.

Her wrinkled hands grabbed some Mskwodewashk[14] sage from the bowl, rolled it into a little ball, and placed it on the hot coals. The children watched her prepare the medicine, and once it

139

began to smolder, the smoke rose. She smiled at the children and gestured to come and smudge themselves. She stood beside them and patiently waited for them to finish, and she smudged them from bottom to top. When one child was done, she pointed for them to sit on the leather pelt. One by one, each child was ready for their lesson to begin. She took a pinch of each medicine and added it to the pan.

The children watched as she lowered herself to the leather pelt. For her age, the children could see she was more agile than they thought she would be. She closed her eyes for a moment and spoke:

"Gizhemanidoo[29] Creator, please guide this lesson. Remove all fear and doubt from these young ones. Bless the day with love and open minds. Let no fear enter this space, for we are safe in your protection. Miigwech [30] Thank you, Miigwech [30] Thank you, Miigwech [30] Thank you, Miigwech [30] Thank you,"

The children's eyes grew wide. They hadn't heard the language in many years. Their teacher opened her eyes to see the children looking back at her. She smiled at their surprised expression.

"The language is the key to our magic. You must learn the language again. Here, you should have no fear of speaking your tongue. Chavo, you're from another tribe, but we are all Native blood. I only know my language, and I will instruct you the best I can. My belief is that your blood will understand and transform it for you. Peter, I know you can't speak, so you will have to feel the words and speak them out loud in your head. Like a silent prayer. Sarah, you were so little when they took you. I don't know how much you'll remember, but your parents spoke fluently to you throughout your life, with this, it may be easier for you to learn. In this building, please use the language you know. You are to become the best person you can be. The language fortifies you and who you are." instructed the old crone.

The children sat in their spots, considering the old lady's words. This classroom was far different from the one at the boarding school. They would no longer be beaten for their language. They could be free to be who they are, a Native student.

"Zaagasi Geezis ndonooziwin[31] My name is Shining Sun. Mshiikenh ndodem[32] I am from the turtle clan. I grew up in Cross Village before being sent to a boarding school in Harbor Springs, Michigan. I know the terrors you may have faced, and you are free to talk to me about them. Then, we will use our medicines to help you heal and let go of the pain. The memories will remain, but what happened to you is not your fault. You were powerless over the pain they inflicted on you. Each time a memory emerges, feel the pain and send the pain back to the one who caused the pain. Each time you do so, you'll gain your power back. They tried to take our power away, but you three must learn to build back that power in you. I know so much of our culture has been stripped from you. It is time to rebuild." stated the old crone.

There was a silence in the room. Everyone sat in their own minds for a moment. Each one lived a little bit of their nightmare in their memories. Zaagasi Geezis[13] Shining Sun took a deep breath and shifted on her leather. She waited for the children to return to her.

"I have been brought here to discover who you are." Her dark eyes scanned each little face as she continued, "I have been told that Sarah has wind magic, Peter is earth and fire magic, and Chavo is earth magic. I, I am earth magic, as you can see, as she gestured at the plants on the walls. When I was released from the boarding school, I had to control myself. I had to remove the brokenness the school caused. I found peace in growing and tending to plants. Plant medicine is what I have come to love," she said as she looked at the children.

The children sat in silence. They listened closely to the old crone as she talked. They watched every move she made. Zaagasi Geezis[13] Shining Sun shifted on her leather and leaned over to grab a pinch of medicine and laid it on the coals; the children watched the medicine burn.

Zaagasi Geezis[13] Shining Sun began, "Each one of you has shown that you are not under control. You get angry or sad, and you set things amuck. Snowstorms, fire shooting out of the

141

chimney, and the earthquake last night show me that you are not in control."

The children lowered their eyes, for they knew she was right. They glanced back and forth at each other, not knowing what to say. They sat there in silence, and soon Zaagasi Geezis[13] Shining Sun rose to her feet and drew open the window. The sun-splashed into the room and fell across the children. The sun's warmth felt good on their skin, and Zaagasi Geezis[13] Shining Sun turned and sat back down.

"Inner stillness. Our first lesson is inner stillness. All one must do is surrender to a quiet mind. At first, it is hard to stop your thoughts from running in your head. Today, I hope you discover a little bit of peace and control. This is key to effective magic."

The children closed their eyes and sat in silence as Zaagasi Geezis[13] Shining Sun showed them. Sarah took a deep breath and let it out slowly. Sarah began to think about her mother, and she remembered Zaagasi Geezis[13] Shining Sun coming to the house. Sarah was certain she was the older woman who came for visits. She didn't remember her much, but she remembered the one day the two ladies lay laughing on the floor. Sarah sat with the memory of the two with happiness as she sat and breathed.

A gasp came from Zaagasi Geezis[13] Shining Sun, which caused the children to open their eyes. When they looked at their teacher, they could see a tear in the corner of her eye as she looked upon a vapor-like person standing in front of Sarah.

"Niijaanis[33] My child," Sarah's eyes opened to look upon her mother, Maptoo Waawaashkeshii[34] Running Deer, "You are safe with Zaagasi Geezis[13] Shining Sun. She will love you as her own." Her mother turned to smile at their teacher, "Zaagasi Geezis[13] Shining Sun, my best friend, I know you will teach her well. I wish I could but that was not the will of Gizhemanidoo[29] creator." She shifted back to Sarah, "Your path is going to be difficult, my child, but know that the ancestors are behind you. Be strong always."

Sarah sat looking at her mother's shape-shifting in the sunlight. Her long hair lofted wispily around her smoke-like face, and her eyes looked lovingly at Sarah. Her mother's clothes were the same as the last time she had seen her. The white shirt hung on her frame, and the brown skirt flowed as her mother's form moved towards her. Sarah stood and looked up to her mother and reached up to touch her. With disappointment, she found that the smoke was not touchable; her hand passed through. A tear formed in Sarah's eye and rolled down her cheek.

"Don't cry, my little one. I am happy with my visit with the ancestors." Whispered Maptoo Waawaashkeshii[34] Running Deer." She looked at Zaagasi Geezis[13] Shining Sun and said, "Please add more Mashkodewashk[14] sage. Others want to visit too." Maptoo waawashkeshii[34] Running Deer's form floated over to Peter and spoke, "You know what to do."

Zaagasi Geezis[13] Shining Sun smiled and rolled up Mshkwodewashk[14]sage and placed it on the coals. Peter leaned closer and blew slightly, and the medicine began to burn. The children watched the smoke loft toward Maptoo Waawaashkeshii[34] Running Deer. The children's eyes widened as they watched the forms appear around them. Walls of people surrounded them, and the children marveled at how the smoke exposed their forms. Babagwaashkini ezibikenh[35] Jumping spider, Sarah's dad, walked upside her mother and smiled.

Chavo's expression changed from awe to grief as he watched his grandmother and his parents appear before him. The reality of their deaths caused Chavo to stop breathing; he couldn't catch his breath from the shock. While he was at school, the village was attacked, and his family perished. He could see they were no longer here on earth for him.

"Grandson, you were not supposed to be here yet; perhaps there is a reason why." She looked over at Sarah, then steadied herself and looked back at her grandson. "Protect her, grandson; it is obvious you two are supposed to be together."

The smoke began to shift in the room. Faces in the smoke shifted, and some disappeared to allow another form to take shape. With another puff of air, Peter blew on the smoke. Peter's eyes

143

Wind Witch

lifted to meet his father's eyes, and a smiling face appeared in front of him. Peter's mouth moved the word, 'oo-si-min[36], Father.'

"My son, don't hold on to my death. You did the best you could to save me. You are earth magic. You can wield fire magic because you saw me wield it. You can use both, but earth magic is needed the most. Nguhsh-we a-ki, gashi-aki shkakimikwe[37] Mother Earth, she is waiting for you to join her." With a smile, the smoke shifted, and Peter's dad dissipated into the air.

The schoolroom door opened on its own, and the smoke exited through it; forms of ghostlike beings smiled and waved as they exited the cabin. The children sat peering at the door, watching the spirits as they exited the cabin. With stunned expressions, they sat in silence, pondering the events. Zaagsi Geezis[13] Shining Sun stood and walked over to the opened door and closed the door behind the leaving guest. With a smirk of a smile, she turned back and became amused at the children's expression. The first time one sees the ghost of an ancestor is always one of great mental complexities.

With a gleam in her eyes, Shining Sun turned to assess the children in her charge. The children were visibly disturbed by the ancestor's visit. Zaagsi Geezis[13] Shining Sun signaled for the children to sit down on their leathers and instructed them to close their eyes and breathe. She began to drum to soothe their being, and the children settled into their feelings. Zaagsi Geezis[13] Shining Sun watched the children as they slowly gained control of themselves. After the tears were cleaned up and their faces washed, she dismissed them for the day. As she watched the children leave the cabin, she closed the door and allowed herself to mourn the loss of her friend.

Ralph sat on the top of the hill, keeping a watch on the cabin below. He watched the children follow as the silly crow led them to the cabin, and he laughed as he watched the silly bird dance across the snow. He watched the crone greet the children and smiled as he smelled the clove-laced tobacco loft up through the air from her pipe. Ralph watched them walk into the cabin and sat in amazement as the dark, cloudy day transformed into a bright, sunny day. After a while, he watched the schoolroom door open and watched the ancestors depart from the cabin. His eyes were wide

Wind Witch

with amazement. He smiled as the children safely emerged and walked to their cabin. All was safe.

The sun glistened off the snow, and Ralph shifted his vision to the horizon. Over the westward hill, he could see the dark clouds were gathering again. Churning dark clouds were forming, and the wind began to rise. Snowflakes were blowing in on the wind, and the smell of stench lingered on the breeze. He scoffed and searched the tree line for any hint of danger. Nothing unusual was visible, but his nose knew different. Ralph could smell the change in the winds, and he grunted at the disturbance he smelled. He settled into the null in which he sat and kept alert.

The darkness settled in on the cabin, and Sarah sat in her room. The vision of her mother taunted her mind as she sat with the memory of her. She listened through the walls as Marshal came into the house, talking about a storm heading towards them. Sara shrugged and returned to her thoughts of the day she was taken from her parents. She grew angry as she remembered being carried away by Jacques. She remembered watching her parents being overcome by men and women. Anger rose as she remembered being hit with branches. As her anger grew, so did the storm.

Sarah's dreams were tormented as she relived the long drive she endured to get to the school. She remembered the fear she had experienced as people sneered at her through the door of her cage. She visited the dark cellar, where she spent nearly a year in darkness. She woke and shook off the nightmares and sat at the side of her bed. Sleep was not going to be her friend tonight.

Sarah wandered to the kitchen to get a drink of water. After a few sips, she heard the crow knocking at the window. Sarah set her glass down on the table and walked over to greet the bird. Snow settled on its body, and he shook off the snow looked at Sarah and cawed. Snow was swirling around the bird, but it stayed steady and knocked on the window when Sarah turned from him. The crow tapped on the window again and fluffed the snow off its body as if he was determined not to give up.

Once again, Sarah turned to look at the bird. A light began to shine in the night sky, and the bird's shadow fell across the

145

windowsill. Sarah walked to the window to see where the light was coming from. Sarah squinted her eyes as she focused on the glow. The brightness of the light caught the whipping snow, and Sarah could see the storm raging through the glass. The light was so bright that it burned through the snowstorm. Sarah watched it approaching the valley and she could see it was steadily growing.

Sarah watched the light, and it stopped near Zaagasi Geezis[13] Shining Sun's cabin. The crow knocked on the window and flapped the snow off his wings. Its head turned from side to side, coaxing her to follow him. Sarah saw movement through the snow, and she could see the form of Zaagasi Geezis[13] Shining Sun emerge from her cabin. Sarah thought it was odd to watch her kneel in front of the light.

Sarah hastily got her winter gear and dressed. She flung open the door to greet the crow on the stoop. The crow was grounded by the fuzzy snow, and Sarah took him up and covered him in her jacket. The snow became deeper as she walked, making walking harder, but she persevered through the snow to the light. A scream sounded out from the hills, followed by a stomach-ripping shriek. For a second, fear ripped through Sarah's soul. She flinched for a moment but turned her eyes back to the light. The light drew Sarah in the direction of the crone's house, and she decided to go to it.

The wind pushed at Sarah's clothes and dragged her body off position. Yet, she kept her eyes on the light and adjusted her path. She raised her hand to cover her face to stop the wind from biting and stinging her skin. Her nightgown tugging at her knees hindered her laborious steps, causing her to struggle more. Sarah didn't stop, no matter how hard she tried.

"Boontaan[38] Stop Sarah! An-wah-tin mahn-duh nchee-wuht[39] Calm this storm!" yelled Jamison from his broom, lofting above her. "Stop the storm and calm yourself."

Sarah paused for a moment and considered the man and then the storm. She felt the rage of the wind matched the rage in her soul. She closed her eyes and felt the fury of wind biting at her exposed skin. A stubborn stance set in inside her, and she willed

146

the wind to wrap itself around her and not touch her. The storm raged, but the storm did not harm her any longer. The crow cawed and jumped on her shoulder and pranced and flapped a little victory dance. It snapped at Sarah's ear, prodding Sarah forward. Sarah adjusted her stance and stood strong and continued forward with ease.

Flashes of lights began to flare all around the valley; Jamison landed next to the crone and kneeled. Sarah fixed her eyes on the light and pushed forward. She stood strong, and with each step, she struggled through the snow on her path to meet the light. Somehow, she felt knowing that she was being summoned. She knew this was a test that she mustn't fail. She stopped and released the crow, who flew to the old crone. She thought, 'Just a little more. I am almost there.' She pushed through the snow until she stood in front of the White Buffalo.

Flashing lights grew heavy around the protective barrier, but she did not dare to look away from the light. She heard the screeching howls of the wendigo as it battled the yetis in the forest. A moment of fear set in, stopping her in her tracks. Thoughts of fear ran through her head, and yet, out of nowhere, a loud crack sounded, and Oboodashkwaanishiinh[10] Dragonfly appeared with his bow in his hand. She smiled at him over her shoulder and gave him a nod of hello and thank you. Sarah listened to the wendigo and the yetis' yell and didn't flinch; she just pushed on with Oboodashkwaanishiinh[10] following her, watching for danger. Together, they made their way to the light.

Lights turned on in the cabin, and the company therein emerged. Marshal and Mary watched Sarah with their wands in their hands. A company of wizards landed their broom inside the protective circle. Their eyes scanned the tree line for the creature as they gave Sarah a side-instiring glance. Sarah paused just ten yards from the white light and stood tall. A sudden burst of light vibrated through the valley, blinding all who were there for a brief moment. Sarah's hand covered her eyes until the flash no longer hurt. Her eyes adjusted, and she continued on.

Through the darkness, Sarah's eyes adjusted to see a white buffalo there waiting for her. Sarah walked directly toward the

147

buffalo and kneeled like everyone else. Another surge of light occurred, and a beautiful white lady appeared. The glow of her beauty was enticing and alluring. The visiting wizards turned to view the lady and stood there in awe. Many of them began to approach her, for they wanted her for their own. They desired her so much that they approached her with lust. In a matter of seconds, they exploded into flames and lay in a black pile on the white snow. Sarah watched wizard after wizard burn, but she remained strong and walked firmly toward the woman.

Another howl came from the hills, and a second, third and fourth howl came sounding through the woods. The hairs on everyone's body stood on end as the symphony of the wind played in their ears. The howls of the yeti and the screeching of the wendigo had everyone at the edge. Yet, they all held strong, kneeling with their eyes lowered out of respect for the White Buffalo Woman. They listened and glanced up to watch Sarah as she approached the old one.

"Bi-zahah Gah chin ba-zhik bizhaangaachi-binoojiinh[40] Come Little one. Bizhaan maampii[41] Come to me." Said the White Buffalo lady. Her voice was musical to Sarah's ears, and Sarah did not fear the request.

Sarah walked closer, kneeled in front of the lady, and stated, "I am sorry, I do not know you."

Oboodashkwaanishiinh[10] Dragonfly sided up with Sarah, "She is the White Buffalo Lady. She is from the old ways and old beliefs." He whispered into her ear. "Listen to her carefully." He backed away with a bowed stance, slowly leaving Sarah to her guest.

"You have been sent here at this time to prepare for the end battle. My little wind witch, you need to learn many things before then. You will have many years to prepare, and I trust you will do so." The lady walked up to her, leaned over, and placed a black arrow in front of her. "Ralph is on his way down the hill. You must not fear him. Take the arrow with you. He is coming, so don't be afraid." The White Buffalo Woman looked to the heavens, and a moment later, she flew through the air like a shooting star and ascended into the heavens.

Darkness filled the valley as the light faded from the lady's visit. Howls sounded, and screeches answered them. White forms emerged from the wood and narrowed in on the wendigo. A white wall of fur surrounded the beast as it hacked and slashed at their fur. White chunks of fur clung in its claws, but no harm was done to the yeti that fought the beast.

Ralph ran through the protective barrier and rushed to Sarah. Sarah grabbed the arrow just in time for Ralph to scoop her up, and he made a mad dash for safety. Sarah's body was wrapped in a blanket of fur, and she held on tight to the arrow, and the beast hung onto her. Sarah could hear the snow crunch under the beast's feet as it traveled easily through the storm.

Sarah could hear the beast's breathing become more laborious as he ran through the forest. The storm raged on, but Ralph wasn't bothered by anything the north wind threw at him. Snow began to cling on his fur as ice clung to strains of his fur from Sarah's freezing breaths. Sarah clung on tightly as the beast ran on to morning.

With a sudden downward slide, Sarah could feel Ralph's body skid down a hill and into a ravine. With a sudden stop, he placed Sarah on the ground in front of a cave and directed her to follow him inside. Sarah's eyes adjusted to the lack of light, and she followed him into the half-lit cave. Ralph sat down and looked at the child and her possessions with awe.

"Well, now," a ruffled deep voice growled, "I was not expecting this turn of events." He leaned back on the wall. "The White Buffalo Woman gave you that arrow. You, little one must be important for the Lady to appear with such a gift for you." His eyes fixed onto Sarah as his heavy chest heaved with exhaustion. "I guess I have no choice but to take you to our hovel. It is a day's travel, but I think I better take you to see the elders." His eyes grew tired as he pondered what to do next. "Here," he lifted his massive arm, "Crawl in here to keep warm, and we can get some sleep."

149

Wind Witch

Sarah crawled into the crook of his arm and settled in. She was tired and welcomed the chance to sleep. With the arrow tucked in her hand, she drew the arrow up to her chest and snuggled into Ralph's fur. With the warmth of the beast's body and with the rhythmic rise and fall of his chest, she was soothed into a deep sleep.

Chapter 16:
The Council

QR Codes: Chapter 16

Scan to hear the language

#	Chapter	Anishinaabemowin	English	QR Code
1	Ch. 16	Noodin Me-koom-maa-senh[1]	The wind witch has returned.	

Wind Witch

Chapter XVI:
THE COUNCIL

The night was full of activity at the cabin. The boys sat near the fire as they listened to the adults talking at the table. The wind had lessened, and the snow had stopped once Sarah and Ralph ran into the forest. The yetis were in pursuit of the beast pushing Father Unis in the opposite direction of Ralph's and Sarah's trail. Jack arrived, and Jamison greeted him at the door.

"Well, my brother, we have a tale to tell you." Jamison took Jack's parka and hung it near the fire.

Robert paced the floor as he thought about the chain of events he had witnessed. Jack wandered over to him and placed a hand on his shoulder. "My friend, tell me what has happened tonight."

"The old one, The White Buffalo Lady came to Sarah!" Robert said. His expression was one of disbelief. "I thought her story was just a myth."

Jack stared at Robert for a moment, "You mean, the legend is true?"

"We have five dead wizards to prove it." Robert began to pace once again. "What am I going to tell the council in the morning?"

"Tyrone met me on the way here, and he told me that his troupe was pushing the wendigo south again." Jack rubbed his tired eyes, "He had said that Ralph would probably take Sarah to the Hovel of Elders because of the black arrow."

Jamison quickly turned to the group, "Why would he take her there?"

.

Jack pulled out his drum and began to consult the ancestors about the meaning of the event. Everyone watched as Jack synced his soul with the collective ancestors. In his usual practice, the spirit

153

began to speak, "The Nodin Me-koom-maa-senh[1] Wind Witch has returned. Train her well and prepare a bow for she will need to be a master archer. Build a bow of the sacred Black Ash." Jack's drumming slowed and everyone could see the spirit leave, and Jack returned to the room.

"The Noodin Me-koom-maa-senh[1]Wind Witch, my great grandfather spoke of that name. The last time one returned, she caused a great freeze that destroyed a pestilence occurring across the land. She drove the people south for the summer. Lakes, rivers, and streams all froze to kill off the bugs that rose from the waters and brought illness to the land. Many people died before she came to power, but it all ended with her."

There was a knocking on the windowpane; Marshal turned, walked to the window, and opened it. Snow scattered from the sill and landed on the floor when the bird shuffled his feet. Marshal grabbed the letter from the beak of the owl. Once the owl's beak was cleared, it began to squawk, and Verna walked to the cupboard, opened the door to grab a piece of meat and took the treat to the bird. The bird danced on the windowsill, scattering the remaining snow, and flew to the barn to rest.

Marshal presented the envelope to Jamison. "We knew this was coming."

With a groan, Jamison took the envelope from Marshal. He took a deep breath, broke the seal, and drew out the letter. As he read the letter, his face showed concern. He looked up to his waiting friends and began to read the letter to them.

Dear Mr. Jacko,

You and your company are required to meet with the council at 1 p.m. on Friday afternoon. Please arrive early and be prepared to relay important events of the evening. Families of the fallen have been notified of their child's fate.

Sincerely,
Mistress Gaagaapshiinh[24] Raven.

Jamison looked up at the group and smiled at their expression. They glanced around the room at each other and nodded. Some of them chose to stay the night at the cabin, and some went home. A night's rest was needed, and it was clear that everyone needed to process their thoughts. A night's rest would give Marshal and Mary a chance to deal with the loss of Sarah. That night, Chavo and Peter drifted off to sleep listening to Mary's grief and Marshal's consoling her. They went to sleep knowing that they were important to their caretakers.

The next morning, Mary woke and began to cook breakfast. Her eyes were all puffy, and her skin appeared pale and careworn. Her heart ached as she looked at Sarah's chair and knew she would not be there this morning. Tears once again began to fall silently down her cheeks. She was thankful for the moment alone, for she didn't want any witness to her grief. This, after all, was the first heartache she would experience as a "mother" type figure. It weighed heavy on her soul, and she wondered if she was really built to be a mother.

The smell of bacon lofted through the air, and the coffee pot began to percolate. The vapors of the brew began to loft the lovely smell of coffee through the air. Mary knew it would be a matter of minutes before everyone would stir. She wiped her tears away and blew her nose as she busied herself to finish the morning meal. She ladled a scoop of pancake mix onto the griddle, and as she waited, her thoughts drifted to Sarah and the yeti. She lingered in her thoughts until her nose alerted her to the burning smell of the pancakes on the stove. She quickly waved her wand, and the pancakes disappeared and she started a new batch.

Marshal scuffled through the room and settled himself into his chair as a worried expression began to appear with a glance at Sarah's chair. He laid his head on his hand and smirked at his wife as the burnt pancakes were swept away. He said nothing to her and just smiled wearily at her. He didn't have to speak, for the tear rolling down his cheek said more than words to Mary.

Mary's lips were pursed together in an attempt to hold back her tears as she watched her husband's loss. In a soft almost squeaky voice she said, "Jack had told me last night that he trusted

155

Wind Witch

Ralph. He confessed to having Ralph keep watch over the cabin because he had a vision that more protection was needed. He didn't expect the White Buffalo Lady to appear, but I am glad he had Ralph watching." said Mary as she settled herself in the seat near Marshal. She reached out her hand and offered her comfort. Marshall looked at his wife and reached out and took her hand into his. He patted it lovingly as if he were patting a sleeping baby's back. Tears fell and stained the table in front of him, but he didn't care. All he wanted was his Sarah back.

"Robert, Jamison, myself, and Oboodashkwaanishiinh[10] Dragonfly will go to the council meeting today," said Marshal in a contemplative tone, as he thoughtlessly stroked his wife's hand.

The morning buzz began in the cabin as people emerged from their slumber. The boys picked a corner and stayed out of the way of the bustle of the feeding frenzy. They whispered amongst themselves as they were watching Mary and Marshal. They have never seen a couple support each other through their loss like they did. The wizards and witches of the room consoled and hugged each other when tears fell. Grief wasn't something new to the boys, but the caring affection the wizards shared with each other was new to them. They just watched and learned that love was deep in the cabin that morning.

Day clothes were adorned, and the men prepared to leave the cabin. Jack took place in the opposite corner of the room and pondered what the Universe had in mind with these children. Their sleeping magic will awaken, and they will come into their powers. Every one of the children has their own purpose and power. He looked at the boys with wonder, for the ancestors hadn't told him much about them. He rose from his seat and walked out the door with the men and bid them goodbye, as the men left the valley to go their meeting.

At the council building, Joseph stood in the corridor of the council chamber and waited for the men to arrive. He had been there long enough to see the families of the fallen come and go. Cries of loss rang down the corridors as the mother's wails burned into his soul. Young men lost and are no more. He knew their parents' dreams had been shattered in a second. He sighed and

156

toyed with his thoughts as he pondered the night. The loss had been so great already, and he knew this would not be the first time he would be summoned to explain the events in regard to these children.

Joseph heard a slight cough ringing down the corridor. He turned to see the four men walking down the hallway to the chamber door to meet him. When they took their space at Joseph's side, the Chamber door burst open again. The men were instantly silenced as they watched those who walked out of the chamber scowl at them as they passed by. Grief and anger lingered in the air, and the parents of the dead's eyes burned hate into them as they walked by. Their anxiety increased, and they stood as if they just experienced what a firing line must have felt like. As the last family was leaving, the little man waved them to enter the room.

"Mr. Jacko. This collaboration is out of control. Five, five dead wizards. Five mourning families. What has happened?" said Mistress Gaagaapshiinh[26] Raven.

Jamison walked to the chair provided for him and sat at the table. His companions joined him, sitting at each side of him. Oboodashkwaanishiinh[10] Dragonfly climbed up onto a chair and stood so he could be seen by the council. Jamison took a couple of deep breaths and began to collect his thoughts.

"There are many details of the day. The old crone, Zaagasi Geezis[13] Shining Sun, had a very upsetting lesson for Sarah and the boys. Sarah's emotion caused a snowstorm to hit, and we all settled in to rest for the evening. We are still not sure why Sarah woke in the night, but she did. The chain of events is unclear, but Sarah went out into the storm." conveyed Jamison.

Marshal cleared his voice, "Peter woke and saw his medallion glowing, so he came in to wake Mary and me. He showed us the glowing medallion, and we rose to get ready to defend the kids. As we dressed in our coats and boots, we could see Sarah through the window walking towards a white light hovering near the old crone's house. We watched helplessly as there was a good distance between us and them. Then I saw Oboodashwaanishiinh[10] Dragonfly appear next to her. His arrow would

157

be greater than our wands so I told Mary that we should watch the event."

Oboodashkwaanishiinh[10] Dragonfly spoke, "I arrived at the time when the white light turned into a massive white buffalo. I knew that this moment was one of importance. I stayed close for I knew she was not in danger."

Robert shook his head, "It was an amazing sight to see the beast of the legend appear before her like that. The old crone was kneeling, and Jamison was yelling at Sarah from his broom."

Jamison butted in, "She is the wind, so she can control it. I instructed her to control the storm. Zaagasi Geezis[13] Shining Sun and I watched Sarah kneel and form a snow circle around her. No wind or snowflakes touched her, and the glowing light of swirling snow surrounded her. The barrier looked like a ball of whirling wind. It was obvious that the bubble protected her from the raging storm. She moved to the lady without fear."

"The old one came to Sarah." hissed Oboodashkwaanishiinh[10] Dragonfly. "I was amazed to witness the transformation of the buffalo into the White Buffalo Lady. I told Sarah to keep her eyes lowered and to listen carefully."

"The death of the men came at this time. If they looked upon the lady with lust, they would burn up from ill intent and desire for her. Obviously, those five men lusted in her beauty, and the loss was instant." recalled Robert.

"Many of us knew not to look upon her, but we needed to see the chain of events occurring. Howls of the yetis and the screech of the wendigo sounded over the blowing wind. Yet, we knew we had to witness the event and let the yetis do their job." shared Jamison.

Oboodashkwaanishiinh[10] Dragonfly hissed, "Then, with a lowered eye, I watched the ancient one's beautiful glowing hand lower the black arrow and place it in front of Sarah. I am the keeper of one, but Sarah was gifted another. There have never been two together in a long time. Then the White Buffalo lady told her not to fear Ralph, for he was coming to get her."

Wind Witch

Jack shifted in his chair, "I watched the campaign of yeti's circle in on the wendigo. The beast slashed at them, but their fur was so thick, they only lost fur with very little damage to their being as they pushed the beast out of the area. Anyway, by the time I turned around, Ralph had already grabbed Sarah and ran off with her into the woods. I didn't see the arrow because I was working with the yetis. I missed that part. What a sight that must have been."

The council was listening intently to the chain of events. A screeching, soaring owl swooped down and dropped a letter in front of Robert. He opened and read it silently, then to the council:

"Robert, it is confirmed that the yeti is heading towards the hovel with Sarah in tow. Tyrone."

Confused faces stared back at the men. Oboodashkwaanishiinh[10] Dragonfly leaned on the table, pulled his body up, and tucked into a crouch. He reached over his back, slid the black arrow out of his quiver, and laid it on the table. Everyone stopped and stared at his position and yielded in respect of the title. They readied themselves to listen to the ancient one.

He stood to his full stature and began, "Two battles, one will win, after a time of peace and times of battles among them, others would come to battle to destroy the victor and his descendants. This, dear council, was a curse put in place during a battle of the Two Brothers. My ancestors are from the old dwellers, a time before man came here and were witnesses to this battle. My father told of the two men who came to us to live with their families in this land. It is said that they were descendants of the lost tribes of the far East. They settled here, and their numbers grew throughout the nation. They fought each other for territory and resources. The story told is that each man had a black arrow in their keep. One day the two brothers and their armies battled a brutal, deadly battle. It was clear that they would fight to the death. Before the final battle, my great-grandfather was tasked with guarding the arrow, and he pledged to safeguard the victor's remaining family. That arrow is this one.

The council looked at the arrow as Oboodashkwaanishiinh[10] Dragonfly continued, "Our kind has watched

Wind Witch

generation after generation of the prophecy unfold. It all started with the arrival of the settlers. The slow destruction of the surviving brother's line began. The battle between the two brothers and other generations' disputes has been playing out through the ages. Sarah's arrow is an unexpected turn of events and is of great importance. Bringing the two together, there must be a reason."

Jamison leaned back in his chair, scratched his head, ran his fingers down the full length of his braid, and began, "One thing is clear, the wendigo could not get through the protective barrier. What is strange is the fact that he did not burn up the moment he hit the shield. He just bounced off it. I do know the children are safe while they remain inside the barrier. However, I worry about Sarah being away from the cabin."

Jack's sideways smile emerged and chuckled as he spoke, "There is nothing to worry about there. Let's say the yetis are capable of great things when protecting another. Sarah is in safe hands."

The room grew heavy as everyone pondered the events, and Mistress Gaagaapshiinh[26] Raven broke the silence, "Why are the arrows so important?"

Oboodashkwaanishiinh[10] Dragonfly lowered himself to stand on the chair and stood to answer her, "I am sorry, Mistress, we do not know. They never miss their mark, so clearly, they will be needed in the near future." Oboodashkwaanishiinh[10] Dragonfly lowered himself down in his chair to rest.

Mistress Gaagaapshiinh[26] Raven tapped her long fingernails on the tabletop. "How do we stop the beast and destroy it?"

Jack cleared his throat and spoke, "I have been told that we will need Father Unis' full name. It needs to be spoken as the beast is felled."

With a wave of a wand, Mistress Gaagaapshiinh[26] Raven summoned her owl. Through the window flew a black owl. Grey and white speckled its chest. Mistress Raven chuckled as the bird bumped its head playfully at his mistress. She stroked the black feathers lovingly, and the bird responded accordingly.

160

"We'll have Father Lyons search the records at the Vatican for his name. This may take a while." suggested the councilor.

Thank you, Mistress Gaagaapshiinh[26] Raven, Jade is still at the boarding school, and we will have her search there too." ventured Robert.

After a moment, the two leaders penned a note to their inside people. Each note requested that the records be searched for the father's name. Mistress Gaagaapshiinh[26] Raven's owl took both letters and flew off by the way it came. Everyone watched as the owls left the space.

"There's hope in the winds, now, let's see if there is help on the way." sighed Robert as he placed his coat about him. "This is the best that we can do for now. Please keep us updated."

With that, the council dispersed. The four men began to leave and noticed they were missing a person. They looked around the room and didn't see Oboodashkwaanishiinh[10] Dragonfly, so they walked up to the chair where Oboodashkwaanishiinh[10] sat. They had found that Oboodashkwaanishiinh[10] Dragonfly had fallen asleep, and Jamison picked him up and carried him in his arms.

"Poor guy, he ran miles and has been up all night watching the cabin. I guess rest had caught up with him. Let's take him back to the cabin. He can rest there." whispered Jamison.

Chapter 17:
The Hovel

Chapter XVII:
THE HOVEL

Ralph's large body shifted, and Sarah's eyes opened to a wall of white fur. She tried to wiggle away from Ralph's heavy arm, but she couldn't move. She surrendered to the warmth and cozy feeling and snuggled back in. Ralph's heaving chest kept rocking her softly with each breath he took. Sarah just reveled in the safe and secure feeling of the warm hug. With a snort and a rumbling snore, he woke himself up. He looked down his snout-like nose to see Sarah's dark eyes looking up at him.

"Good morning, Sarah," he said as he raised his arm to let the little girl loose. "I hope I didn't snore all night."

Sarah leaned up against the cave's wall and said, "If you did, I didn't notice. Thank you for keeping me warm. I slept alright."

"Good, we traveled a long way in the night. I'm getting old and too fat to keep doing things like that." Ralph tried to smile, but Sarah only saw exposed fangs.

The yeti stretched out his legs with strained difficulty. One foot nearly hit Sarah as he stretched himself out, but Sarah hurried out of the way of the massive foot that landed near her. Thick fur covered the top of his foot, and the bottom was dark and leathery in appearance. Sarah looked up to her capturer.

"I was told not to fear you, but why did you take me away from the cabin?" inquired Sarah as she walked closer to the beast.

"Jack had me watch over you. I have been sitting on top of the hill, waiting and watching. Most of the time, nothing significant happened, then, I saw the spirit elders leave the crone's cabin, and I knew something was about to happen because the air stunk with decay. When the snowstorm hit, I knew something wasn't right so I kept a close watch. Throughout the day the wind smelt so not right and stunk of a disturbance. You, young lady, need to get that anger under control." he contemplated the girl for a moment and continued, "As I sat amongst the blowing and raging snow and

163

listened to the orders of my brothers echoing through the valley. I knew danger was setting in. I saw a white light heading toward the valley, so I began to head down the ravine to the cabin. In the distance, I heard my friends howling their battle cry followed by the wendigo's screech, and I knew you were not safe. As I was running, I saw the old one transform into her original shape, and I picked up speed. Then I saw the glow of the black arrow being placed in front of you, and I knew I had to get you out of there." he shrugged.

Sarah pulled the arrow from her coat and turned it over in her hand. There was no glow like the night before emitting from it, but the blackness of the shaft and point seemed to catch the scant rays of light, and its surface seemed to shift on its own. The long black shaft was cold to the touch but unbelievably smooth. The arrow's point was well-flinted to sharp edges, and the feathers on the fletching were of a black swan.

"I do not know how to shoot a bow and arrow." she frowned as she continued to study the treasure.

The beast scoffed, "Have you ever tried?"

Sarah thought about that question for a moment. When she was little, she tried to shoot once with the boys. She remembered being chased away because she was a girl. She walked over to the beast, sat on his thigh, and pondered the question a moment.

"No, well, I wanted to. I really wanted to learn, but the men chastised me for doing so." She chewed on her lip slightly as she played with her thoughts. Her stomach growled in protest, and she looked up to the beast with a smile. "I guess I am hungry," she interjected.

"Yeah, I didn't think of that." He scratched his belly fir and said, "I didn't grab food before I grabbed you."

He shifted his body, and Sarah got up off his log-like limb. Ralph hoisted his massive haunches onto all fours and proceeded to stand. Ralph was so tall that his head hit an ice cycle that hung from the cave entrance. He rubbed his head, and he bent over to exit. Sarah watched the beast's body turn one way, and then his feet

164

shuffled in the other direction. He stooped back down and entered the cave again.

"I don't smell anything cooking for miles. I guess we will have to wait until we get to the Hovel. Now, young lady, we have to find a way to get you there. It is a long walk, and I think I better travel it in a trot or run. I can't carry you that far, and you will not be able to keep up with me on foot. Stay here; I have an idea." grumbled Ralph.

Once again, the beast exited the cave, and Sarah could hear his large feet crunch through the snow. While he was gone, Sarah sat holding the arrow. She thought, 'I am wind magic. The arrow rides in the air. Air is a part of me and is me. I guess I have something to learn. I don't even have a bow to shoot with. I don't understand why I should have this gift. She stood and began to pace the sandy cave floor. I am just a kid. What is a kid going to do with such a thing?' her thoughts ran wild with confusion.

Ralph called out to Sarah, "Come, child, it is time to go."

Sarah walked through the entrance and out into the sun. The light was so bright that she covered her eyes to protect them. As her eyes adjusted, she saw a little birch bark sled in front of her. White sheets of bark were lashed together with Ralph's white fur. Sarah's eyes surveyed the workmanship of Ralph with awe. She ran her fingers over the white fur that strapped the pieces of wood together and marveled at its beauty. Thick white knots tied in a peculiar fashion were holding the bark together. He even had fashioned a handhold on the sides for Sarah to hold on to during the ride over the snow. Sarah marveled at the sled, and smiled at Ralph's impressive gift.

Ralph yowled, and his voice rang through the trees. On the top of the hill, a white stag appeared and stood tall and proud. Puffs of frozen air poured from his nose as he trotted towards them. His fur was so white that he blended in perfectly with the snow as he approached. It came to a stop in front of Ralph. Ralph walked up to the beast, wrapped it in his arms, and rubbed his face into its fur. The beast gave a welcoming snort and nudged Ralph's body in greeting.

165

Wind Witch

The massive deer was white from head to foot except for his eyes and a few darker spots on his nose. The eight-point buck's size was impressive. Sarah marveled at how small it appeared next to Ralph and how big the buck was to her. The full of his back reached up to Ralph's waist, and Ralph laid his hand on his back as he talked to the stag. After some grunts and groans, the stag's head nodded and backed up into the sled. Ralph hooked up the sled to the deer and turned and lifted Sarah into the sled.

With a giant jolt, the deer and Ralph began to trot away from the cave, and Sarah held on to the sides as best as she could. Sarah sat watching the beast and the deer take stride for stride over the snow. With each step they took, Sarah's head would pull back against the tree bark. At first, the cold air was refreshing, but soon, it began to bite at her exposed skin. She hunkered down into her jacket and tucked herself into a little ball.

Ralph looked over to the balled-up child in the sled, halted the deer, and said, "You know, that bubble you made last night to protect yourself from the wind?" He waited for Sarah's response, "Make that bubble again, and you will warm up in no time."

With a nod, Sarah began to concentrate on the air around her. The cold air began to move. Ralph watched the air as it toyed at the fir on the deer's tail, and Ralph chuckled as his fur shifted in the blowing wind. Sarah was in a moment of silence as she focused on pulling the air around her to form an air shield. Ralph stood in amazement as he watched a ball of air surround the child in an egg-like fashion. She shifted in the sled and opened her eyes. All around her was a bubble of ice and snow stuck in patches on the shield. She smiled through the ice glass at the yeti. With a slap on the white deer's backside, they continued on their journey.

Sarah watched as the landscape slid by her. The pine trees were laden heavy with snow, and the branches hung with their weight. There was no sign of habitation anywhere, and soon, she drifted off to sleep. There, in her dreams, she dreamt of her mother and her father as they laughed together as they worked. Her father was cleaning fish to smoke. Her mother worked on a black ash basket, carefully weaving a design. With a smile, Sarah woke with

166

Wind Witch

a moment of happiness. The first happy memory she had in a long time.

The next thing she knew, Ralph was lifting her out of the little sleigh. He set her on the ground and held her until she steadied herself. She rubbed her eyes and tried to adjust her vision. As she awoke from her slumber, she noticed the White stag fleeing into the distance. With a tug on her jacket, Ralph led her to a rock wall. With a melodic howling song, a small rumble began, and a pebble or two fell to the ground as the wall opened to expose a cave. Ralph easily walked into the cave entrance and ascended down a lit cavern. She saw many shapes shifting in the distance, and they were all shaped like Ralph.

"Where are we?" asked Sarah.

"We are at our hovel. We winter here. In the summer months, we hunt and gather as your parents did." growled Ralph as he offered his large hand to Sarah, "Come with me. There are others whom you need to meet."

As the pair walked through the cave, she could see many corridors leading off in different directions. The chill in the air cooled her nose, and she stopped to adjust her jacket to keep her warm. The path wound down into a cavern, and a wide stretch of water flowed lazily through the rocks. Ralph and Sarah followed a path that ran next to the river until a bridge came into view.

When the two approached the bridge, another yeti advanced upon the two. The yeti came at a dead run across the span of the river. When he noticed Ralph, he came to a halt; he paused for a bit, kneeled, and apologized to Ralph for his behavior.

"Your honor, I am sorry to have approached in such a manner." Tyrone bowed and turned his head to look directly at Sarah. "There must be a good reason why you brought a human here."

Stand Tyrone and meet Sarah. The reason she is here is business of my own." His eyes leveled on his friend. "I believe you should follow us to the chambers. You need to witness the chain of events that are about to occur."

167

Tyrone stood and followed the pair to the chamber as he continued, "You know, she will not remember anything when she leaves here. So, why risk her visit?"

"You need to be patient, my friend. I do not want to tell the tale many times. All will be revealed in time." growled Ralph as he scratched at the fur on his face.

Sarah watched the two beasts stand face to face, talking to each other. All she heard was a series of grunts and growls coming from the two. She looked around the cavern as the beasts spoke to each other. Seeing that she couldn't understand what they were saying, she distracted herself by looking around the space. Tyrone peered at Sarah, and his gaze was stern, and Sarah backed into the safety of Ralph's tree-trunk legs. She didn't know what was going on, but it was clear that Ralph was one of power.

"Look now, you scared her, you big Olaf," growled Ralph.

Ralph grabbed Sarah's hand and began to lead her across the stone bridge. Tyrone called another sentry from the side to take charge of the bridge. Soon, Sarah watched two smaller sentries take their spaces at the bridge. As she passed the two yetis, they growled, and she assumed they said hello. With a nod, they allowed her and her companions to pass.

The walls glistened in the torch's lights. Sarah could see gold strains in the rock, and they grew in width as they traveled deeper into the earth. The light grew, and Ralph stopped just outside an opening as they traveled. Light streamed a golden hue, and Sarah's eyes danced with awe.

"Tyrone, announce Miss Sarah and I." asserted Ralph.

Tyrone dutifully turned and entered the room. The yeti took a knee, and his voice rang loud and clear through the open space. Sarah could hear Tyrone complete a series of grunts. In reply, another voice rang through the open space. Sarah watched as Tyrone took a stand and carefully retreated from the room in a respectful manner.

Tyrone turned and smiled at his friend, and Ralph nudged Sarah and they entered the room together. Ralph kneeled, and he gestured to Sarah to do the same. She lowered her eyes and shifted her tired legs to the ground. In front of Sarah was placed a medallion with a white eagle on it. She lifted the emblem from the ground and looked up to Ralph.

"Put it on; you will be able to hear all we say," whispered Ralph.

Sarah picked up the medallion and placed it around her head. She held it in her hands and looked at the fine piece of work. She felt the smoothness of the porcupine quills that formed the picture. The features of the white eagle were so detailed that they brought instant awe to the child. The white eagle was framed with darker quills that made the bird stand out magnificently. Her fingers drew across some fancy hatched work design along its edges and looked up to Ralph with a smile. As she placed the medallion around her neck, the grunts and groans were transformed into words. Her eyes widened as she listened to the whispers around her.

"My Lady Lashier and Council," Ralph spoke respectfully.

Ralph rose to his feet and walked up to the wall, where an etching had been engraved. He stood looking at a hooded woman with a bow in her hand. The image was painted white and tinted with golden threads in her robe. In the archer's hand was a black arrow like the one hidden inside Sarah's jacket.

"I believe she has returned." insisted Ralph as he gestured to the picture then turned to the council.

Sarah peered at the picture on the wall. She had never seen such beautiful work. She looked around the room, and she could see other decorated walls with similar paintings and carvings that she did not understand. Her eyes danced from picture to picture and acknowledged the serpent's image that was stationed over Lady Lashier's head.

"My dear Ralph," snapped Lady Lashier, "Why would you think that?"

169

Wind Witch

Ralph walked back over to Sarah and said, "Little one, show them your treasure."

Sarah unzipped her jacket pulled out the arrow, and held it out in front of her, and the room came alive. The chamber members began to gasp, and whispers echoed through the room. Some chamber members began to growl, and some howled, almost an angry sound. Sarah covered her ears and closed her eyes, for fear was bearing in on her.

"Ladies and Gentlemen of the chamber, you are frightening the young one. COLLECT YOURSELVES AT ONCE!" Lady Lashier yelled to the others sitting in the circle.

Lady Lashier rose from her seat and approached Sarah. Her large frame sided up alongside Ralph looked him straight in his eyes, and grunted a displeased growl. She drew herself to full height and turned and approached Sarah in a controlled manner. Sarah's eyes widened as she watched the massive form advance towards her. She kneeled to get closer to the frightened child standing in the middle of the room. She lowered her head close to Sarah to look at the arrow up close.

She smiled up at Ralph and inquired, "How did she get this?"

Ralph sighed, "As many of you know, I have been watching the cabin where Sarah has been staying. Sarah is capable of controlling the weather enough to conjure a snowstorm. During the storm, I saw the light present itself. Once I saw the light, I began to head towards the cabin. As I ran to the clearing, the White Buffalo Lady presented herself to Sarah; then, I could see the Lady laying this arrow down in front of her. The wendigo was making every attempt to get to her. Tyrone and the brothers were busy fighting the thing off. I ran in and grabbed her and went to the west tunnel, and we rested until this morning."

"My child," she said softly, "I need to see if you are the Nodin Me-koom-maa-senh[1] Wind Witch." She pointed to the wall, "Take your arrow and touch that picture with it. I don't know what will happen, but don't be scared. Go now, let's see."

170

Sarah looked around the room. Lady Lashier and the council members stared at her as she uncomfortably walked to the hieroglyph on the wall. She lifted the arrow to the picture and touched the gold inlaid rock. A low rumbling began, and a low level of shaking rock caused Sarah to step back. A light began to glow around the lower section of the pictograph, and the shaking wall began to expose a hidden drawer. Sarah watched as the rock drawer slid out, and she stepped in closer to look inside. Sarah saw a black quiver and another black arrow tucked inside.

Carefully, she reached inside and lifted the quiver in her hand. She admired the ornate decoration on the leather. An etching on the leather matched the hieroglyph on the wall. She smiled, and then she reached for the arrow. To her surprise, it jumped into her hand. Sarah startled at first then fastened her fingers around the shaft of the arrow. Slowly, she turned around to face the council. Their expression matched the stone walls, and Sarah lowered her eyes as they collected their thoughts.

"Ladies and gentlemen of the council, it is clear the Nodin Me-koom-maa-senh[1] Wind Witch has returned," announced Lady Lashier.

Sarah's eyes steadied on Ralph, and a scared smile appeared. She could see that Ralph had kneeled next to Lady Lashier. She steadied her eyes onto her friend and walked up to him. He opened his arms, and she fell into them. When she pulled back from his hug, her quiver wiggled itself from her grasp and strapped itself to her back. The arrows took flight and took a celebratory flight through the massive room and found their resting place inside the quiver. Lady Lashier held out her arms, and Sarah accepted her warm hug.

Lady Lashier pulled Sarah back to look at her, "Sarah, you are being hunted, and we need to keep you here for a short time. That pendant is yours from here onward. Once you leave here, you won't have to wear it all the time but know that you must wear it in times of need. Keep it with you."

171

Lady Lashier rose to her feet and turned to the council, "From this day forward, wherever this child is, a troupe of us must be nearby."

"My Lady Lashier, allow me the privilege of being the leader of the troupe," growled Ralph proudly.

Mistress Lacier walked up to her husband and growled, "Ah, so NOBEL of you." She turned her back on him with a scowl on her face. "I suppose you will be gone more if I approve this."

The yeti lowered his eyes at his wife, "My love, I suppose I would be gone a little more. However, I will make you a priority when my schedule allows. For now, I will have to give my time to assist the Nodin Me-koom-maa-senh[1] Wind Witch. This is important. I will train the young to be able to take my space, and then, I swear, I will return to you."

Lady Lashier turned and faced her husband, sighed and said with a nod, "Granted. Begrudgingly so. You are right. You need to be the one in charge of this mission. Train the young ones. We have no idea what is coming."

The council members began to howl and cheer. Lady Lashier lifted Sarah and placed her on a rock near the center of the room. Sarah turned to face the council, and they all bowed their heads in reverence. Ralph walked up to Sarah and stood next to her. The agreement bound the two together, and together they stood.

Chapter 18:
The Boarding School

Chapter XVIII:
THE BOARDING SCHOOL

Marcus lay in his bed as the sun rose. Another day at the hands of the nuns was not something he was looking forward to. Once Sarah left, he seemed to become Sister Mary's target. He pulled on his trousers and shirt and stood with a yawn. He paused for a moment to watch the snow as it was lofting down to land agilely on the branches of the evergreens outside. He laced up his worn-out shoes and went to find Jade so he could start his daily chores.

Jade was in the kitchen when Marcus arrived. She was leaning over a pan of water, preparing the oats for morning breakfast. She was deep in thought as she stirred the contents. Marcus walked up to her side, and Jade jumped in fright. She jumped so much that oatmeal flew through the air and littered the floor. Her eyes were wide as she steadied her gaze onto Marcus.

"Goodness boy, don't sneak up on me like that!" exclaimed Jade as she grabbed a broom and swept up the mess.

"I am sorry, Jade; I didn't mean to scare you. So, what are my chores today?" he said with an apologetic smile.

Jade stopped and stared at Marcus for a moment, "We must clean the father's office and get rid of his things. A new priest will be arriving soon." She leaned in closer to Marcus, "We have an important mission to do. I will explain more later. For now, get the bowls ready for breakfast."

After the morning chores were done, Jade grabbed Marcus and led him down the hallway and through a classroom to a closet in the back of the room. They entered the closet and closed the door behind them. Jade nudged a board loose from the wall. She placed the board aside, and Marcus could see a small hole in the wall. With her finger, she slid the wallboards aside to expose a passageway. She reached into her boot and pulled out her wand, and the black open space began to illuminate to show a space filled with boxes. She gestured her head to direct Marcus to enter the room.

174

Marcus stepped inside and walked down a hallway as Jade closed the door behind them. Marcus passed the boxes to find a library tucked away in the back of the room. His mind was full of questions because he had never seen such a library, let alone one tucked away in the back of the classroom. Jade walked up to him, smiled, and sat down in front of a burning fire. She motioned for Marcus to sit down in a chair near her.

"Marcus, you have been a great help, but I need to ask more of you." she shifted in her chair, "Next year, you will be old enough to leave the boarding school. I know you had seen me work magic when I scry and when I fought the wendigo. Your magic is different. I wish I had your brain. You see, dear boy, everything you read you never forget. This skill may be an asset in the future."

She watched the boy nod in agreement, and she rose from her chair and took a box off the shelf. She walked over, placed it on the floor, and sat back down. With prying hands, the box opened, and she looked at the papers inside.

"We have one year for you to spend as much time in here looking over the papers in these boxes. You never know which paper will be the key to solving an issue or dispute." She hesitated as she watched the boy's eyes search the bookshelves behind her. "I know this is a lot to ask, but your chores will be here. A new boy will take your place in the kitchen. I need to keep you away from Sister Mary's reach." She leaned over the box, "Today, we need to go and clean up father's office. We are looking for any hint of his full name. It may be here, in one of these boxes, but the new priest is coming, and we have to clean out his things and the important papers brought here." She rose and walked over to the fire, and the flames extinguished themselves in a muffled puff.

"Let's go and get the office done. Grab a box or two, and we will head out." Jade said in a wary tone.

The schoolchildren were heading into the schoolroom as they exited the closet. The nun looked up, and Jade smiled and said, "I need Marcus today for cleaning father's office." She held up the box in her hand, grabbed the boy's shoulder and began to lead him from the room. The nun protested and stood in front of the door

175

with her arms crossed. Jade lowered her eyes at the nun and squared her shoulders. Jade threw the box at the nun, and the nun darted out of the way. Jade's hand grabbed Marcus' shirt and she dragged him along with her through the hallway. The nun scowled at the two as Jade led the boy down the hall.

The pair opened the office door and looked at the piles of papers recklessly placed around the room. With a sigh, they began to sort and clean and process the papers into piles. Marcus and Jade worked through the day, hoping to find the father's full name on one of the documents. Pile after pile went into boxes with no name to be found. In the evening, they hauled the boxes back to the secret room.

Day after day, Marcus spent his days in the secluded room. Box after box, he viewed each sheet. Names of old and names of current attending students were written on sheets of paper. Old names of nuns and priests were handwritten in eloquent script on browning papers. The dingy, dusty smell of decay bothered his nose, but he kept on committing the information from the boxes to his memory.

In the corner of the room was a leather-covered chest that was perfect for reading. Jade put a nice reading lamp next to it and laid a makeshift cushion on top of it. Marcus spent a lot of time lounging on that chest as he paged through books and Paper. Jade watched Peter consume the contents of box after box. She loved his determination to complete the job he was given.

Marcus stumbled into their room, and Jade sat there waiting for him to arrive. She watched the boy stroll past the shelves in a downtrodden way and sat next to a slow, smoldering fire. She smiled a small smile as she admired how tall he was getting. He began to rub at his eyes, and he yawned and stretched and flopped back to rest against the chair's back. She noticed how tired he seemed to be. Her brow creased in concern as she looked at him. Even with reduced chores, Marcus always seemed tired. She wondered why.

Marcus sat with his eyes for a moment, just soaking in the warmth of the fire. He took a few deep breaths and opened his eyes and looked over to Jade. She held a box in her hands, and Marcus cocked his head sideways and looked at his friend. Jade smiled and lifted the box towards him, offering it to him. He leaned forward and grabbed the box from her.

As he took the box, she smiled, and Jade's off-tune melody of the happy birthday song commenced. Jade was so proud to be celebrating Marcus' birthday with him; she just glowed as she looked at him in a celebratory manner. She stood and belted out. 'Happy birthday to you." Marcus' smile was one of thank you. Then the tune turned onto a crying cat yelling through the room. Marcus watched her continue the tune with a half-thank-you smile on his face.

"Thank you, Jade; I had forgotten that today was my birthday." said the boy as he looked down at the box.

Jade stood watching Marcus as he shifted the box in his hands and shook it a little. He could tell it was something soft. He could hear that it didn't clang, nor did it hit on the side of the box. Jade's disposition became impatient as she waited for Marcus to open it. Her eyes feasted on Marcus' excitement as he took his sweet time opening the box.

"Aw, come on. Just open it!" she said as she bounced impatiently on her toes.

Marcus lifted one corner of the box and peeked in. The darkness inside the box revealed nothing to him. He sighed with a wide and happy expression when he peeked and lifted the lid to see the blanket lying on the bottom of the box. The woolen brown blanket greeted him. His eyes looked at Jade's fine knitting and ran his fingers gently over the knitted knots. So even and perfect. He stood and lifted the blanket out of the box to get a better look at it.

Jade smiled at the boy when he pulled the knitted blanket out of the box. She watched his eyes feast on his new blanket. Her heart soared as he swung the blanket to fly around his shoulders that wrapped itself around him and encased his growing frame in its warmth. She stood proudly, looking at the boy who was slowly becoming a man.

Wind Witch

"I made that so you can keep warmer as you read," she said.

"I appreciate this, Jade! This winter has been cold, and the trunk is too far away from the fire." Marcus muttered.

"Would you like to move the trunk?" she inquired.

"Oh no, the little nook is so comfortable. I have everything just right. Everything is in their rightful place. This blanket is the icing on the cake." he said as he snuggled into the blanket's warmth.

"CAKE!" said Jade as she suddenly jumped up and ran to the corner where she had hidden it.

Jade rushed back to Marcus with a chocolate cake in her hands. Marcus smiled at the smooth brown mountain of sugar in front of him. His eyes danced from candle to candle. He counted each of the ten candles circling the top of the cake. He smiled up to Jade with the happiest smile she had ever seen. He took a deep breath and blew the flames out one by one in a giant sweeping blow.

Jade whispered, "Don't forget to make a wish."

Marcus closed his eyes and searched his mind, and he thought, "I wish to leave this school."

The day had passed, and Marcus spent many days snuggled in his reading spot. One day, he settled himself on the top of the chest for a quiet afternoon. In the corner of his eye, he saw something small pass by the shelving. He shook his head and went back to reading. Two paragraphs later, again, there was a sudden rush of movement at the end of the shelf. Marcus was certain he saw something move.

Curiously, he got up from the chest and slowly navigated his way to the end of the shelf. He peeked around the corner, and nothing was there. He shook his head in confusion and went back to work reading. He pulled his blanket over his legs, staring down the aisle hoping to see what was in this room. Marcus' eyes did not leave that spot as he leaned mindlessly to grab the book on the table. Suddenly, a sharp pain rang through his hand.

Marcus' head snapped quickly to where the book rested, and there he stood. A little man about two feet tall with a fur hat and buckskin jacket. Marcus quickly scanned the little man's form from his hat down to the little man's moccasin-like shoes. The little man gave Marcus a little wave, bowed and disappeared in a dead run into the darkness of the room. Marcus looked down at his hand and noticed a set of little teeth marks lying on his skin. He thought, 'He bit me.' Marcus began to rub his finger and scowled down the aisle as he picked up his book to read.

Whispers filled the room, and Marcus thought he could hear people talking. At first, he thought he was missing class again and went to check the classroom. No one was in there. He wondered what the voices were he was hearing. He closed the closet door and then the sliding door and retreated to the room. He shook his head and walked back to take a seat on the chest. As he rounded the end of the shelving, he saw him again, sitting on the trunk. The little man smiled, waved, jumped up onto his feet and ran off in another direction. Marcus heard whispers and giggles come from behind him, and he turned to see the little man again. Marcus took a step in his direction, but once again, he ran off. Who was the little man, he did not know. Quickly, he grabbed his things and left the room for the day, feeling as if he was losing his mind.

Dreams of the chest interrupted his rest night after night. The little man came to visit him in his dreams, taunting him and laughing at him. One night, the little man made the chest explode, causing Marcus to wake up. The following night, the little man hung the chest up in the air, and no matter how hard Marcus tried to get it, he couldn't. In his dreams, he could hear the little man laughing at Marcus as he tried to catch the trunk in a cat-and-mouse-style game. Marcus came to the point where he didn't want to sleep anymore because his dreams were so bonkers.

Jade watched Marcus one morning from across the room as she ate. Marcus' eyes drooped, and she could see he was about to fall asleep in his bowl of oatmeal. Unfortunately, Sister Mary saw him too. Jade watched as the old nun rounded up on the boy and hit him squarely across his head, sending him to the floor. He

179

landed on his side, and the long-faced nun leaned over him and glared down at him.

"You're a lazy little gimp. Skipping work in the kitchens, are you?" She pulled Marcus up to his feet and, bent him over the table and beat him in front of the whole group of students. "There she said with a smile, maybe that will wake you up so you can get to work on your chores." She spat in his food and left the room.

Jade didn't dare to move from her place to help Marcus. She watched him as another nun forced him to sit down and eat the bowl of spit-laden food. Her stomach turned as she watched the whole scene defensively. Her soul ached when Marcus started heaving vomit. She covered her ears at the nun's cackling laughter. Helplessly, she watched the boy's torment as the nun scooped a spoonful of defiled oatmeal into the defenseless boy's mouth. The helplessness she felt at that moment, she will never forget. Once the nuns left the boy, Jade took him to her room to clean him up.

"Marcus, why are you so tired? Your chores have lessened, and the nuns say your studies haven't been very good." She said as she removed the vomit-covered shirt from his body.

Marcus' downtrodden eyes were clouded over from the trauma he just experienced, but he met his gaze in Jades' eyes, "My dreams keep waking me up. I can't shake them. This little man keeps playing tricks on me in my dreams. He won't leave the trunk alone. Last night, the trunk chased me all through the school. I just fear going to sleep because I don't know what that little man will do next."

Jade walked over to the cabinet, drew out a bag of chamomile tea and set to prepare a cup for Marcus, "A little man? I don't understand."

"Jade, he runs all over the back room playing tricks on me. He pokes me and runs away while I am reading. One day, he even put a toad in the box. The thing jumped out and hit me in the face when I opened the box. Now, the little man is in my dreams. I just don't want to go to sleep." scowled Marcus. "I definitely don't sleep all night, thanks to him."

Jade handed him a cup, "Little people are tricksters. He's tricking you for some reason. This didn't start until you made the trunk your reading spot. I find that very odd, don't you?"

"Yes, that's when it all started." as he sipped on his tea.

Later that evening, Jade and Marcus ventured to the box to see if they could figure out what the small man wanted. They ventured to the room but found that the chest was locked and no key was near. Jade used an unlocking spell, but the chest just shook, and the locks stayed fastened. With a shrug, they left the space to return to Jade's room. She prepared a tonic for sleeping and sent him to bed with the medicine's warmth soothing his body.

Marcus' slumber was peaceful at first, then his nightmare began. The little man once again showed himself; this time, he had a clump of keys in his hands. Marcus knew immediately they were Sister Mary's keys. The little man smiled, threw the keys at him, and ran away. As not to get hit by the keys, he tried to catch them. The startled jump his body made woke him from his dream. He looked around his bed and didn't find the keys, so he knew it was a message from the little guy. He knew what he had to do.

In frustration, Marcus rose from his bed and slipped on his shoes in the dark. Boys in the room slumbered, and no one noticed him move from his bed. Carefully, Marcus opened the door to the hallway to find it barren. Slowly, he made his way out and closed the door behind him. A sudden stream of light showed through the window. Marcus followed its beam back through the window to stop his sites on the moon. He lingered in her light for a moment, then turned back to his chore.

The moon's light faded as the clouds passed her, and darkness filled the hallway. Marcus blinked a few times to help his eyes adjust to a darker room. As he stood there, he thought, 'Now, to get those keys. I know that's what he wants me to do.' Marcus smiled a little mischievous smile, for he had an idea how to get them, too. He made his way down the darkened hall to retrieve the sister's keys.

Marcus rounded the corner of the nun's room when he heard her snoring through the door. He reached for the doorknob and gave it a twist. 'Locked,' he thought. He passed the door and made his way to the basement area. Near the washtub was a dumb waiter who went right up to her room. He opened the little door that concealed it and found a full set of clean clothes for the nun to dress in in the morning. Carefully, he placed the folded clothes on the chair, crawled into the small box and began to hoist himself up to her room.

Pull by the pull of the dumbwaiter's rope, the sister's snoring became louder. Carefully, he tied the rope to the side to secure his escape. Slowly, he opened the little door in her room to look around. In the corner sat her bed with a little nightstand nearby. He could see the outline of the keys nestled there. Slowly, he emerged from the waiter and tiptoed to the nun's bed. The little man appeared next to the keys. He smiled at Marcus, and Marcus' heart began to beat hard. He didn't know if he was going to help him or play another trick on him. Sister Mary startled awake, and her eyes opened and focused in on the little man standing on the table.

Marcus froze to watch the pair. Sister Mary's eyes were wide as she looked at the little man. The little man took a bow, reached into his side bag, and pulled out a pouch. He poured some powder onto his hand. He walked over the edge of the table and blew the dust into the sister's face. Instantly, her body collapsed onto the bed, and snoring commenced. Marcus stifled a laugh as he looked at the couple in the moonlight.

Marcus' eyes met the little man's, and he nodded. The little man walked to the keys and made the keys levitate in midair. Silently and swiftly, the keys drifted over to Marcus and landed in his hand. The little man bowed and vanished into thin air. Peter returned to the waiter and exited the room, leaving the snoring nun undisturbed.

Carefully, Marcus navigated his way to the classroom and through the hidden door to the room of his studies. Marcus lit his lamp, approached the chest, and came to a stop in front of it. He looked down at the loop of keys and wondered which he needed to

182

get it open. Key after key, he was met with no success. After the seventh key, he found the one that unlocked the trunk.

His tired body yelled from weariness, but his excitement increased when the key turned. With a click, the first latch flung open and the second one unhinged. He lifted the heavy lid and shifted the lamp to expose old moth-eaten clothes tucked inside. One by one, Marcus pulled its contents out of the trunk. Letters and pictures of Father's Unis' childhood unfolded in front of him. Baseball cards, an old glove, pictures of his parents and siblings, and an old trophy. With a yawn, Marcus continued to look through the trunk.

At the bottom of the trunk was a large envelope. Marcus picked it up, slid out the papers, and laid them out in the light. Marcus picked up the Father's parents' death certificates to find out the cause of death. He nodded in sympathy because he lost his parents the same way, consumption. He placed the papers down and grabbed the next object. On the front of the envelope were the words, 'To my grandson.' He opened the ornate envelope and took out the card. On the front flap was written 'Happy birthday!'. His fingers worked to pull out the card with gaudy painted dogs on the front. He began to skim over the writing inside, and with a quick breath, he stopped to read the inscription written inside. Marcus paused with wide eyes and thought, 'I must show Jade.'

With the help of the little man, he found the Father's given name. He tucked the letter into his shirt, threw the contents back into the trunk, and latched it. He grabbed the lamp and rushed out of the space to go and wake Jade. He rushed out of the darkened classroom and down the hallway. He carefully navigated through the corridors and made it safely to stand next to Jade's bed.

Marcus lit a light in the room and shook Jade's shoulder to wake her. Jade struck Marcus across his face out of fear. As soon as her mind cleared, she saw that she had just struck Marcus. She threw her body up out of bed, grabbed the boy, and held him tight.

"I am so sorry, Marcus. I, I, I just. I didn't know it was you." she began to sob as she held him.

Wind Witch

"Jade, it is alright. I should have been more careful. Please stop crying; I must show you something. I found out what the little man wanted," stated Marcus as he rubbed his cheek.

Jade's eyes grew wide as she watched the boy unbutton his shirt. She watched him as he drew out the card and placed it into her hand. Her eyes rose to meet Marcus, and he smiled with a look of success. She turned the card over in her hand and opened it to read it.

A smile appeared on her face, and she peered at the boy with a smile and said, "Amazing. You are amazing. Where did you find it?"

Marcus smiled at her and set Sister Mary's keys on the side table. Her eyes went wide with acknowledgement, and her eyes fixed on the boy with fright. I snuck into her room through the dumb waiter to find the little man waiting for me. Sister Mary woke up and saw him standing on her table. He blew something in her face, and she passed out face down on her pillow. She didn't see me at all, and the little guy helped me by floating the keys to me. I made my way out of the room to the trunk, opened it, and found the trunk belonged to Father Unis. In the trunk was this. This is what we were looking for, right?"

Jade grabbed the boy, gave him a huge hug, and twirled him around mid-air. She placed him down on the floor, fluffed his hair, and rushed out the door to the main room. Marcus regained himself and stood watching Jade's shadow enter the other room. She rushed around her room, gathering supplies. He followed her to the soap rack and watched her take down the black soap, and she rushed to get some water. With a plunk, the soap rested on the bottom of a mason jar. Jade stepped back for a moment and began to watch the water.

The water began to stir. Black ooze began to sluff off the bar and began to churn its darkness into the water. Swirls of darkness danced through the water and consumed the whole cup with blackness. Marcus' eyes glanced up at Jade, and she returned his glance with a smile.

"It is ready." She explained as she lifted the soap out of the jar and placed it back onto the shelf.

"Ready? Ready for what?" replied Marcus.

"To conceal the truth, to hide the words, to make a secret message. Only the one who needs it will be able to see it." murmured Jade as she reached for a cloth on the table.

"Just watch," explained Jade.

Marcus watched Jade dip the cloth into the blackened water. Jade's fingers wrung out the drippage and carefully began to rub the material over the words. Letter by letter, Marcus watched Father Unis' name disappear in front of his eyes. As his eyes focused on the card, he could see no evidence of the inscription inside.

"How is that going to help? You can't see his name," exclaimed Marcus.

Jade smiled at him in excitement, "Oh, my dear boy, there are ways to see this message. When it is time, his name will be revealed."

Jade walked to a bedside table and opened the drawer to pull out her wand. She made a quick flick, placed it back into her drawer, and walked to the window to wait. As she waited, she wrote the name 'Sarah Shingwak' on the envelope. She also wrote, "black soap." A moment later, Jade's brown owl landed on the windowsill. She walked over to the opened window, gave the letter to him, and sent him on his way.

Wind Witch

Chapter 19:
The Christmas Tree

Chapter XIX:
THE CHRISTMAS TREE

Marshal stared at the empty seat at the table where Sarah sat. Weeks had passed, and there was no news of her safety. Jack had assured them that she was totally safe at the hovel with Ralph. The boys were unusually silent as they picked at their roast beef dinner. The days with the crone seemed to challenge them for some odd reason, and they sat silently, considering the daily lesson. Marshal scooted his chair back, creating a loud noise with his chair.

"I know we are all missing Sarah, but it is time to get ready for Christmas." he mumbled, "quickly eat so we can go and get a tree."

Mary smiled at her husband as she watched the boys shove food in their mouths and leave the table to get ready to go. Verna glanced sideways at the couple and smiled. She turned and listened to Chavo's laughing as he dressed, and they could hear Peter shuffling around. Soon, the boys came out of their room bundled up in heavy sweaters and layers of pants for trudging through the snow. With a small spurt of chaos, the guys headed out the door, leaving Mary and Verna behind.

The moonlight shone bright, and the cold air stung their exposed skin. Marshal inspected the boys and pulled their hoods up over their heads. He could see that their breath was already collecting ice on their scarves. With a wave of his wand, an axe, rope, and saw appeared and floated near the boys.

"Will you two carry those for me?" Marshal said. "I'll carry the rope. I want you two to hang on to it so we don't lose each other."

The snow glistened in the moonlight, and the path to the crone's house was clear. Step by step, their boots crunched through the snow, announcing their position as they proceeded through the woods. Sarah's snowstorm brought in so much snow that trudging through the snow was difficult for the guys. As they passed the crone's cabin, they could see her tending to some of her chores. She smiled and waved as they walked down the path.

Soon, Marshal drew to a stop. He waited for the boys to catch up with him. The moonlight glens spread before them. The trees' shadows spilled across the snow, and the men just stood for a moment to take in its beauty. After a while, Marshal took a knee and coaxed the boys to do so too.

Marshal bowed his head and closed his eyes. The boys watched him as he began to shimmer. At first, the boys thought the moon's light was glowing on his back until the light spread out in front of them. Radiating light traveled through the snow and into the trees. The boys watched as one tree began to glow. Marshal opened his eyes with a smile to view the tree that agreed to be their Christmas tree.

"There we go, boys. Let's go and meet our Christmas tree," said Marshal with a gleaming smile.

Chavo stood staring at Marshal and whispered, "You are glowing. Marshal, you are glowing!"

"Of course I am. I am connected with the trees. I asked them to choose one to be our tree this year." he smiled as he looked at the tree. "Just so you know, it hurts all the trees and me when a tree is cut. I chose to stay connected so that I could ease their pain. As you cut, I can reduce the pain for the others. So, you see, it will be your job to cut as I work to soothe them." He looked each boy square in the eyes. With a nod, he set off for their Christmas tree.

Marshal pulled out a pouch from his pocket and opened it. With his large fingers, he reached inside and took a pinch of (A)Sema[15] tobacco and offered it at the trunk of the tree. The boys watched the man with new appreciation. He offered them the pouch, and they followed his example.

"Thank you for giving me your life," Marshal reverently spoke.

As Marshal remained kneeling at the tree's trunk, he nodded to the boys. The boys began to cut at the trunk. With each blow or cut they made, they could see Marshal flinch, and a few times, he groaned. The boys worked as quickly as possible to cut and sever the tree. Once in a while, the boys had to stop to watch Marshals' energy surge through the woods. His groan would cause them to pause, and he would signal them to keep going. Once the tree was cut, Marshal once again laid (A)Sema[15] tobacco in thanks, rose from his knees, and led the boys from the woods with the tree dragging behind them.

Mary and Verna were busy popping corn for decorations when the boys entered the cabin. The cold air lofted in as the boys entered the room. Coats and boots moved to their place next to the fire and dried themselves. The boys sat at the table where thread and needles were laid for stringing popcorn.

"So, Marshal, did you show off for the boys?" whispered Mary as she handed him a bowl of popcorn.

"Yes, seeing that they were here, I could help the other trees. You know I don't like to hurt them. What I do helps them." Marshal said with a smile. "I love to give thanks that way."

Verna settled next to Chavo, "Isn't it an amazing thing he can do?"

Chavo's eyes widened. "He glows. His light just spread across the forest. Waves and waves of light coming from him." The excited tone was accented as he thrashed his arms about.

Peter's arms flew in the air as if he was cutting at a tree, and he tried to show light traveling across the snow. Mary stood smiling as the boys shared their version of the event. Verna's eyes danced back and forth between them, and giggled.

"I was amazed the first time I had seen him do that, too." chuckled Verna as she picked up her needle and thread. "We were much younger when I saw it for the first time." She picked up a kernel of corn and pushed it onto the needle. "And I had a hard time staying on task because I was amazed by the light."

"Oh, I remember that. I practically had to cut the tree down myself," murmured Mary.

189

Wind Witch

"Everyone has their magic. I just never saw magic like his." Verna said as she looked at the boys who were concentrating on stringing corn. "You know, energy magic, as you saw tonight, is different than the energy we use with our wands." The boys lowered their popcorn to listen, "Everyone's energy is different. Different wands use different energy sources. Marshal must be part Native American because he connects to the earth's energy without his wand. Trees are his friends. He communes with them and learns from them."

"Isn't that why Zaagasi Geezis[13] Shining Sun can grow plants even in the winter?" asked Chavo.

"Yes, she does indeed have that understanding, but with plants," said Mary.

"So, I am earth magic." wrote Peter, "I should be able to do something like Marshal or Zaagasi Geezis[13] Shining Sun?"

"We don't know yet." Marshal shook his head. "We know that you can work with the fire skills, but you really haven't focused on your earth abilities. There are so many things on the earth that you may be able to work with." He yawned and stood up. "The old crone said you have shown promise with plants, but she thinks there is more to you." He walked over to the tree and began to work to get it to stand. "I can help, but right now, the earth sleeps. We'll play more with your skills in the spring." He stood back, admiring the tree as it stood in the living space.

Mary sided up to her husband's side hugged him, and said, "Another beautiful tree, my love." and walked back to the table and began to help string the popcorn.

Chapter 20:
Black Ash Tree

Chapter XX:
BLACK ASH TREE

In the distance, Mary could see the form of a man emerge from the distance. As she watched the man approach, she could see that he was limping along on snowshoes. He neared closer; she could see Jack was coming for a visit. She smiled and called out to Marshal.

"Well, well, well, my love, we have a visitor. Oh, wait! There are two!" She turned to look at the men sitting at the table.

With a rush, the men stood from the table and pushed each other aside to peer out the window. They watched as the figure approached, and behind him was a white wall of fur following him. The boys fixed their eyes on the approaching pair and became excited. They quickly began to pull on their jackets, slipped on their boots, and rushed out the door.

They ran up to Jack and Tyrone and became immediately disappointed when they saw that the beast was pulling a tree behind him and not a sled. They had great hope that Sarah was coming home, and the heavy disappointment caused them to go silent. They stood still as they watched the odd couple pass by them. The boys became confused by the tree. They thought it must be important because the odd couple wouldn't have brought it.

Jack stooped down, unfastened his snowshoes, and then went to work untying the rope. The boys watched the pair discuss the place to set the tree. With a nod, Tyrone lifted the tree and tossed it next to the barn like it was a piece of firewood. The boys stood in awe at the beast's strength. Silently, they watched Jack turn and walk to the cabin. Tyrone grunted and followed behind him, and the boys followed the large beast.

Mary and Verna waited for the men to return from the cold. They didn't hear cheering and merriment and knew that Sarah hadn't returned. An odd silence filled the kitchen as each woman dealt with their disappointment. A mother's disappointment runs deep, and the two ladies' emotions reeked in the air. They tossed

192

and turned their thoughts in their heads. Pouts and held back tears threatened to burst from their beings. Sniffles and wiped-away tears sounded silently from the pair in the kitchen as they waited for the men to return.

Loud thumping sounds began to sound on the porch. Quickly, the ladies dried their tears and pulled themselves back to reality. They smiled as they heard the boys kicking snow off their boots, and they knew the men would arrive soon. Mary turned to greet her friends and stopped immediately as she watched the wall of fur enter the door. The beast's massive body had to shift to make its way through the entryway.

"Well, Tyrone, that is one impressive entrance. It's been ages since I have seen you," smirked Mary as she waved her wand to make the ceiling rise to accommodate his size.

With a nod, Tyrone smiled and said, "Yes, at least a few years. I am here with Jack to bring you news of Sarah."

"Finally, we have news! Sit down, everyone, and rest. Let Verna and I finish setting tea so we can all listen to you." suggested Mary as the two women continued their work.

A knock sounded on the door, and the two boys jumped up and rushed to the door. Peter turned the knob and peeked through the crack. Zaagasi Geezis[13] Shining Sun stood staring at the boy and smiled. Peter opened the door wide, and the old crone wandered through the door.

"I saw the two of you coming through the clearing. I hope you have news about Sarah," she said as she slid her coat off her shoulder.

"We do, and it is nothing little," sneered Jack as he removed his smudging tools from his bag. "I will need your assistance again, young man. The yeti's news is of much importance."

The company of the cabin knew the news was of significant weight, or Jack wouldn't smudge the company and ask Peter to assist. Everyone took their place at the table as Jack

193

prepared the smudge. Smoke lofted into the air. Jack worked to clean everyone's spirit. Once the ceremony was complete, Jack offered (A)Sema[15] tobacco to Peter for his work, and Peter took it willingly. Jack cocked his head at Tyrone, and Peter understood.

Everyone watched as the boy carried the (A)Sema[15] tobacco to stand next to the yeti. Once he grabbed onto the beast, he laid the (A)Sema[15] tobacco on the smudging pan's coals and added Mshkwodewashk[14]sage into the pan. The smoke began to rise, and Peter's eyes closed.

Smoke enveloped Peter and Tyrone, and soon, the smoke took shape. A circle of yetis stood around Sarah and Ralph. They heard the story and watched as Sarah retrieved the quiver and another arrow from the drawer. It was apparent that confusion was creeping in on those who were watching. They gasped when Lady Lashier presented Sarah as the "Nodin Me-koom-maa-senh[1] Wind Witch" to the council.

"Did the council know what is a Nodin Me-koom-maa-senh[1] Wind Witch?" muttered Mary.

"We don't know, but this is very old magic. One we are not sure of," growled Tyrone.

"Sarah is in need of training," replied Jack as he turned to face the crone. "You know we are children of the stars, and she needs to consult the ancient ones." He walked over to the fire and peered into the flames. "The ancients are awakening, and Sarah is the sign of their return." Jack turned to his friend, "Marshal, Tyrone, and I have brought you a black ash tree; please prepare a bow and some arrows for Sarah's return."

The door cracked open, and Oboodashkwaanishiinh[10] Dragonfly appeared through the door. "I have been sent. I dreamt that I was needed here." The old creature removed his sheepskin coat and laid it on a drying rack. "In my dream, the old ones woke. I saw Sarah; she was given a second black arrow." As he looked at the faces around him, "You mean to say that there are three Black arrows?" Oboodashkwaanishiinh[10] Dragonfly said slowly as he gawked at his friend's expression. He pulled his hands to his head in disbelief. He turned to face Tyrone and said, "So, it is true; the Nodin Me-koom-maa-senh[1] Wind Witch has returned."

Jack walked to his friend, "Sarah will return here in 2 days. Ralph and she are on their way back at this very moment. I just ask you to train her to shoot and help Zaagasi Geezis[13] Shining Sun to help her connect to the ancient ones." Jack turned and sat at the table and rested his hands on his feather, "I fear for Sarah. To practice our ways could mean that she could be imprisoned if she is discovered. Our ways come with a price; many medicine men have paid their price with death. We must be careful to keep her safe as she grows into her powers."

Zaagasi Geezis'[13] Shining Sun's eyes were wide with acknowledgement, "Peter's dad, my cousin, paid dearly with his death." Zaagasi Geezis'[13] Shining Sun walked up to Peter and said, "You, boy, know very well that they will never stop hunting you for your skills." The fire sparked, and a loud crackling noise shot out from the embers. And she looked at Peter, "My boy, we have work to do. Grieving your dad is natural, but one must keep those powers under control, or you'll set the forest ablaze by accident."

Oboodashkwaanishiinh[10] Dragonfly slithered over to Tyrone, "Is that ash tree for constructing bow for Sarah?"

"Yes," growled the beast. "Black ash trees sacrificed a tree for the making. The old ones spoke that the bow must be made from it."

The creature limped over to Marshal, "My friend, your skills will be needed. I will instruct you in its construction." He looked at the crone, "My lady, your teaching will be needed in making a bowstring once we are done. He took out the arrow from its quiver, "Three, I only thought there were two. I didn't know there were more than two. I do not know what will happen when the other two arrows come to life with this one. Uncertain times we have here."

The tea kettle sang and snapped everyone out of their heavy thoughts. The air was thick with uncertainty as everyone took a seat at the table. Tea and treats were served to the group. No

195

Wind Witch

one seemed to notice the silence as they settled into their thoughts as they sipped and snacked. Once they finished, the men rose to go out and inspect the tree. They hauled the tree to the work shed, and the boys followed behind them.

Chapter 21:
Sarah's Return

Chapter XXI:
SARAH'S RETURN

Christmas Eve, Marshal rose with a start. Wolves were howling through the woods. He quickly grabbed his gun and pulled on his pants. He rushed through the house to the front door and squinted to peer through the darkness. He could see wolves darting back and forth, playing in the snow. In the distance, he heard another howl ring through the trees, and all the wolves came into the clearing, continuing their midnight dance.

In the distance, Marshal heard another howl ring through the trees, and all the waiting wolves sat down on their haunches and waited. The wolves sat panting with a smile on their jowls, and Marshal's excitement grew. A moment later, Marshal could see a sled team coming towards him. Alongside the sled, he could see Ralph jogging along with it. With a quick turn, he ran back into the house.

"Wake up, everyone! Sarah! Sarah is home!" rang his loud voice through the cabin.

The rush of movement inside the cabin was complete chaos. Coats, boots, and hats were retrieved from the fireplace. People's arms flew over each other's heads as they stretched out their arms and pulled on their jackets. The boys pushed each other out of the way and ran to the door and rushed to the porch.

The two boys watched as the wolves pulled the sled across the valley. When the team passed, the pack that lined the path bowed their head out of respect. When the sled passed the waiting members, the brethren of the pack howled as if they were singing to them in honor. Marshal had never seen such a sight and marveled at the event. Once the sled slid to a stop, Ralph unfastened the tethered wolves, and they ran off the join their pack. He smiled as he watched them hop, skip, and play with the other pack members. The two young boys just stood in their spaces, taking in the night's events.

198

Ralph uncovered the sleeping child, and she rose sleepily and stretched. As she rose to her feet, Marshal could see the child did indeed have a quiver tied to her back. Sarah straightened her jacket and turned to face her friends with a smile. She jumped out of the sled and ran to greet the onlookers. She flew into Marshal's arms and held him tightly. The boys stared in amazement as they watched the wolves run into the woods. They approached Sarah, but they didn't hug her. They just bounced around her and turned her around to look at her quiver. With a ruffle of her hair, they stood aside and let Mary and Verna join in the hugs and celebration of Sarah's return.

"What an adventure that was," growled Ralph. This child has caused great wear on me." His smile-like grin shone brightly. When Jack asked me to watch over her, I never had any idea that I was taking on this huge job." He lowered himself to the ground in exhaustion. Marshal, can I rest in the barn for the night? I need room to spread out."

With a chuckle, Marshal turned and looked at the barn and said, "Let's go, my friend; I think we better get you rest. I know you and Sarah have traveled a long way."

The two women tended to Sarah. In the midnight hour, they escorted her to her room. The quiver would not unfasten for them, so Sarah helped them to remove it. When Sarah touched the buckle, it loosened at her touch. Sarah laid the quiver by her bedside, and she allowed them to continue to dress her in her nightgown. Verna summoned a late-night snack, and Sarah ate with vigor. With a yawn, she snuggled into her bed and fell asleep almost instantly. As the ladies closed the door, they gave each other a hug and celebrated that their family was once again together.

Wind Witch

Chapter 22:
Nibaanimaang[43]

Christmas

QR Codes: Chapter 22

Scan to hear the language

#	Chapter	Anishinaabemowin	English	QR Code
42	Ch. 22	Nibaanimaang	Christmas	

Chapter XXII:
NIBAANIMAANG[(43)] _{CHRISTMAS}

Sarah woke to the smell of breakfast. She could smell bacon, biscuits, sausage, and coffee lofting through the air. A sudden hunger and pain bit at her insides, causing her to cringe a bit. She thought, 'All right, Stomach, I'm getting up. No dried nuts and berries today!' She flung off her blankets and jumped out of bed. She smiled at her comfortable slippers and slid her feet into them. She smiled and did a little victory dance before leaving her room.

Though her excitement of being home pushed her feet into moving, she really felt like going back to bed. She shrugged off the feeling and thought, 'I have more important things to do,' and exited the door. Sarah stumbled down the hallway, she was so surprised about how foggy her head was. She could feel that she needed rest, but the drive to move into action drove her more. She was home, and she craved the companionship of her friends. The time with the yetis and the long travel wore on her, but she drove herself to push her feet down the hallway. She was home, and her soul thirsted for human companionship.

The boys were at the table, and their merriment filled the air. They seemed to be happier than Sarah ever remembered. As she walked out to the kitchen, the quiver followed behind her and fastened itself to her. The boys watched in amazement as the clasps of the quiver's flashings fastened themselves to Sarah. They stood still until Sarah settled into her seat.

As her eyes cleared, she could see that the cabin was decorated for Christmas. She looked around the room and realized how long she had been gone. Weeks had passed since she left, but she didn't know it was that long. She realized that she had no sense of time while in the cave. Her head whirled at the thoughts of the time she had lost.

Sarah's eyes searched the room and smiled at the sparkling Christmas tree in the corner. Underneath the tree were packages wrapped in fancy paper. Sarah's eyes danced around the room with

202

Wind Witch

all the decorations. Christmas did not look like this at school. She smiled at the boys who were watching her intently. She gave a slight giggle because she could see they were about to explode with questions.

Sarah took a bite of bacon and let the tastebuds revel in its salty goodness. When she opened her eyes, the boys were at a dead stare. She looked down at the straps around her and touched the buckle to remove the quiver. The boys watched as the quiver unfastened itself and settled on the table next to her. The boys eyed the black feathers resting above the quiver's top. Their bodies shifted back and forth as they inspected Sarah's gift. Their eyes feasted on the blackened leather, and their eyes danced across the gold-plated leather design etched into the black quiver. Sarah took notice of their expressions and smiled.

"Would you like to see them?" inquired Sarah as they quickly nodded. "I never thought I was meant for these," she said as she retrieved one of the arrows from the quiver and laid it on the table.

The long black shaft seemed to shift and move, almost like shifting clouds. Once the boys watched them closely, they could see that it was only the light catching on the shaft. The black fletching was trimmed into sharp points. Chavo reached out to touch it, and the arrow lifted itself and returned to the quiver.

"They don't like to be touched. I can touch them, but no one else can." shared Sarah as she watched the arrow settle back into the quiver.

"We have heard that you are being called the Nodin Me-koom-maa-senh[1] Wind Witch," stated Chavo.

"Yes, the yeti's made sure I knew my new name." frowned Sarah.

"It's Christmas! No frowns are allowed here!" said Verna with a giggle.

Wind Witch

"Christmas? Nibaanimaang[40]?" Sarah looked around the house. "Today is Nibaanimaang[40] Christmas? I have been gone for four weeks?" exclaimed Sarah.

"Oh yes, we waited a long time for you to return," said Mary.

Marshal wandered out from his bedroom and plopped down in his chair. Mary poured a cup of coffee for him and sent it to settle in front of him. He rubbed his eyes groggily and looked around the table. It was obvious he had a long night for sleep, and it was still lingering in his eyes. He glanced over at Sarah and smiled, then glanced down at the resting quiver. He smiled then with a spark in his eyes; his grin grew wider when he looked at the boys. Marshal sat up and admired the young lady.

"Well, let's eat breakfast and then unwrap gifts." chuckled Marshal as he watched the boys' excitement.

The meal was devoured in minutes, and the dishes were washing themselves in the sink. Mary and Verna sat down at the table to relax and sip their coffee. Marshal sat in his chair, and, with his full belly, sleep threatened to lull him back to bed. The boys sat as patiently as they could, but excitement overtook them.

Peter wrote, "Is it time?" he nudged Marshal, who startled awake.

Marshal stretched and yawned, and he slid the note over to his wife. Mary read it and passed it on to Verna. She smiled, and with a wave of her hand, gifts lofted up from the air and settled in front of the kids. The kids hadn't received gifts on Nibaanimaang[42]Christmas for a long time. So, seeing the shiny gifts in front of them brought them such excitement.

A long package landed in front of Chavo. He smiled up at Mary and Marshal and smiled and opened it instantly and held up a spear. The spear was long and lean with a flint tip. He held it in his hand and found it to be well-balanced. He stood up and lifted it over his head with a smile. Thrusted a few jabs into the air and smiled at Marshal, ran over, and gave him a big hug. Chavo sat back down at the table to watch the others open gifts.

Wind Witch

Peter looked at his gift before him and began to unwrap the treasure within. He pulled and ripped at the paper and found a bundle inside. Slowly, he unrolled the bundle, and he found a belt woven with beads and knotted decorations sewn into the leather. There was an empty space in the centre of the belt in the very front, and Peter wondered why. There was a letter inside the package, and he opened it and read,

"Merry Christmas, Peter,

This belt was made with knot magic. Once you place the spider coin into the open space, it will stay safe in the belt. If you wear the belt, you will never lose it. Also, the knots are knots of protection.

Sincerely,

Zaagsi Geezis[13] Shining Sun."

Peter retrieved the coin from his pocket. He slipped the spider coin into the open spot. Before he could look away, he saw the loose threads wrapped around each other and securely cinched together. He watched as the ends of the strings tucked themselves into the weave and disappeared. Peter smiled as he looked at how nice the design and the coin looked together. He slipped the belt around his waist, and he cinched the buckle tight. If the old crone was there, he would have given her a thank-you hug.

From the corner, a long package lofted through the air and came to rest in front of Sarah. The boys and Marshal began to smile from ear to ear. Their eyes watched closely as Sarah's hands unwrapped the package. She could see the wooden longbow emerge through the paper. Her eyes widened as she picked up the bow. She smiled and admired the fine work the guys had done. The ash longbow was the finest thing she had ever seen. On the limb, there were designs imprinted on them, and the leather on the handgrip was soft to the touch. Her hands ran over the length of it, admiring their work.

"Thank you! How did you make this?" reverently expressed Sarah.

The boys talked about Jack's and Tyrone's visit when they brought the ash tree. They re-enacted the beating of the wood into strips. Then, Marshal used his magic to dry the strips so they could be glued together in the proper shape of the bow. Chavo showed Sarah how each layer was stacked on each other to give the bow its strength. The boys recounted the moment Oboodashkwaanishiinh[10] Dragonfly drew the runes on the limb. The boys didn't miss a step, and Marshal beamed with pride.

A knock on the door sounded, and the yeti folded himself into the cabin. In his giant pawlike hand, he held a package. With a silly smile, he handed the package to Sarah, "Here, little one. This is for your bowstring."

Sarah opened the package to see strains of long white fur. Strains and strains of fur lined the paper in front of her. She looked at her friend and could see the areas where his fur had been cut. The yeti shifted in an embarrassed manner and smiled lovingly at her. Sarah's eyes widened, and her heart filled with love. She rose from her chair and ran to hug him. Ralph pulled her back, kneeled in front of her, and gave her a big hug.

Sarah whispered in his ear, "Thank you, Ralph, for everything." She looked over at the package sitting on the table and back at her friend, "You shouldn't have. I am thankful. But your fur."

Ralph said, "It will grow back soon. The wind will be a little colder for a while." he said with a sly smile.

Sarah walked to the table and, with a confused expression, asked, "How do I make a bowstring with this?"

With a wave of his hand toward the old crone's cabin, Ralph smiled and chuckled, "With knot magic. The old crone will teach you."

"That old bat has made us do nothing but tie knots. I know we are making a fishing net, but that's all we do in silence. We tie knots and say the abundance incantation as we do so. Non-stop." stated Chavo in a disrespectful tone.

Ralph snapped and turned towards Chavo and growled, "That old crone is not to be disrespected, young man." He took a couple of steps toward Chavo and scoffed, "She is a well-respected elder. Don't you forget that!" He lowered his large face to Chavo and snapped, "Next time I hear you say something disrespectful about her, I will feed you to my wolf friends." The beast stood to his full stature and glared at the boy, who wouldn't make eye contact with the beast.

Chavo stared at his feet and quakingly spoke, "I'm sorry. I will be more mindful." He sighed and looked at his hands. "Imagine sitting there for hours tying knots. My fingers as so sore they bleed most days."

Verna stopped and turned to look at the boy and asked, "Are you telling me that you have sores on your fingers? Why, in the love of god, didn't you tell me? I have a salve for that ailment." She rushed off to her room, brought back a bottle of ointment, and began to treat the boy's fingers.

"Chavo, why wouldn't you tell us about your fingers? These are a mess!" she said with a scowl.

"I guess I learned that there was no point in getting help. I just had to tough it out." the boy said with a shrug, "No one cared about you at the school. They probably wouldn't do anything about it if they knew." His eyes rested upon Verna's face, then on Mary's. "I guess I better unlearn that."

Chavo sighed and looked at his hands and noticed the dry and cracking skin felt better almost instantly. Verna handed him the bottle and told him to use it in the morning and then again at night until his hands were better. With a nod, he settled himself back into his seat at the table. The spear slid when the setting bodies bumped the table and Chavo caught it and instinctually tucked it into the crook of his crossed arms.

Sarah smiled as she watched Chavo stand as a warrior with his spear. She thought, 'It fits him.' Chavo stood watching the events of the room take place and Sarah observed something a little different about him. Over the weeks, he let his tough, scared side fade away, and Sarah was surprised by the way he was enjoying the moment. Then, in a brief second or two, Sarah saw a rare event where the person's real shows through. She liked the boy he was becoming. He was tough on the outside, yet he was becoming happier and more open to talking and participating with the group. In school, he was always scrapping in the yard with the older boys. She liked the softer side of Chavo.

Sarah watched a moment longer as he sat there in his own unscripted space in his thoughts. She watched as he looked at his hands in amazement that the soreness was gone. Then, he would watch the room for a bit and return to his hands in awe. Apparently, he could feel her watching and glanced over at her. With a sheepish smile, he held up his hands. Suddenly, his eye caught the movement of the spear falling. With a quick turn of his body, his hand flew through the air, catching the spear as it fell. With wide eyes, he caught the shaft just in time. Sarah's eyes widened to see the tip of the spear was only half an inch from Verna's head. With wide eyes, the two children looked at each other. Their breathing quickened, and they scanned the room to see if any of the adults had seen it.

Chavo stood with his spear, walked towards his room, and came back empty-handed to sit at the table. No one knew of this event, nor did either child speak of it. They just smiled at each other knowing it was a story they shared between the two of them.

Sarah watched as the others opened their gifts. She marveled at the trinkets and objects they made for each other. She could see that Zaagsi Geezis[13]Shining Sun had a great influence on the designs and techniques used in their gifts. For a moment, Sarah was saddened that she had nothing to give. However, she could see that everyone was happy. No one seemed to notice that she didn't have presents for them. She felt so warm inside, for she knew she was not forgotten while she was gone.

Verna rose from her chair and lifted a lovely basket Mary had made her and smiled. She slightly chuckled at the way the basket leaned to the left, even when it was in midair. Verna loved how imperfectly made handmade things were. Mary was so proud of her first basket, and Verna was proud of her, too. Even more so, she loved that Mary made this basket just for her.

Verna stood at the hallway entrance and turned to look at her friends and the kids. She could see Marshal and Mary beaming as they watched the children. She sat in her room behind a closed door, and she smiled as the radio crackled to life and Christmas Carols rang through the air. Verna settled into her blankets as the day's celebration continued in the other rooms. She drifted off to sleep with the words "Silent Night" singing in her head, and slowly, she faded into a restful sleep.

209

Chapter 23:
The Bow String

QR Codes: Chapter 23

Scan to hear the language

#	Chapter	Annishinaabemowin	English	QR Codes
3	Ch. 23	BiZhaan Maampii	Come and give this old lady a hug	

Wind Witch

Chapter XXIII:
THE BOW STRING

The old crone, Zaagsi Geezis[(13)] _{Shining Sun}, had traveled to her family for Christmas and returned after the New Year. The children woke to see the smoke lofting into the air from her chimney. After nearly three weeks with no lessons, the children were stir-crazy, so they were eager to go back to school. They wasted no time eating and getting dressed that morning. Once the crow came to get them, they threw on their coats and boots in record time. Sarah grabbed the package with Ralph's fur and tucked it inside her jacket.

The sun sparkled across the snow, and the kids shielded their eyes from the brightness when they stepped out the door. After a moment, their eyes adjusted, and they ran to the cabin. As the children approached the cabin, a snowball flew through the air and hit Peter square in the chest. The old crone laughed as she tucked herself behind a tree. The kids could hear her laughing like an old loon. She emerged with another snowball and lofted it through the air. She watched it hit Chavo in the leg, and she hid.

Sarah took cover behind a woodpecker-riddled tree trunk. She couldn't risk losing Ralph's fur. She peeked around the tree and watched the three of them laughing and playing with each other. The boys ran and hid behind shrub-like bushes and began crunching snow into balls. When their ammunition was ready, they began throwing snowballs at each other. She watched as they laughed and played, and she laughed along with them. After a short scuffle, Sarah saw that Zaagsi Geezis[(13)] _{Shining Sun} was tired, but her laughter was warm and joyful. Sarah knew it was safe for her to come out of her hiding spot.

Zaagsi Geezis[(13)] _{Shining Sun} stood panting from the play and turned to look at Sarah. A smile grew wide, and her arms flew wide when she saw her friend's daughter. Smiling at Sarah, she walked through the snow towards the young girl and said, "Goodness, aren't you a sight for sore eyes." She stopped and admired the girl for a moment and walked towards her. "BiZhaan Maampii[(43)] _{Come here, and give this old lady a hug}."

212

Wind Witch

Sarah smiled and made her way to the old lady and wrapped her arms around her. Zaagsi Geezis[13] Shining Sun held her tight for a moment. She pulled Sarah back with a puzzled look on her face and poked at her belly. Sarah giggled when she jumped at the sound of crinkling paper.

"What do you have there?" questioned the old crone.

"Yeti fur. Ralph said we are to make my bowstring with it," exclaimed Sarah.

Zaagsi Geezis[13] Shining Sun's eyes were wide, and her mouth fell slightly open in astonishment. She looked down at Sarah's mid-drift in amazement. She turned her head sideways in thought. She turned and paced for a moment, then stopped. She turned to the boys and raised her arms in praise-like fashion.

"OOKAYY! Well then. I guess you three better get inside. I am so curious." She stopped and said, "Peter, I will need your help today. I want to see everything you three have been up to while I was gone. I don't want to miss any part of it."

In the corner of the cabin, there was a workstation where the boys were working on a net. They wandered over to the benches and prepared to work. The two boys snuggled down into their seats. They looked over their progress and began to tie the knots.

"Oh, come boys, I must hear your tales. Seeing that Sarah is back with some impressive gifts, I am sure the story must be good. At this rate, it may take all day." pondered Zaagsi Geezis[13] Shining Sun.

The boys got up from their stools, walked to the circle, laid their pelts on the floor, and sat down. Sarah laid the package on the floor and followed the boy's example. The old crone pulled out her smudging tools and lit the Mshkwodewashk[14] sage. She washed herself in the smoke and passed the pan to the next person. Chavo was first, then Peter, and lastly, Sarah cleansed herself. Together, they sat silently for a moment and took in the moment of togetherness.

213

Wind Witch

"Well, now, my young ones, let's join hands. Peter, you know what to do," whispered Zaagsi Geezis[13] Shining Sun.

Peter leaned in on the smudging bowl, and soon, the smoke rose. The old crone chuckled as younger she appeared in the smoke. She and Peter's dad were sitting near each other, chatting about escaping from the school. In the background, an old nun overheard them and threw them into the darkroom in the school's basement.

"Your dad and I were very close. I see him in you all the time. I went to visit his grave while I was home," she shared in a silent tone as the smoke showed the visit. "Once we left the school, we went our ways. This is one of my greatest regrets."

"Is that why you made the belt for me?" wrote Peter.

"This is a wampum belt. One day, you will find your voice again, and you will tell the tale of your friendship. Until the ancestors free your voice, you must listen, learn, and watch the events so your tale will be true." asserted the old crone.

The images shifted, and Sarah's tale began. They watched the chain of events unfold. They watched as the golden image opened upon the arrow's touch. She watched as Sarah retrieved the arrow and quiver. The old lady's eyes fixed onto Sarah, assessing the girl before her. She watched the boys assist Marshal as the bow was being made. She watched as Oboodashkwaanishiinh[10] Dragonfly etched symbols of the ancient ones onto the wood. She watched as the wolves ran over the frozen snow with the yeti following. She watched as each child opened their gifts the next morning and smiled at all the happiness of the day. She stopped and took a deep breath when she saw the yeti's gift of fur, and she turned and looked at the girl.

Sarah lifted her package and opened it and laid its contents on the floor in front of her. The old woman reached over and grabbed the corner of the paper, and slid it to her. She peered down at the white fur in a moment of disbelief. Slowly, she lowered her wrinkled hand and touched the white strain with a loving smile.

"Ralph told me that you could help me build a drawstring for my bow with this," said Sarah.

214

Wind Witch

The old one stood and walked to the window and spoke, "My child, this gift of his fur is an honor that no one has ever known. With that hair, no one will ever be able to cut the bowstring, nor will it fray. I do not know what else may come from this. Yed's magic is different, and I do not know it at all. Jack may, but I don't."

Zaagsi Geezis[13] Shining Sun's shadow cascaded across the paper. She turned and stepped out of the sun, letting the light hit the fur, and the fur glistened in its rays. The children looked at the hair on the paper with a new appreciation. They hadn't known that there might be magic contained in the strains. They were glowing as if it were indeed magic. Zaagsi Geezis[13] Shining Sun placed her hand on Sarah's shoulder and squeezed as if saying, "Okay, let's begin!"

The old crone instructed the children to sort the pieces of hair by length. Long, short, and middle lengths were divided into piles on the table. She sent the boys to retrieve the bow so the proper bowstring length could be measured. With the precious fur, no mistakes could occur. When the boys returned, she held the bow in her old, wrinkled fingers. Her eyes checked the symbols on the bow's limbs, and shook her head.

"The symbols are those of the old ones, Child; you are well protected," she said as she ran her fingers over each rune.

The old crone measured the proper length of string that would be needed. She grabbed a long strain of fur, grabbed a second piece of hair, and twisted the two strands together to join them into one. The children watched her work her skill with amazement. After she joined a few strands together, she passed the hair to the children to inspect it. At first, Sarah was amazed that she could not see where the strands were joined. When it was her turn to take a closer look, her eyes ran down the white strand until she came upon the most beautiful sight. She drew in closer and noticed swirls of white wrapped and twisted together. Each swirl was frozen in time and at the perfect moment when the two ends were joined. She smiled up as Zaagsi Geezis[13] Shining Sun. The old crone smiled down at Sarah and then snapped her attention back to the boys.

215

Wind Witch

"While you tie the knot, you say the following incantation: 'Two become one, bound together forever.'" added the old crone. "Then you slide your pinched fingers over the knot. They should mend together if you get it right."

Peter wrote, "I can't speak; how do I speak the incantation?"

"Ah, my boy, your mind is stronger than words. Feel the incantation. If you notice, I did not say anything either. I just spoke to the spirit, and they bound them for me. Just practice, you'll get it." she softly spoke to Peter.

Zaagsi Geezis[13] Shining Sun showed the three how to combine multiple strands to make them stronger. Then, she grouped many into a bundle and wrapped the length of the bowstring from top to bottom to sinch them together. With a final, binding incantation made, the four of them stood and admired their work.

A loud knock sounded on the door. The old crone screamed out of fright as the knock sounded. The kids chuckled, and Zaagsi Geezis[13] Shining Sun held her chest and took a few breaths. She rose from her chair and let Marshal through the door. The room was dark, yet the light of the lantern over the table showed the bowstring's brilliance.

"Are you four about done? Mary has been waiting for the kids for hours." He smiled at the old crone.

I believe we are," shared Zaagsi Geezis[13] Shining Sun. "Please come and look at what we have learned today."

Zaagsi Geezis[13] Shining Sun led Marshal to the table where the kids stood smiling. Marshal looked at the opal-like rope sitting on the table. The kids stepped aside and let him view their work. Marshal ran his finger along its length and admired their work. His eyes danced across the details with delight.

"That, Zaagsi Geezis[13] Shining Sun, is a fine piece of work." he admired, "So smooth and not one knot can be seen." He looked up and smiled at the children. "Nice work indeed. Now, let's not keep Mary waiting any longer."

216

Wind Witch

As they cleaned up their workbench, they pulled on their jackets and bid Zaagsi Geezis[13] Shining Sun goodbye. Sarah carried the longbow in one hand and the bowstring in the other. The day was tiring but productive, and the kids could hardly wait until they could rest.

The children ended their long day by telling Mary and Verna about the lesson. The ladies smiled and slurped sips of soup as they listened to the children debate about who was the first one to join a knot. Then, who was the best? Finally, who completed more? Peter sat in his chair with his grin growing wider as his boastful friends' stories grew wilder. He reached for his pad of paper, and with a shake of his head, he flipped to the page where he wrote the words, "Two Become One, bound together forever." Under the inscription, he smiled to see that he was the first to tie the knot. He slid the book to Verna and smiled.

Verna giggled and slid the book over to Mary to read. Chavo and Sarah's eyes met Peter's book as it slid across the tabletop. They glanced at the book and back at each other. They knew they were busted. They knew Peter was the best and the score on the paper shows it. Like most kids, they got lost in their moment of boastfulness and got burned. Over a hot bowl of stew, Peter found the power that silence brings, the value of his integrity, and the power and validation of the written word as he smiled triumphantly at his friends. Verna and Mary giggled at the two blushing kids, who were caught in an innocent tall tale.

Sibling fights were beginning to happen more and more, and most of the time, Chavo and Sarah were the two most likely to grumble. Peter usually stayed out of their way and listened. Peter sat back and wrote all he had witnessed. Sometimes, like today, they asked him to keep score. They didn't think of doing so until Peter was the first one to show he could do it. After that, the kids kept track of the task at hand. Even though Sarah tied the most knots, Chavo was the only one who was able to make one continuous strand while wrapping.

Mary and Verna looked from the book and back to each other. When they were done reading, their faces were that of concern. Mary pointed at the words, "Two become one joined

217

together forever." Verna nodded, then scanned the section that said, "We found that if we work together, we can move quicker. I would find the right length and line up the pieces for them. Sarah ties the knots, and Chavo smooths them out. After Zaagsi Geezis left us to work by ourselves, we began to chant together, and the joining always worked the first time. It really sped the process up." Mary slid the Book to Marshal.

Marshal cleaned his glasses with his shirt and placed them to balance on the tip of his nose. He cleared his throat, looked down at the book, and read it over and over. Confusion covered his face until his head snapped up, and he looked at Mary and Verna.

"Do you suppose that spell works the same way with Natives?" Verna slid the book back to Peter as she asked Mary.

"Now there's a bonding experience for the history books." Blurted Marshal as he burst out in a laugh.

The children sat clueless at the table, watching the adults laughing their heads off. They knew something hit them funny, and they just watched as tears ran down their cheeks. The children shrugged their shoulders, and they just chucked up the experience to be a wizard joke. Nonetheless, the kids appreciated their happiness and went to bed with happy hearts.

Chapter 24:

Oboodashkwaanishiinh[10]'s Lesson

QR Codes: Chapter 24

Scan to hear the language

#	Chapter	Anishinabemowin	English	QR Code
44	Ch. 24	Nish-kah Nodin Me-koom-maa-senh[1]	Wake, Wind Witch	
45	Ch. 24	ah Binoojiinh	Ah Child, we have our answer.	
46	Ch. 24	Bizhaan	Here (come)	

220

Chapter XXIV:
Oboodashkwaanishiinh⁽¹⁰⁾'s Lesson

Sarah woke the next morning with a small tap on her shoulder. At first, she just shifted and stirred under her blankets. A moment later, she felt another tap that she could not ignore. She rolled over to see who was annoying her before the sun rose. She opened her eyes to see Oboodashkwaanishiinh⁽¹⁰⁾ Dragonfly looking at her. She pulled the blanket up and tucked it securely under her chin.

"Nish-ka Nodin Me-koom-maa-senh⁽⁴⁴⁾ Wake, Wind Witch." murmured Oboodashkwaanishiinh⁽¹⁰⁾ Dragonfly.

"The sun isn't up yet. I am so tired. Just a little longer, please." whispered Sarah after a deep-chested yawn.

"There is no time to spare. My yeti brothers tell me that the wendigo is determined to get back here. We must work hard to get you ready to defend yourself." hissed the creature as he crawled up on her bed and crossed his legs.

Sarah shifted her body and sat up and rubbed the sleep from her eyes. With a stretch and a yawn, she began to clear her mind as she focused on the old grey creature. A low vibration began to emit from her quiver, and Oboodashkwaanishiinh⁽¹⁰⁾ Dragonfly looked at it curiously. Sarah pulled the quiver and arrows from under her covers and held it in her hands.

"That has never happened before." she said in curiosity.

"It is time. You need to learn about your arrows." hissed the creature.

Sarah watched the creature unstrap his quiver and lay it in front of her on the bed. Oboodashkwaanishiinh⁽¹⁰⁾ Dragonfly rose to his feet and opened the curtains to expose the moon shining brightly in her full glory. Her light showed through the window and lit the covers on Sarah's bed. As Sarah's eyes adjusted, she could see many arrows tucked in the shaft of the quiver. She covered her eyes as the black arrow started to glow brightly.

221

The light from the arrows pulsated through the room as Oboodashkwaanishiinh[10] Dragonfly retrieved his arrow and held it in his hands, and he hissed, "Show me yours."

Sarah lifted the two arrows from her quiver and laid them in front of her in the moonlight. The three arrows lay on the bed, and their light pulsated through the room. The pair watched the obsidian arrows' shafts shimmer and shift in a mist-like fashion. It was such a sight that the two just watched and witnessed their celebration in awe.

"I can't believe that there are three of them. I had always thought there were only two. I find it very odd." whispered the creature to the young girl.

"If there are three arrows here, I wonder if there are more. I serve one. You have two. I am bound to this one, and it will serve me until I fulfill my vow to protect Peter's line. For now, it will remain loyal to me. The other ones will stay loyal to you." slurred Oboodashkwaanishiinh[10] Dragonfly.

Sarah's deep dark eyes peered upon Oboodashkwaanishiinh[10] Dragonfly and questioned, "How is it that yours has come to you?"

"Well, I am an excellent archer, just like many of us. However, I was able to take down a short nose bear. When I defeated it, I was given this one by my father." he proudly spoke.

Sarah hesitated, "Those big bears that are told in the stories? The ones that are as big as the cabin? Aren't they instinct?"

"Ah child, I am from an ancient culture." Oboodashkwaanishiinh[10] Dragonfly trailed off as he scratched the top of his head. "I was very young with men came. I have no idea how old I am."

Sarah sat looking at the creature's old hand and the wrinkles on his face. It was clear that he was indeed very old. The hairless body was adorned with furs to keep him warm. She remembered how much he struggled to stand and walk. Is he older

222

than the men's arrival? She couldn't wrap her thoughts about the creature in an understandable manner.

"It's time to tell you what I know." hesitated Oboodashkwaanishiinh[10] Dragonfly. "Humans were not always here. There were two brothers and their families that came to this region. Each brother had a black arrow. There was a curse set during a great battle between them. The victor would be cursed with destruction by intruders. When the battle was done, my father was given this one to protect medicine men and their families."

"How did the yeti's get this one?" queried Sarah.

"I have been told that an ancient one came and spirited it away." sneered Oboodashkwaanishiinh[10] Dragonfly.

"I wonder if the ancient one was the carving in the wall in the yeti's cave." replied Sarah.

"Perhaps. I didn't see her so I couldn't confirm. I wonder." his thoughts drifted off.

Oboodashkwaanishiinh[10] Dragonfly stared at the arrows. With his left hand, he held it over each arrow. One arrow's vibration was firm like a drum. The second one felt high and tinny. His arrow's vibration was a low growling tone. Oboodashkwaanishiinh[10]'s Dragonfly's eyes rose to look at Sarah.

"Place your hand on the arrows. Their energy is distinct from one another. They are all so lively in their own ways. "I'm curious whether they serve various functions," he spoke in a deep tone of wonder. "It is clear that this chain of events is meant to be unknown."

Sarah's eyes grew wide as her hand came to rest over each one. Her eyes searched for each arrow. She couldn't see any difference between them all. They all had the same sharp tip and the same shaft and feathers. The only difference was the way they felt.

223

Wind Witch

"I will tell you this: One must not use them for hunting animal flesh. Don't disrespect them. One must not anger the ancestors," he commanded.

Sarah shifted under his gaze and muttered, "I am just a girl. I haven't even come into womanhood yet. This is a lot to take in."

"It is normal to doubt yourself, young one. Humility is a good thing for you to practice. You should understand that you are the Nodin Me-koom-maa-senh[1] Wind Witch and let doubt go on the wind. Learn, listen, grow, and practice what you are being taught. This is time for you to come into your power. That mark on your arm, that is, the kiss of the wind. You can wield the magic of all winds. Northern wind, which you seem to favor, brings in the winter months. Western wind drives the weather. The southern wind is dry and hot. The eastern wind drives the oceanic weather, mainly the great winds and storms. There is a purpose for each wind. Study what men have learned and use it." stated Oboodashkwaanishiinh[10] Dragonfly.

The two individuals were startled by an owl knocking on her window. Oboodashkwaanishiinh[10] Dragonfly slid from the bed to the floor, climbed up into the chair, and let the bird in. With a flutter, the bird lofted over to the bed and flopped the envelope down in front of Sarah and flapped out the window. Sarah picked up the envelope and read, 'Sarah Shingwak. Black soap'. Her forehead wrinkled as she could see the card was a birthday card. Addressed to Father Unis. Oboodashkwaanishiinh[10] Dragonfly looked upon the card over Sarah's shoulder.

A smile stretched wide, and Oboodashkwaanishiinh[10] Dragonfly slithered around Sarah's side and hissed, "Ah Binoojiinh[45] child. We have our answer."

Oboodashkwaanishiinh[10] Dragonfly reached over to his arrow, and it jumped into his hand. His eyes glistened with so much excitement. He raised his finger and motioned for Sarah to lean closer to him. His eyes shifted down to the card, then back to Sarah. They tucked in close, and Oboodashkwaanishiinh[10] Dragonfly lowered its tip to the paper.

224

Wind Witch

"De-bwa-min-aa-gwa-se   (18)   Reveal" ordered
Oboodashkwaanishiinh[10] Dragonfly.

The glow of the arrow began, and it illuminated the faces
of the unusual couple. Oboodashkwaanishiinh[10] Dragonfly shifted the
arrow back and forth across the card as the light grew brighter.
Sarah's eyes squinted as her eyes focused on the paper. Black ink
began to reveal itself, and the shaky scripted words began to appear
after a moment. Soon, Sarah and Oboodashkwaanishiinh[10] Dragonfly
could see the script completely.

"Just in time. When you face Father Unis, you must speak
his name at the moment you release the arrow." instructed
Oboodashkwaanishiinh[10] Dragonfly as he rose to his feet and began
pacing. "Shingwak, medicine men and women." he slurred as his
eyes fixed on Sarah. "Keep that with you," I remember the name
that must be spoken when you shoot the beast. If you fail this time,
I will protect you from death. Not injury, but death." lisped the
creature as he made direct eye contact.

A knock on the door interrupted the pair's concentration.
With startled expressions, they quickly rose to open the door.
Verna's eyes widened as the two exited the room together. She
smiled as they passed and chuckled when the quivers brushed by
her. She paused for a moment as she watched their quivers fasten
onto each owner, and the arrows flew through the air and settled in
to rest in their chariots.

"What have you two been up to? Did I hear an owl
knocking on your window? Are you hungry?" blurted Verna as she
followed the two to the kitchen.

Sarah shrugged, then nodded and smiled at the thought of
food. She could smell breakfast cooking on the stove and took a
deep breath when she smelled the percolating coffee. She made her
way to her seat and settled in. She still had the card in her hand,
and she laid it on the table. A dish of pancakes and scrambled eggs
were set in front of her. A hot cup of tea landed near her, and the
honey pot slid to stand next to her cup. Her eyes fixed on
Oboodashkwaanishiinh[10] Dragonfly as he made a beeline for Marshal.

Wind Witch

"It is time, my friend; she must learn to shoot. Tyrone said the beast was heading this way again. It actually stowed away on a boat and is crossing the water and heading this way." informed Oboodashkwaanishiinh[10] Dragonfly. "We have no time to waste."

Marshal's eyes widened, and, for a moment, he considered this news. He absently minded chewed on his lip and stroked his beard simultaneously. He rose from his chair and walked outside. A moment later, he sat down pensively at the table.

"I think we better use the barn for practice. It will be warmer. With help, we can lengthen it to fit a range inside." he sighed and continued, "I sure wish we had a few more wands. Kinda late to summon help."

After Marshal finished his meal, he and Oboodashkwaanishiinh[10] Dragonfly exited the cabin. The boys dressed and followed them. Sarah sat sipping her tea and warming her hands on the warm cup. She slid the card from under her plate and held it in her hands and opened it up. The ink on the inside was gone and concealed. She held it in her hands and placed it back down.

"May I see what you have there?" asked Mary.

"Is that what the owl brought you?" queried Verna.

Sarah held up the card with a smile, and Verna dashed over to retrieve it from her. Her excitement turned to confusion in a matter of seconds. She turned the card over, hoping to see something of interest. To her, it was an ordinary card. She handed the card to Mary, who also shared in the confusion.

Sarah chewed and swallowed and muttered, "Oboodashkwaanishiinh[10] Dragonfly showed me how to see its secret. Jade used the black soap to cover the name." she trailed off for a moment then continued, "It's a card from his grandmother. The handwriting was so shaky that it was hard to read at first. It is clear that his grandmother was pretty old when she wrote it."

Oboodashkwaanishiinh[10] Dragonfly and Zaagasi Geezis[13] Shining Sun walked into the cabin to retrieve Sarah. Sarah quickly

226

dressed and followed them to the barn. Marshal was putting on the finishing touches on the range when they walked in. Bales of hay were stacked at the end of the barn. In the center of the stack hung a piece of paper no larger than a doorknob. The old crone and the master archer admired Marshal's work and smiled.

"Here, Sarah, use these to practice with." Said Marshal shyly.

Sarah's eyes fixed on the arrows, and she took a deep breath when she saw Marshal handing her a dozen arrows. She took them in her hand, and the bright yellow band crowned the nock end. Her eyes danced with the sight of black lines painted on its crown. She hugged him, and his face turned a scarlet color.

"I will leave you three to your lessons." He said as he stood with pride.

Zaagasi Geezis[13] Shining Sun stood next to Oboodashkwaanishiinh[10] Dragonfly and smiled at Marshal's gift. Sarah lowered them into her quiver and smiled at the pair in front of her. She lifted the bow and bowstring bag to her teachers, and they looked at her gifts. A slight chill rushed in through the cracks, and Zaagasi Geezis[13] Shining Sun pulled her shawl around her.

"Oh child, I know you are scared. This is a lot to take in. With practice, you will become a fine archer." Zaagasi Geezis[13] Shining Sun insisted.

Oboodashkwaanishiinh[10] Dragonfly began to pace. His feet moved quickly back and forth in front of her. He mumbled under his breath as he processed his thoughts. Every now and then, he threw his arms up into the air. He seemed to be talking to others who were not in the room. He kept glancing over at the bowstring pouch, muttering.

"How is it that the other wizards didn't erase your memory when you left the hovel?" hissed Oboodashkwaanishiinh[10] Dragonfly.

"The council agreed that I would need to have contact with my protecting sentries." she shrugged. "If I remember them, I won't be scared of them. Well, human friendly ones at least."

The creature tilted his head from side to side shaking it as he cleared his thoughts. "I don't understand what is happening at this moment, but I will not question it either. Let's get you ready Noodin Mekoom-maa-senh[1].

"Not to mention the fabulous gift of the bowstring. The children worked hard to get it ready. Sarah, I need to see your card. Let's make sure you can read it when you need it." stated Zaagasi Geezis[13] Shining Sun.

Sarah pulled out the card and struggled to retrieve the black arrow from her quiver. They seemed to slip past her hand when she tried to grab them. Oboodashkwaanishiinh[10] Dragonfly watched with a smirk on his grey skin. He seemed to enjoy the moment. Zaagasi Geezis[13] Shining sun watched in a confused manner.

"Ah child, you must call them." hissed Oboodashkwaanishiinh[10] Dragonfly as he walked over to her chuckling. "Now that you put regular arrows in the quiver, they will only come on command." He chuckled as he looked at the mess of arrows in the quiver. "You see, they move out of the way so you can grab the others easily." Oboodashkwaanishiinh[10] Dragonfly said with a chuckle. "They are not toys nor hunting tools. To retrieve them, hold your hand over the quiver and say, "Here."

Sarah steadied herself and followed his directions and commanded, "Here!"

The arrow shifted slightly in the quiver. Sarah frowned at the lack of success. She tried again and failed a second time. She looked at her teachers and frowned.

Zaagasi Geezis[13] Shining sun smiled and walked over to Sarah and began, "Use our language, dear child. Say Bizhaan[46] here!".

Sarah straightened herself up and lifted her hand over the quiver, and sternly said, "Bizhaan[46] Here!"

One of the black arrows jumped into Sarah's hand. She looked up at her teachers and smiled. She pulled the arrow over her shoulder and looked at it. Slowly she lowered her arrow to the paper and said, "Reveal."

"Oh child, say: De-bwa-min-aa-gwa-se [18] Reveal." suggested Zaagasi Geezis[13] Shining Sun.

Sarah followed suit and said, "De-bwa-min-aa-gwa-se [18] Reveal."

The glow of the arrow began, and everyone leaned in close to watch. The light's intensity grew, and the words began to show. Sarah concentrated and mentally repeated the words in her mind, and more script could be seen. She smiled as she read:

"My Dearest Eugene,

It is hard to believe that another year, 55 to be exact, has passed since Eugene Johnathan Unis was born. Happy Birthday, my grandson.

Your Loving Grandmother."

"Learn that name, little one. Commit it to memory if you can. Keep that card with you at all times. Memory seems to run when it's needed the most." commanded Zaagasi Geezis[13] Shining Sun. She turned to Oboodashkwaanishiinh[10] Dragonfly with a sly smile, with a flick of her eyebrows, and added, "Would you like to see the bowstring of yeti fur?"

Oboodashkwaanishiinh[10] Dragonfly turned towards Sarah and walked to her. His eyes were leveled at the pouch that held the string. He watched Sarah reach for the bag, and she pulled out the string, and the yeti pendant fell on the ground. Oboodashkwaanishiinh[10] Dragonfly stopped in his steps. Sarah reached down and picked it up. Oboodashkwaanishiinh[10]'s Dragonfly's expression was of exasperation. He stood there with his mouth hung open, and his eyes were wide as he looked at the Pendant. He looked over the Zaagasi Geezis[13] Shining Sun and shook his head.

The creature approached the child and laid his hand on hers, "It is very clear, you are very protected. Now, it is time. Let's begin."

229

Wind Witch

Oboodashkwaanishiinh[10] Dragonfly wore his bow over his shoulder, and he lifted it from his body and held it in front of him. His small arms were thinner than the limbs of his bow. He unstrung it and held his bowstring in his hand. Sarah watched as he slid one end of the bowstring on one side then hooked the other end with the bowstring loop on the other. He waited for Sarah to copy him. Once she was ready, he showed her how to bend the bow's limbs so she could hook the opposite end. Sarah struggled to bend the arms of her bow, but after a small struggle, she smiled at Oboodashkwaanishiinh[10] Dragonfly when the bowstring was in its proper nook on the bow.

Oboodashkwaanishiinh[10] Dragonfly stood aside from her and said with a nod, "If I were you, I would leave it strung. It's not healthy for the bow, but you will need to be ready. That is until the wendigo has been destroyed. Now, it's time to shoot Nodin Me-koom-maa-senh[1] Wind Witch".

Sarah's day was long. Oboodashkwaanishiinh[10] Dragonfly drilled her as her muscles strained to pull the bow and release the arrow. Her aim was miserable. Out of multiple shots, she only hit the target twice. She felt deflated that she was not a natural shot. Oboodashkwaanishiinh[10] Dragonfly worked with her on her form and chastised her for forgetting to slow down and concentrate. By the end of the day, she had had enough and stormed out of the work shed and into the house.

Sarah stormed into the cabin and said nothing to the curious onlookers. She unrobed, shed her boots, and proceeded into her room. She threw her quiver onto the bed and stared at them in disgust. She thought, "I am no Nodin Me-koom-maa-senh[1] Wind Witch." She changed into her pajamas and heard Marshal and Oboodashkwaanishiinh[10] Dragonfly talking about the day. Sarah climbed into her bed, exhausted and ready for a night's rest. She closed her eyes and drifted off to sleep.

230

Wind Witch

Chapter 25: Snowman Army

QR Codes: Chapter 25

Scan to hear the language

#	Chapter	Anishinabemowin	English	QR Code
47	Ch. 25	Kaa, call the Muh-kuh-da mtig-wah-wi	No, call the black arrow.	

Chapter XXV:
Snowman Army

Morning came and went. Sarah woke to the noon sun's rays. She rolled over in her bed, and her muscles stung, and her arms rebelled against use. Still, she rose and painfully reached for her quiver, and she wrestled her sore body to the kitchen and seated herself in her favorite chair. No one seemed to be around, and no movement could be detected. Sarah wondered where they were.

The card sat on the table, and she picked it up and read it again. She shook her head and thought, "If only his grandmother knew how he treated the kids at school. He wasn't sweet at all. He was always mean and nasty. However, he did like to punish us." she thought as she put the card down on the table and pushed it away.

Outside, she could hear Chavo laughing, so she went over to the window and peeked out to see what he was doing. Sarah smiled as she watched Peter place a head on a snowman. Marshal and Mary were building a snowman of their own, and they chatted with each other as they did so. Verna emerged from the old crone's house and inspected everyone's work as she passed by. Sarah rubbed her sore arms and turned to sit by the fire. As she listened to the outside chatter, she mindlessly waited as sleep exited her head.

Verna entered the cabin, "Oh Sarah! You're awake!" She took off her jacket, shed her boots, and walked to Sarah. "I was just at Zaagasi Geezis[13] Shining Sun's cabin. We made an ointment for your arms. I am sure you are very sore today." she said as she took off her coat.

Sarah went to yawn and stretched but recoiled in pain. "Yes, I am very sore."

Verna walked over to Sarah and escorted her to her room. Verna worked on her sore muscles by firmly rubbing the ointment in. The warm, soothing ointment soaked into Sarah's sore arms and chest, and the pain seemed to diminish. Verna worked diligently

233

Wind Witch

rubbing in the ointment across Sarah's back in a loving motherly way.

"There you go, little Noodin Me-koom-maa-senh[1] Wind Witch; you should feel better in no time," Verna said as she helped Sarah dress for the day. "Now, let's get you fed." She said as she showed Sarah from her room and into the kitchen.

The boys rushed into the cabin and greeted Sarah and Verna. Verna smiled over her shoulder as Mary and Marshal entered the cabin. They were smiling and chatting with each other. Sarah watched as they helped each other knock the snow off their clothes. Chavo and Peter sat down near the fire to warm.

"Did you two have fun?" Verna smiled at the couple.

"We did; the fresh snow that fell overnight was perfect for snowmen today," said Mary.

"I have already used the ointment on Sarah. She was very sore this morning," said Verna smiling at Sarah.

Marshal turned and studied Sarah, "I am sorry to say, Sarah, you will have to try again today. Those muscles need to build in strength." He watched Sarah frown, "You will get better in time, and the soreness will go as your muscles build."

Sarah looked over at the quiver with a frown. "I don't know why. I can't even get close to hitting any target."

Marshal looked over his shoulder to the boys and smiled and chuckled, "We've spent hours getting ready for your lessons today. The boys are planning on joining you. Chavo can't wait to skewer a snowman."

"My hands are a bit cold, but they will warm in time to go back out this afternoon. He rose to his feet and retrieved his spear from the corner. "I am going to see what I can do with this!" said Chavo.

"You three will have to wait. It will be a few minutes before the food will be ready, so you might as well rest until you

234

have eaten your noon meal," said Mary and Verna nodded in agreement.

The sunny skies began to cover with clouds as the three kids stepped outside. Their eyes still squinted with the brightness of the sun's rays reflecting off the snow. The boys looked at each other and ran off ahead of Sarah. With a sigh, she followed the boys to one of the snowmen. They made a mark on the snowman and turned and smiled at her.

"You just need to have a little fun! I mean," he scuffed his feet, "I remember being watched by my father, and I couldn't hit a thing. Once I started practicing on my own, I wasn't too bad of a shot. Let's give it a go. " Chavo smiled, and Peter nodded in agreement.

The sunny skies began to cover with clouds as the three kids stepped outside. Their eyes still squinted with the brightness of the sun's rays reflecting off the snow. The boys looked at each other and ran off to their snowman ahead of Sarah. With a sigh, she followed the boys and wished she felt as excited as they seemed to be. They made a mark on the other snowmen in the clearing and turned and smiled at her.

"You just need to have a little fun! Come on Sarah, let's have some fun." Chavo smiled, and Peter nodded in agreement.

With a sigh, Sarah readied her bow and arrows as Chavo and Peter readied the spear. Sarah leveled her eyes at the snowman's mark. She reached over her back and grabbed an arrow and slid it out. She placed her left foot forward with her right foot in the back. She lined up her shoulder to face the white lump of snow smiling at her. With her eyes fixed on her target, she knocked her arrow and drew the bowstring back, resting her hand on her jawline. She lowered the arrow's tip to match up to her arrow point to the mark in the snow. She pulled her hand back, and her fingers brushed past her ear as she released the arrow. The arrow flew through the air and struck the snowman many inches below the mark.

"Ugh, I am never going to get this!" she yelled to anyone willing to listen.

She shot off four more arrows, one after another. Each arrow landed in places that were not even close to her mark. Sarah stared at the arrows sticking out of the snowman's belly with a frown. Once again, she drew another arrow, lofted it into the air, and landed near the X, and she smiled.

"Sarah, Bizhaan[46] come." said the old crone exiting through her cabin door in an old shawl.

The boys looked at each other in concern as Sarah headed towards the old crone's cabin. After knocking snow off her boots, Sarah entered the cabin. She could see that Zaagsi Geezis[13] Shining Sun was sitting on her leather pelt waiting for her. Sarah's eyes adjusted to the darkness of the room and made her way to Zaagsi Geezis[13] Shining Sun. Sarah retrieved her pelt and laid it on the floor, and lowered herself upon it.

"My dear, those arrows fly on your wind. As you breathe in, you breathe in your magic. You need to pull in the energy from the air. As you exhale, you give their flight new life. "Those are magical items," she said, nodding to Sarah's bow and arrow. You must use your magic to make them work well." She lifted a wooden arrow from the quiver. "The fletching feathers need feather medicine. They will celebrate having some wind work done on them while you are shooting." The old crone stroked the feathers and blew on them as she did so. "See, the wind is what they ride on. Do you understand?"

"So, I use my magic to breathe the life back into them?" said Sarah as she was eyeing the crone blowing on each feather. "As a thank you, they send magic back?"

She leaned in closer to Sarah, "Enh[19] Yes, you do understand. Now, let's go and try it."

Sarah and Zaagsi Geezis[13] Shining Sun stepped out of the door and chuckled when they saw the boys taking turns throwing the spear at their icy friends. It was clear that Chavo did indeed have talent in landing a good stick with the spear. He and Peter laughed

236

Wind Witch

as they removed the spear out of the head of one. Peter's skills were dismal. Half the time, the spear hit the snowman sideways or bumped and skidded off the snowman's round body. Zaagsi Geezis[13] Shining Sun laughter was so round and happy as she watched the boys at play. Zaagsi Geezis[13] Shining Sun just loved to play, and she rushed off to join in the boys' fun. She tried her hand to throw the spear.

After a brief moment, she turned to Sarah. "Now, my dear, try it again."

Zaagsi Geezis[13] Shining Sun watched Sarah ready herself to shoot. Once Sarah was ready to draw, she sided up to her and said, "Breathe in and draw. Have a focus, then exhale as you release." Sarah let loose; the arrow flew straight and hit near the target. When Sarah saw the result, she turned and smiled at Zaagsi Geezis[13] Shining Sun.

The boys watched as Zaagsi Geezis[13] Shining Sun coached Sarah again and again. The arrows flew straighter and straighter as Sarah got the sequence down. Snowman after snowman wore an arrow, and Sarah and Zaagasi Geezis[13] Shining Sun were beaming with pride.

Once again, Zaagsi Geezis[13] Shining Sun instructed her to shoot. Sarah began to pull an arrow from the quiver, and the old crone stopped her, "Kaa, Call the Muh-kuh-da mtig-wah-wi[47] No, call the black arrow."

"Call the Muh-kuh-da mtig-wah-wi[12] black arrow?" Sarah said in a confused manner.

Zaagsi Geezis[13] Shining Sun smiled and walked up to Sarah, "It's simple. Hold your hand over your quiver and say, 'Bizhaan[46] here'!"

Sarah lifted her hand over her shoulder with an open hand, "Bizhaan[46] here!" she spoke. The arrow jumped into her hand. Her fingers wrapped around the arrow, and she pulled the black arrow into her view. With a smile, Sarah beamed at the old crone.

"Well. What are you waiting for?" said the old crone.

Sarah took her stance, notched the arrow, and drew her breath and bow. With pull, release of breath, and release of the arrow, the arrow flew and pierced a one-inch hole straight through the snowman. The arrow did hit its mark, but its power caused everyone to gasp. After a moment, cheers went up from everyone who came to watch Sarah practice.

The old crone turned to Sarah with a smile, "Now. Call it back! Hold out your hand and say, 'Bizhaan[46] here.'".

Sarah turned her attention back to the arrow. She held up her hand and said, "Bizhaan[46] Here!".

The Muh-kuh-da mtig-wah-wi[12] black arrow was buried under the snow yards away from the snowman. It jumped up out of the snow and turned itself around and flew through the air to land in Sarah's hands. Marshal began to clap his large hands, and his clapping rang across the glade. Sarah smiled as Chavo and Peter ran to her, smacking her back in celebration. Their eyes shifted back and forth from the arrow to Sarah.

Peter reached into his pocket and retrieved a pencil and paper. "Shoot another one! That was awesome!"

Sarah read the note out loud. She began to line herself up with her target and reached over her shoulder and said, "Bizhaan[46] Here." Like before, the arrow landed in her hand.

Oboodashkwaanishiinh[10] Dragonfly was watching from the shed and yelled, "NO! Do not use them until they are needed!"

Everyone watched the old creature make his way to Sarah, "Remember, child, magic items need much respect." he hissed and looked at Peter. "The black arrows are not toys." he said as he turned to Sarah. "Use the regular arrows. Get back to practice!" said the grumpy creature as he went back to the shed.

The afternoon crept into darkness as the children gave up their imaginary fights. The snowmen were tattered with the day's play, and the kids felt very victorious! With laughs and giggles, the children went to the cabin for a hot bowl of soup before the night's

Wind Witch

rest. As Sarah reached the door, she turned back around and smiled at the snowmen and the fun they brought to her work.

239

Chapter 26:
Gashi-Dibik-Giizis[11]

Mother Moon

Chapter XXVI:
Gashi-Dibik-Giizis[11] Mother moon

"Wake up, Sarah!" Exclaimed Chavo as he and Peter shook her awake.

Peter held out his belt, and the spider coin was glowing. Sarah looked at it and closed her eyes in fear. The last time it shone so brightly was when the wendigo was near. She nodded and told the boys to go and get ready, and she turned to dress. Quickly she pulled on her clothes and grabbed the quiver. With a tug of her boots and a fling of her coat, she was ready for the quiver to fasten itself to her. She reached for the card on the table and shoved it inside her jacket and waited for the boys to come out of their room. Peter's spider coin pulsated as if it was urgently yelling out a warning.

"Go and wake up Marshal and Mary. " commanded Sarah.

Wolves howled through the trees, and Sarah shivered as she listened to them. Quickly, she checked her quiver and stationed it to make sure everything was within reach. With a mental nod, she steadied herself and took deep breaths to calm herself.

Yeti's howls began to sound in the night's air, and Sarah's anxiety grew. She placed the medallion around her neck, and she listened to the yeti's orders to each other ring through the trees. She closed her arms around her chest and pulled them tight. Marshal walked up to her and kneeled in front of her. He opened his arms wide for Sarah. Sarah tucked into his shoulder and just lingered in his strong love, and she could feel his concern. For the first time she felt very wanted. She felt love and care all pass through a twenty second hug. Sarah jumped as Yeti's call alerted her that they were near.

She pulled back and looked into Marshal's eyes and nodded. She leaned forward, pressed her forehead against his, and took a deep breath. The strength of the trees filled her, and she stood and opened her eyes to see the others looking at her with

241

pride and love. Oboodashkwaanishiinh[10] dragonfly walked up to Sarah, and she lowered herself to her teacher and now protector.

"I have your back. I know you can do this, Noodin Me-koom-maa-senh[1] Wind Witch. "Go get that bastard." he said as he levied his eyes at her.

Ralph burst into the cabin and yelled, "It is near. The wolves have lost many in their pack. Get ready, Sarah. Now is your time."

A loud crack rang in the snow-covered valley. A few seconds later, Jamison and Jacques entered the cabin. The two men walked over to Marshal and Sarah hurriedly. Their faces showed helplessness, and each one was flustered. Howls rang through the air, and their heads tilted to listen to the yells and screams ringing through the valley.

Jamison paused and began, "We've lost our lines. We lost two men. The damn thing ate them. Our wands are just no match."

The old crone opened the door and yelled for Sarah. Sarah left Marshals' arms and went over to see her. The old crone wrapped her arms around Sarah and held her for a moment. She stepped back and admired the young lady standing in front of her.

"Amazing how you look like your mother. She is proud of you. Now, remember to call his name when you release the arrow." spoke Zaagasi Geezis[13] Shining Sun as she looked down at her. "I am glad to see that you are wearing your pendant. Listen to the brothers for into battle you go. Trust that you are protected."

The yeti's yell alerted Sarah that the beast was at the top of the ravine. Sarah looked over to Ralph. He nodded his head towards the door. Sarah walked over to him and hugged him. He smiled down at her. His white-covered hand patted her on the head in his loving way.

"It is time for us to go." he exclaimed as he led her out to the clearing.

The door hung open, and Sarah stood staring at her fate. She faced the darkness outside and shivered as the wind kissed her cheek when she crossed the doorstep. The full moon shone brightly, illuminating the figures of her friends as they searched for the signs of the beast. She walked out of the cabin and let her eyes adjust to the light of the moon.

The woods were dark and silvery shimmers of the moon flickered across the snow. Footsteps of others crunched in the snow as they paced and waited with wands in hand. Chavo stood with his spear, and Sarah marveled at his warriorlike stance. So proud he stood. With a nod of her head, she stood next to him. Oboodashkwaanishiinh[10] Dragonfly took his place next to her. She smiled down at her teacher and nodded.

"I know you are scared, but just think of all the things he has done to you at the school," Chavo said. "Use your anger to beat the beast."

A stench rose in the wind, and a screeching yell rang through the trees. Shapes of men came from the woods and stood around the barrier that surrounded the cabin. Clouds began to form and began to block the light of the moon. Everyone concentrated and scanned the woods, looking for the damned beast.

Oboodashkwaanishiinh[10] Dragonfly tugged at Sarah's coat as he pointed at incoming clouds, "Child, now is not the time to call in the wind. We need the moon. Calm, take deep breaths and calm yourself. Push the clouds away. The wind can do this too. "

Sarah closed her eyes and took a few deep breaths. The wind whirred, and Sarah opened her eyes to see the silvery moonlit clouds traveling across the moon to exit out of sight. In the moonlight, Sarah could see Ralph and Tyrone holding the beast back. She watched as locks of fur were being ripped off her friends. The wendigo reeled its blood-covered head and bit down on Ralph. Screams and a deep roar rang in her ears as she watched Ralph fall. Tyrone knocked the beast aside, and it flew into the barrier. Sarah watched as the creature bounced off the barrier.

243

Wind Witch

Sarah took off for a run, reached over her shoulder, and yelled, "Bizhaan[(46)] Here!"

The Muh-kuh-da mtig-wah-wi[(12)] black arrow flew into her hand, and Sarah stopped to knock it and drew her arrow and let it loose. The arrow flew through the barrier and struck the wendigo in the chest. The wendigo stumbled back a few steps, and it looked down at the arrow sticking out of his body. He stood motionless until he could see that the arrow did not affect him.

A dark laugh began to sound from the decaying beast, "You stupid child, you can't stop me!"

He rose to his feet, turned and walked over to Ralph, and threw the arrow on him. Slime and drool began to drip from the wendigo's jagged teeth. His eyes narrowed in on Sarah as he circled Ralph's body. He looked up at Sarah and back down to Ralph.

Sarah slowly approached the barrier and hissed, "Father Unis, you foul soul." She began to pace as, and she continued, "You have no power here." Her eyes never left the beast as it hovered over her friend. She continued, "You're filth, a damned loathsome beast you have become. Rapist of the child, abuser of youth, flesh-eater to become one of the damned. No longer will you hurt any of my people."

Sarah turned and called her arrow, and she drew out the card and faced the damned creature. She touched the arrow to the card. For a brief moment, she closed her eyes and concentrated on the word, "De-bwa-min-aa-gwa-se [(18)] Reveal". She opened her eyes and watched it as the Muh-kuh-da mtig-wah-wi[(12)]black arrow began to glow. From a distance, Sarah heard a drum's beating sounding over the clearing. Jack and Zaagasi Geezis[(13)] Shining Sun's drumming sounded with a loud thump, thump, thump, thump ringing through the air. Sarah fixed her eyes on the wendigo as it lowered its body to crouch over the yeti. Sarah fixed her eyes on him, watching every move he made.

The beast lowered itself to Ralph's neck and wrapped its retched teeth around its curve. Ralph screamed at the pressure of the wendigo's jaws, but his fur stopped the sharp teeth from

Wind Witch

penetrating his veins. Out of frustration, the wendigo began to tear the white fur away from Ralph's neck with its sharp claws.

The glow of the arrow reminded Sarah of the card. With a glance, the name reminded her of what she needed to do. Her eyes fixed on the father's name and a new resolve began to burn in Sarah. Strength began to surge with each thud of the medicine man's and woman's drum. He is man no more and no more will I allow him to harm. A part of anger burst open from her soul and Sarah reveled in the moment of newly found strength. She smiled down to the glowing arrow and thought, 'Never again.'

With the fortitude of an empress, she resolved herself. As the card dropped to the ground, Sarah knocked and drew. As she drew in a deep breath, she could feel the cold bear in her chest. The cold wind rushed in and she let out a yeti bellowing howl. As she howled to the sky, she and her yeti brothers began to howl to the moon in unison. In the distance, the wolves answered their cry by sending their song through the midnight air. The hairs on Sarah's skin stood on end as she smiled at the moonbeams brightening the sky, and the snow glowed as bright as day.

Oboodashkwaanishiinh[10] Dragonfly whispered over her shoulder, "The shield is lowering so get ready. He can run very fast, and you must move quickly. I have your back. Now, get the bastard."

The crackling sound of the fading shield stopped the wendigo's assault on the yeti. Its hideous bloodstained face was lit as the dissolving line of the barrier passed by him. It stood at full stature and grabbed Ralph's body and dragged it to the edge where the barrier should be. He laughed a hideous screech as he flung Ralph's body at the shield. When the yeti landed with a thud on the other side, the wendigo steadied its eyes on Sarah and he began to charge.

With a dead on look at the advancing beast, Sarah drew the bow and screamed, "Gashi-Dibik-Giizis[10] Grandmother moon, I call thee now!"

245

Wind Witch

The arrow began to pulsate white in the moonlight. Sarah drew in the cold winter air and felt the sting of the cold hit her lungs, giving her power to her inner being. The steady drums beat fed her with a surge of energy as mother moon and she joined for a brief moment. The yeti's Howl rose and met her howls and Sarah felt another surge of energy enter her being giving her shared strength with them. She steadied the arrow and drew back, blowing on the feathers as they passed her lips.

Her eyes fixed on the beast and released the arrow, yelling, "Eugene Johnathan Unis!"

Instantly, the yeti's heard and yelled his name alongside her. Crackling vibrations snapped and popped their way through the air causing the onlookers to cover their ears. With covered ears, Peters eyes were wide as he watched the flashing white light gathered around the arrow as it flew. The combined magic of the yeti with the Noodin Mekoom-maa-senh[1] Wind Witch magic, caused the arrow to surge as it flew through the air. The arrow was pulsating white, and its light trailed behind it like a shooting star. Straight and narrow the arrow flew and hit the rotting wendigo in the chest. A bright flash of light burst in the dark, knocking the onlookers down to the ground.

Sarah and Oboodashkwaanishiinh[10] Dragonfly stood together watching the light spread and penetrate into the ground. A low rumbling began to occur as the light seemed to shake the ground wherever it traveled. Dust puffed up through cracks of snow and ice. Everyone watched curiously without being able to give a good explanation. Marshal and Mary glanced over to Chavo to see if he was doing anything. Chavo pointed at his chest and shook a vibrant 'NO' with his head. With a puzzled look, Chavo dusted his clothes and stood.

The wizards and witches hurried back to their feet. Many people covered their eyes as they watched as the beast burned to the ground in a fiery blaze. In the end, all that was left was the ash of the Father's body lying on the snow. Everyone stood silently in shock.

246

Sarah stood for a moment of disbelief that the beast was gone. Her eyes searched the area for her friends and saw that everyone was okay except for Ralph. Tyrone called the other sentries to Ralph's side. The cries rang through the woods as they viewed their friend lying on the ground, slowly dying. Tears flowed down Sarah's cheek as she watched others attend to Ralph.

Sarah thought, "He cannot die. He cannot die."

Jacques walked up to Sarah, laid his hand on her shoulder, and spoke, "Child, you are a medicine woman. Look what you have done for me. Let's go and see what you can do for him."

Sarah walked up to her friend and kneeled next to him. Tears began to fall as her fingers touched the exposed gashes of flesh. Jacques watched as Sarah's fingers closed gashes on Ralph's blood-covered fur. Sarah jumped when a spurt of blood shot out of a vein and landed all over his fur. Quickly she searched for the wound tucked into his shoulder. Her fingers tried to seal the wound, but the blood continued to escape. In a moment of frustration, she picked up the Muh-kuh-da mtig-wah-wi[12] black arrow on his chest and held it to the wound.

"Gashi-Dibik-Giizis[11] Grandmother moon, I call on you now!" put fort Sarah into the light of the moon.

Sarah concentrated on Ralph's wound with everything she had in her. The arrow's light was too much for most to watch but Sarah didn't seem to be bothered. She watched the flesh of the wound heal over. Wound after wound healed as she passed the arrow over them. She watched the arrow continue to work to synch up all the smaller wounds. When she saw every wound was healed, she laid her head on his chest and listened to his faint heartbeat.

"He still lives." she relayed to the yeti brethren near her.

"Noodin Me-koom-maa-senh[1] Wind Witch, we are going to take him back to the hovel. He will need time to heal. Thank you. You are an amazing medicine woman." exclaimed Tyrone as he ruffled her hair.

Tyrone bowed and turned away from Sarah. Sarah watched as the men hoisted Ralph onto their shoulders and disappeared into the woods. Sarah fell to her knees after a moment. Took a deep breath and called her arrows back, and she settled into ground herself in that place. So tired she was. She didn't move.

"Come, child; the night is done. Let's go inside." coaxed Jacques' voice.

Verna rushed up to the couple and wrapped Sarah in a blanket. Jacques lifted the exhausted child and carried her to the house. Once in the house, Jacques carried her to her room and left her and Verna alone. Sarah's head hurt with exhaustion, and she didn't fuss as Verna dressed her in a nightgown. Sarah snuggled into bed with a quiver in tow. She took a moment to pull each one out and thanked them for their protection and healing. Verna smiled and left her to rest.

Inside the cabin, the adults gathered at the kitchen table. The air was thick with confusion as conversations blended into one loud banter. Jack and Zaagasi Geezis[13] Shining Sun walked in unnoticed by the others and went to see Sarah. They knocked then entered her room. Both looked upon her, and pride beamed in their smiles.

"Well child, we have never seen anything like that." cried Jack as he threw his arms up in the air.

Zaagasi Geezis[13] Shining Sun sat on the bed next to Sarah and her arrows and said softly, "You know, my dear; I believe I have a great challenge on my hands. I have never known magic like yours. But you learn quickly. So, that is good."

"She needs rest; it is time for you two to go." Insisted Verna.

Sarah settled into her bed, and darkness began to creep in. She laid there for a moment listening to the others talking in the kitchen. The conversation between them echoed down the hallway, and she smiled to herself that her friends were all safe. No more harm would come from that man. Sarah tucked her blanket under her chin, and she drifted off to sleep.

Wind Witch

Chapter 27:
Council's Joy

QR Codes: Chapter 27

Scan to hear the language

#	Chapter	Anishinaabemowin	English	QR Code
48	Ch. 27	Miigwech Migi-zi-wahs for your Mii-gwaanhs.	Thank you, dear eagle, for your feather.	

Chapter XXVII:
The Council's Joy

Sarah woke the next morning to a knocking on her window. She covered her eyes to shield the light as she focused on the window ledge to see an old barn owl sitting outside. Sarah rose and opened the window, and the bird hopped in and placed an envelope in her hand. She turned the envelope over, broke the seal, and took out the contents.

Miss Shingwak,

   You and your party residing or visiting the cabin are required to attend a council meeting at 2 pm. Please arrive early.

   Sincerely,

   Mistress Gaagaapshiinh[26] _{Raven}

Sarah coaxed the owl to perch on her shoulder and headed to the kitchen with the letter in her hand. The kitchen light blinded Sarah, and the noise of people talking caused Sarah's head to swirl as she tried to comprehend their words. Mary stopped and looked over to Sarah and stopped talking to Verna.

"Good morning, Sarah!" Mary said.

The morning greeting to Sarah was an announcement to those in the room. They all turned and smiled at the child with love. The smiles warmed her heart, and yet she felt strange at their stares. Sarah smiled and greeted Mary in return. Sarah jumped when the owl screeched her ear.

"Geeze! Okay! I will show them." She considered the owl, and Sarah lifted her letter, "We, all of us, have been summoned to the council chamber at 2 p.m. today."

Wind Witch

The uncomfortable shifting of her friends' mood clearly showed that the news felt heavy to them. They looked at each other then back to Sarah. The confused look on their faces at her announcement made Sarah smile. She laid the letter on the table and sat down.

"All of us?" Jack said in an astonished manner, "I have never been there."

"Good God. How are we all going to get there in time?" Said Verna.

Marshal and Mary smiled at each other. "Well, we can use the fire." Mary walked to the fireplace and pulled down a jar from the mantle. "I think we would be safe enough to do so."

"Let's get Sarah and that owl fed, and we all need to get ready to go," said Verna.

In a furry, the room began to bustle with excitement and plans. Wizards and witches changed into fancier clothes and stood ready to move at a moment's notice. Verna cleaned Sarah's plate and sent it back to the cabinet. Once her chore was done, she and Zaagasi Geezis[13] Shining Sun, escorted Sarah back to her room.

Zaagasi Geezis[13] Shining Sun tiredly sat on the bed. "I swear, I am getting too old for this." She reached down and grabbed her old backpack and brought it to her chest. "I have a gift for you." She handed Sarah the bag with a sigh.

Sarah opened the bag, and a splash of yellow material emerged through the opening. She reached out and found a yellow and black shirt beaded with the finest decoration she had ever seen. On the back was a turtle hand-stitched into the shirt. The matching ribbon skirt made Sarah gasp and giggle at the gift. Zaagasi Geezis[13] Shining Sun laid the outfit on the bed, and Sarah threw her arms around her.

"Miigwech[15] Thank you! This is the finest outfit I have ever known!" She said as she hugged the old lady lovingly.

252

"Verna, Let's get our little witch ready for the council." Said Zaagasi Geezis[13] Shining Sun as she reveled in Sarah's loving hug.

The ladies began; leggings, a matching skirt, beaded hair ties, and other adornments were carefully placed on her. The two ladies stood back, looking lovingly at Sarah. After a moment, they admired the young woman she was. Sarah beamed from the inside out as she stood proudly as a Native American maiden.

Mary opened the door to see Sarah standing in full regalia; she gasped and said, "Oh, my girl. You are so beautiful." She paused for a moment at the young girl standing in front of her. "The men are waiting, and it is almost time to go."

Sarah smiled and followed Mary from her room. Jacques looked up to see Mary step aside to reveal Sarah dressed in her yellow brilliance. His eyes grew wide, and he held his hand to his chest. The little girl was gone, and a young maiden stood in all her glory. A tear settled in the corner of his eye, and he quickly swiped it away.

Jacques cleared his throat and struggled to say, "Ah, my little one, are you a sight to see!" He reached his hand out to her, and she walked over to him. "I am so proud of you. After all, you have been through, look at how wonderful you have become." He pulled her into his arm and wrapped her in a loving hug.

She leaned back and reached up to his scar and ran her finger over his cheek, "Thank you for everything. You have done so much for me. I had forgotten that I could heal until you reminded me. If you didn't, I think Ralph would have died." She said as a tear rolled down her cheek. "I had forgotten."

Jack stood watching the pair as he took out his drum. He walked to the fire, began drumming a low soft drum, and gazed into the flame. He stopped, then stood and walked to the door and opened it. Through the door's opening, everyone could see a massive eagle flying through the air. It lofted through the air, pulled to a stop, and landed on the stoop. With a loud squawking screech, it walked into the room. It fixed its eyes on Jack and walked towards him.

253

Wind Witch

Jack lowered himself to the floor and offered his arm to the bird. With a hop, the bird jumped onto his arm. Jack took a moment to stroke the bird as the eagle tucked its feathers under itself. Everyone watched as Jack walked across the room to stand in front of Sarah. Sarah's eyes fixed on the magnificent bird, and she nodded out of respect. Jack lifted his hand and turned over his closed fist, and opened his hand to show the brown (A)Sema[15] tobacco being offered to the bird.

"My dear eagle friend, I present to you Sarah Shingwak, the Noodin Me-koom-maa-senh[1] Wind Witch. Last night, she showed us great courage and magic and proved to be an excellent healer. I ask you to bless her with a feather." Jack said to the bird.

The eagle turned its head from side to side. One eye looked at Sarah, then turned the other to look at the child standing before him. His sharp feet dug into Jacks' arm as he turned his back to Sarah. A moment later, it began to shift its wings and opened them wide. Sarah's eyes widened as she looked at the wide wingspan. The eagle bowed its head and allowed one feather to fall from its wing, and Sarah caught it as it fell through the air.

Sarah stood looking at the feather in her hand. Her eyes scanned the feather in disbelief. Softly, she ran her fingers across the tattered edges. Clearly, the feather was torn in battle. Sarah smiled at the dark grey edges of the feather then fixed her gaze on the shifting bird on Jack's arm. For a moment, their eyes met, and Sarah closed her eyes. As if commanded, she held the feather to her forehead. Sarah felt its energy surge through her. Nothing big, just a soft whisper of hello and welcome could be felt. She felt the connection, and she felt loved and honor. She opened her eyes and looked at the bird.

"Miigwech, Migi-zi-wahs, mii-gwaanhs[48] Thank you, dear eagle, for your Feather," Sarah said to the bird.

Jack smiled at Sarah and walked to the door with his friend on his arm. Everyone watched as the medicine man and the birds touched head-to-head for a moment. Jack raised his arm, and the bird took flight. He reached into his pocket and pulled out a

254

Wind Witch

medicine bag and took a pinch of (A)Sema[15] tobacco and released it into the air giving thanks to the sacred bird.

Robert arrived to see the bird fly into the sun, and he turned towards the cabin in confusion. He rushed to those waiting inside and could see that everyone stood silently looking at Sarah. His eyes caught sight of the feather that Sarah held in her hand. His eyes widened as he looked at Jack.

"My friend, the eagle gave a feather?" he said as he walked to Jack.

"Yes, I knew it was time. After all, we saw last night, I couldn't ignore her truth, so I asked the eagle to assess her. He agreed and gave one to her." said Jack to his friend.

Robert shook his head, "If the day didn't get any more epic, I don't know what would." he mumbled and smiled at Sarah and shook his head, "My friends, it is time to go."

People vanished into the flames one by one. Each kid or Native Elder was guided by the magical folk in navigating the journey to the council. Sarah saw her friends vanish one by one. Jacques grabbed some powder and Sarah's hand, and they swirled through the spirit world. Sarah opened her eyes as the fire swirled around her. Faces appeared in flames; each face presented her with an approving smile as the fire drove her on.

Sarah and Jacques ended up in a hallway outside of the chamber. Sarah's eyes grew wide as she peered around the wide-open space at the ornate decorations littering the walls. She saw the boys sitting in the cloth-covered chairs along the side of the window. Peter smiled and waved her over. Sarah glanced up at Jacques, and he nodded in approval.

Peter saw Sarah walking towards him, and he took out his notepad. "Have you ever seen anything so grand?" He wrote and handed the note to Sarah.

Sarah read the note and shook her head as she looked around at the ornate decorations in the room, "no."

Wind Witch

People began to gather. Wizard robes flashed in front of the children, overwhelming them. The din of talk became louder, and Sarah's nerves began to rise. The children huddled closer to each other for support. Seeing the children's distress, Verna walked over to gather them around her. Sarah and the boys stood in her arms and felt safe and secure amid the chaotic nature of such a gathering.

The large door opened, and people started piling into the space. Wizards and witches took their seats. They all became silent as they waited for the summoned group to enter the room. Verna looked at the children and straightened their clothes and stood beaming down at them.

"It is time. Only speak when you're spoken to," she said as she led the children into the room.

Verna took the lead, and Jacques and Oboodashkwaanishiinh[10] Dragonfly followed behind them. The children entered the room. All eyes focused on them. Sarah looked from side to side at the stoic expressions of strangers peering at her. Verna walked them down the aisle to stand in front of Mistress Gaagaapshiinh[26] Raven. Sarah looked up at the beautiful lady sitting in a chamber chair. Her brown skin glowed as she openly smiled at the children.

"Welcome, my brothers and sisters. We summoned you here to discuss the events of last night." She said as she looked at Sarah. "Let's watch the memories of all the witnesses."

A screen of light grew brightly, and all the wizard's chamber watched the events of the evening unfold in front of them. Sarah watched herself take on the wendigo. She won, not only the battle of the monster, but the battle of her self-doubts. As she watched the events unfold; she felt the power she had as she faced the beast. She straightened herself and blushed at her stern words when the witches and wizards heard her. When the beast's body incinerated, Sarah felt a release expel from her being, and the room began to swirl. Jacques saw Sarah falter, and he quickly went to support her. Jacques held her steady as the story faded from the screen.

256

Sarah surrendered to the safety of Jacques's body. She closed her eyes and took deep breaths. The air in the chamber began to swirl around the pair, no one moved. Their eyes were fixed on Sarah waiting for possible consequences. The cool air swirled around the pair for a moment until Sarah took a deep breath and pulled herself away from Jacques' grasp. She looked up at her friend and nodded thank you. Sarah felt lighter and steadier with each inhale and exhale she drew. She turned to face the room again with down cast eyes at the floor. Sarah shivered for a moment for she could feel the eyes of the strangers peering at her. She drew her body up straight and strong like Chavo had done last night. She lifted her eyes to look upon Mistress Gaagaapshiinh[26] Raven.

Robert cleared his throat. "Mistress Gaagaaapshiinh[26] Raven, I must add to the story."

"What do you mean, Robert," she said in an inquiring tone.

Robert walked over to Jack and steadied his gaze on his friend, "Jack called the eagle and asked it to bless Sarah with an eagle feather." He turned to Sarah, "Show them your feather."

Sarah reached into a little side bag and drew out the feather and held it in her left hand. She lowered her eyes and held the feather up for those in the room to see. Mistress Gaagaaapshiinh[26] Raven rose to her feet and walked up to Sarah. She reached down and lifted her chin to meet Sarah's eyes with her own.

"Child, it is clear to me that the three of you need the council's protection as you grow and learn." She smiled down at the child. "I am sorry to say that we might have to bring the three of you into the school for safekeeping."

"You will not!" Said Robert firmly. "They will not be put into another school. They need to be taught our ways. Your school doesn't have the lessons they need."

Mistress Gaagaaapshiinh[26] Raven turned her gaze to Robert, "What do you suggest then?"

Robert's gaze fixed on Mistress Gaagaaapshiinh[26] Raven 's eyes and walked to her. As he walked, he reached into his vest

257

pocket and produced a piece of paper. He unfolded the paper and handed it to her. She took the paper and began to read. Her eyes widened, and she looked around the room with surprise. She briskly turned and walked back to her seat, and she sat down in contemplation.

"Do the kids know?" She said as she surmised the children.

"No, they don't," Robert said gruffly.

Robert turned to Marshal and Mary, "It is time you talk to the kids."

The couple turned to each other, and Marshal nodded to his wife. "It is time."

Mary and Marshal walked up to the children and kneeled in front of them. The children looked down at them, confused. They could see the two of them were nervous as they took hold of each other's hands. Together, they looked up at the children. They glanced at each other and took a deep breath and began.

"We are sorry you have lost your parents. We are so happy to have you in our home. You have become family. We've been talking to Robert, and he is allowing us to adopt you three." said Marshal.

"That is if you want to be a part of our family." said Mary.

The children's eyes searched each other's faces with wide eyes. Peter's smile grew wide, and his eyes showed brilliantly bright. Chavo stood with his arms crossed, looking around the room in thought. Sarah's head began to swim with the thoughts of being a part of their family. They looked side to side in total surprise.

Mistress Gaagaaapshiinh[26] Raven watched the couple and the children with a smile. The air hung still as the children considered the proposal. The silence became awkward, and the children did not speak.

"Well, you three, do you agree to an adoption?" Mistress Gaagaaapshiinh[26] Raven said.

Peter withdrew his notepad from his pocket, scribbled the words, and handed the note to Marshal. The only word written on the notepad was, "Yes!"

Marshals' eyes squinted with a smile as he looked at his wife. "We have our first Yes, my love."

Mary looked up to Chavo, who was standing protectively, "Chavo, we know this will be hard for you. Please, Chavo, know we will make sure to keep the three of you well.

Chavo's eyes met Mary's. "Can I keep my family's name?"

"Of course, you can; we will have to hyphenate it. But yes, if you can accept that?" She said to the boy.

Chavo shook his head, "I do not know what you mean, hyphenate?"

"Well," she flicked her wand, and 'Chavo Dowagiac-Martin' appeared in the air.

Chavo stood looking at his name shimmering in the air. With a smile, he lowered his eyes to Mary and said, "Only," he shuffled his feet, "Only if I can call you Mom and not Mary."

Mary's eyes began to flood with tears as she looked into Chavo's pleading eyes, "I would be honored to be called your mom." She turned to Marshal, "I believe we have our second yes." She said, beaming with love.

Sarah looked over to Jacques. He smiled at her and nodded. She took a deep breath and blew on her feather and closed her eyes to consult it like her mother use to do. She saw a vision of happy moments that she and the boys would have. She smiled and opened her eyes and fixed on the couple.

"I have chosen. I agree to be Miss Sarah Shingwak-Martin," she said with a smile.

A cheer rose through the council at Sarah's announcement. Wizard's wands sent celebration sparks to fly through the air. Jack worked to begin a smudge to sanctify the agreement. Zaagasi

Wind Witch

Geezis[13] Shining Sun began to beat her hand drum, and the children were led to the table to watch as the adoption papers were being signed. They beamed at each other as one happy family.

"It is done!" announced Mistress Gaagaaapshiinh[26] Raven. "Let's feast in honor of this wonderful celebration!"

There wasn't a dry eye in the room as the council members came up to meet the children and to congratulate the adopting couple. After a while, wizards and witches departed full and happy. Verna could see that the day wore on the children and nudged Marshal and Mary to lead their family from the chamber room to go home.

Chapter 28:
An-dah-yanh[49]
Home

QR Codes: Chapter 28

Scan to hear the language

#	Chapter	Annishinaabemowin	English	QR Code
49	Ch. 28	An-dah-yanh	Home	
50	Ch. 28	It is Nmebine-Giizis after all.	It is May after all.	
51	Ch. 28	Mino Dibikatken N'Wiijkiwenh.	Good night my friend.	

Chapter XXVIII:
An-dah-yanh[(49)] Home

The darkness of the woods was lit with celebration when the children landed in the clearing with the adults. Smiles grew on their faces as they saw a bright fire burning in the center of the field. Jack and Zaagasi Geezis[(13)] Shining Sun began to beat together with a rhythmic pattern, and the children ran to the fire and began to step to the beat of the drum.

Wolves howled in the distance, and the children answered their cry. Sarah could feel the wolf's happiness, and she invited them to come and play. They ran into the clearing and jumped and howled with the children. No one feared the other as the pack played together. The howling celebration was heard throughout the woods, and Marshal and Mary smiled as they watched their new family.

A loud crack rang through the woods and Jamison stood in the clearing with a smile on his face as wide as the crescent moon above them. Lyra, Jacques, Joseph, and Verna walked up to him and gave him a hug. The kids could see the men exchanging handshakes in greetings. Together they walked to the fire and joined in with the family's celebration.

Jamison smiled at his brother and gave him a nod. Jack smiled back and nodded. Everyone stopped as they watched the brother's play. The thudding of the drum began, and Jamison closed his eyes and took in a deep breath. He pulled his body up to full stature with each thud of the drum. His feet began to move to the beats. With a celebratory yelp he withdrew his wand from his robe pocket and began to dance. Wand and body stepped and twirled together in a magic dance. He touched the wand to his heart and the robes dissolved and his regalia began to cover his trunk and limbs. Everyone's eyes were alight as they watched Jamison's dance and they grew wider as they witnessed the transformation.

The drumming stopped and Jamison walked to the fire and signaled Marshal and Mary to come to him. He placed them in the east sector of the fire. Jamison walked to the northern direction and

263

Wind Witch

signaled Sarah to take her place at the northern door. The children watched Jamison wander to the western sector and called for Chavo to take this space. Peter smiled as he began to walk to Jamison and met him to stand in the southern door of the fire. The fire illuminated their faces, and the drumming began again. Jamison and Jack worked together in unison. Jamison emptied a bag onto the table and began to prepare to smudge the establishment.

The two men nodded to Zaagasi Geezis[13] Shining Sun and she began a low drumming to call the ancestors into the gathering. The drumming began to increase, and Jamison turned to the fire. In his hand, he held Mshkwodewashk[14] sage, Giizhkaandok[27] cedar, (A)Sema[15] tobacco and sweet grass and he held it to the sky:

"Gizhemanidoo[29] Creator. Tonight, we come to you to finalize the agreement made between Marshal and Mary with Sarah, Chavo, and Peter. We call the ancestors to witness the willing partnership with all those presented to you at the fire tonight. Marshal and Mary have requested to join in union with these children of our descent. We, the protectors of our magic, feel that this agreement has been made with the best intentions for all. Please accept their offerings as good-will and a blessing to those here."

He gathered four bowls to him and broke each medicine into each bowl. Jack and Jamison worked in unison to quickly prepare for the offering. Small pieces of the herbs laid in the bottom of the bowls already for everyone to take a pinch for offering. Each bowl was placed in their respective direction. In the East, Marshal and Mary's door, Jamison placed the (A)Sema[15] tobacco. In the North, he smiled at Sarah and laid a bowl of Wiingashk[28] sweetgrass in front of her. In the west door, Chavo stood proudly as Jamison laid the bowl of Mshkwodewashk[14] sage in front of him. With his free hand, Jamison fist bumped Peter's shoulder and laid the Giizhkaandok[27] cedar on the firepit's stones. With all four medicine's laid, Jack went back to join Zaagasi Geezis[13] Shining Sun to watch the events unfold.

Jamison stood and turned to the fire. Silence filled the valley as he pondered his next words. A Crack rang through the woods, and everyone jumped at the sudden unexpected noise that rang through the trees. The light of the fire didn't reach far into

264

darkness, and they strained to see who would be joining them. The wizards took out wands and prepared to fight. They could hear light footsteps approaching and they levied their wands to the noise. A little light lit and luminated Mistress Gaagaaapshiinh[26] Raven's face. Her dark hair and dark eyes were lit at the tip of her wand.

"Do you mind? Do you mind if I join?" her eyes lowered to the ground as she waited for acceptance.

Jamison glanced over to his brother and walked to her, "Mistress, you are accepted here. You and I, well, there aren't many of us Native Wizards. Here, you belong here too. Just because we weren't raised Native doesn't mean we don't belong. Come into the world that we were taught to be ashamed of. "Please, join us!" he motioned her to take her place with Lyra and the rest. He smiled a faint smile as he watched her take her place next to the others.

The ceremony began and Jamison's eyes lit up and fire seemed to burn in his eyes. His eyes glowed red in the fire as he peered into the flames before him. He took a deep breath and picked up a pinch of (A)Sema[15] tobacco and began to load his pipe. Everyone watched as Jamison prayed with the pipe in front of the fire. He lifted the pipe to the sky and began to whisper to the pipe and held it to his forehead in a loving manner. Jamison walked to each person and lowered the pipe to the adults to take a small drag from the pipe. Then he turned the pipe and touched each shoulder with it to bestow a blessing upon them. The children received a blessing from the pipe and he turned and placed the object next to the fire. He took a deep breath and peered over to Jack with a pale-like expression as he took out his wand. Jack nodded and crossed his arms and smiled at his little brother. His smile was one of, "Show me whatcha got." And Jamison's smile widened to match his.

"Gizhemanidoo[29]Creator , I stand in front of all these people to secure the union between the five individuals standing here in front of you. We do not understand why these children's parents were taken so soon, such truths we do not know. However, Marshal and Mary asked the children to be their family. We ask that this union be blessed in all worlds represented here today." Spoke Jamison to the sky in a sacred stance.

265

Wind Witch

The silence filled the valley as everyone watched Jamison walk up to Mary and Marshal with the (A)Sema[15] tobacco in his hands and said, "Do you Mary and Marshal accept your responsibilities of care for these children?" He lifted the tobacco pouch to them, and they laid their hands on top of the bag and looked each other in the eye and nodded.

"We do!" spoke the two parents in unison.

Jamison turned and peered into the fire and spoke respectfully, "Flames that burn within, seal this agreement between the two. Let them always conduct themselves in a manner that honors, nurture and protect the children in the best possible way including in the wizarding world."

Jamison walked to the fire and burned the bundle of (A)Sema[15] tobacco sealing the agreement between Native and wizards. Jamison lifted the bowl of (A)Sema[15] tobacco and carried it to Marshal and Mary and they took a pinch. Jamison stepped aside and the couple walked to the fire together. They stopped and gazed at the red embers for a moment and turned to look to each other with a smile. Then, together, they took a deep breath and turned their hands over to release the (A)Sema[15] tobacco onto the fire. The fire consumed the (A)Sema[15] tobacco and flames grew to glow an earthy yellow flame.

Jamison looked over to Jack and nodded. Jack walked closer to the fire and began to drum. Jamison took a deep breath and closed his eyes and pulled his wand close to his chest. The wand and Jamison began to glow and everyone's eyes fixed upon him. He walked up to Marshal and Mary with a smile and lifted his hands to rest on their hearts. Mary and Marshal began to glow at his touch.

"Ancestors of Marshal and Mary Martin, I call on thee now! Please join us!" he said up to the Universe.

The shimmer of light around Marshal and Mary grew and Sarah could hear laughter in the wind. She began to look around the glen at the sudden movement of the air. She knew she didn't conjure the wind so she stood there and watched. She began to smile as the skies began to fill with the Northern lights. Her eyes caught site of a falling star falling behind Marshal and Mary. She smiled as she watched it but became concerned as the light grew bigger. A sudden flash occurred, and Sarah covered her eyes. When she opened them, she saw yellow glowing faces and bodies standing behind her new parents. Her eyes widened as she watched Marshal and Mary turn to see passed loved ones standing with them. Sarah's heart burst as Mary fell crying at her mother's feet.

"Oh, stand my daughter. Dry those tears. I have never been so proud of you," whispered Mary's mother as she kneeled down to her weeping daughter.

The smoke began to shift and spirit of a medium stature walked up to Marshal and shifted into human form in front of him. Marshal could see the long braid form around the narrow face of an Indian man. "It is time Great-grandson, to be who you are meant to be. The children need your magic. They need to see you wield it. We needed to keep you safe all these years, but it is time." said the spirit.

Marshal's eyes widen as he watched the spirit turn to Mary, "My dear, a child, not of your own is coming. He comes in the arms of another. Marshal is his teacher. It is time for Marshal to rise." The spirit turned and smiled at his Grandson. "Your mother and I will be with you as you raise these children. Be the dad you were meant to be."

With a stunned expression, Jamison watched Marshal's great-grandfather walk around the couple and take his place with the other ancestors. He shook his head in disbelief and Jamison turned to the east and walked over to Peter who stood proudly in the south gate. Jamison turned to face his brother and stood with fear in his eyes. Jack smiled at his little brother and chuckled. Upon seeing his brother laugh a bit, his brow creased in concern. Yet, he knew he had work to do so he steadied himself to face what was to come.

Once again, Jamison firmly picked up his wand and circled his head in black smoke. A loud howl sounded through the trees and echoed down the valley. Jamison's stood still. Motionless.

267

Wind Witch

Almost frozen in fear for he dared not to move. He knew that She was coming.

Peter's eyes lit up as one wolves' voice answered another. Eyes widened as a black fog crept in behind Peter. The fog shifted and swirled around itself. Swirls of black clouds began shifting into spirit wolves. They danced around until they took shape and set on their haunches. Peter watched as wolf after wolf came to answer Jamison's call to attend.

Peter looked across the magnitude of wolves sitting behind him. Spirit wolves filled every space of the field. A light flashed in the far back horizon and Peter could see one wolf sitting in the light. Alone, she sat looking across the assembly at Jamison. Her gaze remained steady for a long time before she moved. The longer she sat and held his gaze, the heavier Jamison's disposition became. The She wolves' eyes left Jamison and settled on Peter.

Peter's eyes met hers and he found that he could not release eye contact. As she gazed into his eyes, Peter's body stiffened as a burst of light settled around him. The wolf almost smiled as she kept his gaze and she smirked as his body slightly convulsed. Mary screamed and attempted to rush to the boy, but the spirit wolves stepped in and stopped her. The She wolf watched as the others surrounded the others congregation. She wanted to make sure they remained safe. The She wolf rose from her haunches and began to walk towards him. Everyone watched as she made her way to the boy and Jamison.

As she passed Jamison, he kneeled and didn't look up. He could see her shadow pass by him, and he sighed an audible sigh. The She wolf stopped when she heard him and narrowed her eyes. She snapped around and turned a steady gaze upon him. Jamison's eyes widened when he saw her shadow come into his view. He watched as her shadowy nose nestled next to his ear and growled. He didn't dare to move. The She wolf slid her paw into his view and he smiled when he saw her paw still held their star etched into her fur on her paw. Jamison smiled when she presented it to him. Lovingly, he touched the mark to his forehead and his shadow formed into his wolf like form as his body remained in a kneeled position. The darkness of the night matched the black shadow's fur

268

Wind Witch

on Jamison's back and he lowered his front haunches to bow to his She wolf. Her eyes levied onto him and a moment later, she sauntered up to Jamison and gave him a nudge. They nuzzled each other for a moment and then turned to the boy.

The two wolves sniffed the air and circled around the boy smelling every part of him. Peter stiffened body shook with waves of energy surging through his little frame. Everyone helplessly looked on as they witnessed the two wolves working. Together, they stood in front of the child in silence.

"This is a pup. You have brought me a pup?" the She wolf sniffed at the boy.

"They will all be pups who will rise." Jamison whispered to his friend.

"He will be gone soon. Will he not?" She growled softly inspecting the boy's shoes.

"No, the humans will keep him here now. He won't be taken like me." he glanced over to his wolf friend. "If he ever is, it is for his safety, like me. They were taking me away to keep me safe." Jamison held up his paws in an apologetic manner.

"YOU WERE SAFE WITH ME!" snapped the wolf.

"Yes, my Lady but I had to learn to control my magic." said Jamison as he sniffed the boy's butt.

Her eyes leveled at her old master, "You left me with him."

Jamison shook his head, "How could I have brought a wolf to the school. You are way bigger than an owl!"

The She wolf circled the boy once again and leveled an eye at Jamison, "He smells of injury."

With a nod Jamison sat down next her and looked up to the boy and spoke, "He is the storyteller, yet he is unable to speak."

Jamison's eyes slid sideways hoping to catch a glance at the news of Peter's infirmary. Jamison jumped when the She wolf

Wind Witch

began to growl a low tone. He straightened himself up and steadied himself to deal with the old one.

"A messenger. You bring me a mute messenger?" Snapped the old one.

Jamison cringed, "The ways of the old ones are unclear. The old ones saved him but took his voice. What could I do? None of us have been able to bring his voice back as of yet."

"I have no more time to give to you. I must transfer the pack to him. Mute or not, tonight the stars are aligned for this." She stopped and turned to the boy then back to Mary.

The wolf walked up to Mary. Slowly, she nuzzled her way closer to the woman struggling to get to Peter. Mary's eyes widened for a moment and her struggle began to lessen the closer the She wolf came. She shook her head for a moment and focused at the wolf at her feet. Mary watched as the wolf lifted her paw to her and Mary reached down to accept it.

"Mother of the pup, I am leaving him for you." Peter's body convulsed again and the She wolf turned to Mary, "He is alright. The energy of the wolf has been freeing his soul. He is not being harmed. Tonight, he will be free again. Reign him in for wolves are hunted." said the She wolf. "I too have something for you."

The She wolf looked down at her paw and the outline of the star began to lift. Jamison watched as the star tattoo lofted to Mary's hand and affixed itself to her. The She wolf looked up at him and gave him a half smile then back to Mary. Their eyes met and a cold goosebump rushed to cover Mary's body in seconds.

The old She Wolf raised her head and said, "A mother's love. I smell you have it. Jamison's mother and I thought you and Peter should be gifted the same bond that Jamison and I have."

A second tattoo lifted from her mark and lofted and landed onto Peter's hand. "Wherever he is, you can speak to him." She gave Jamison a side glance. "If he will talk to you. I am sorry, but one more energy transfer and you and Peter will be all set to work together."

270

Wind Witch

Jamison turned his eyes away from the She wolf in shame for a moment as she passed by him. The She wolf brushed up against Peter and took his hand into her mouth. Peter's body surged again with energy and fell to the ground. A whimper escaped the She wolf as she watched Peter fall. His body shook with vigor and the She wolf whimpered as she covered his body with hers. She wrapped her paws around his chest and steadied their bodies together. Together, the light grew and fell as the energy settled into his new owner. The She wolf rose and shakily sat next to Peter. She nudged the boy with her snout and Peter struggled for a minute to recover from being hit with her energy.

The She wolf nudged him again and after a moment, he felt oddly strong and thought he could get up. Slowly he maneuvered his body from the ground and stood. Jamison ran up and offered his back and steadied him as he gained his footing. His eyes met Jamison and Jamison led him to his rightful place alongside the fire.

Wolves gathered around him. Live and old brushed past his legs as they retreated to their place behind him. With each wolves' welcome, he could feel himself grow stronger and soon he felt well enough to stand on his own. He looked down at the She Wolf and smiled.

Everyone watched as Peter stood in the midst of the spirit wolves. His breathing was heavy but he seemed to be okay. Jamison returned to his form and stood near the boy assessing him. The She Wolf sniffed him and walked to sit in the glow of the light. She turned and looked at the two men in front of her and sighed.

"Humph" sounded the wolf as she stared at the boy. "You have lost the love of running." She got up and lifted her nozzle to the boys' face and growled, "A messenger must be willing to run." She walked behind Peter and spoke to the pack, "I call on the pack to train this pup to run with integrity and truth and hold him accountable for his words."

Yelping and howls rang through the woods. A rustling occurred in the woods. Wolves began to sound and sauntered to the clearing. Spirit wolves and worldly wolves stood behind him.

271

Wind Witch

Everyone began to clap as more and more wolves appeared in the clearing.

The She Wolf cocked her head sideways and looked up to Jamison. Her eyes met his and she turned her head and looked at the ground. Jamison stood there for a moment staring blankly at the wolf. She humphed again and looked at Jamison and then back at the ground. A spark ignited in Jamison's head, and he finally understood what the wolf wanted. With an embarrassed smirk, Jamison kneeled to the wolf and sat in submission to the spirit wolf.

"Conjure up a pen that never dies, and book that never ends. Peter's life will be long and many stories need to be written." said the wolf as she lowered her nose to sniff at the Wizard. "You, Dear Sir, reek of anger. It is time for you to run as well. Get off that broom and run with the brothers." She turned her back on him and walked a few steps then sat pensively on the dirt. Her tail began to sway back and forth in the dirt leaving streaks in the sand. She stood and walked back to Jamison with a smile on her jowls and pushed her giant head into his stomach. "I miss our play. I miss our adventures. I shall be waiting for you on the other side." she said as she walked away from her childhood master and misted into the pack.

Jamison's eyes welled with tears as he looked back down at Peter and over to Mary. He shook his head and cleared his tears. With a swipe of his wand, a leather book appeared in midair and rested in front of Peter. A moment later, a stick-like object shimmered into being. A long pencil-like object began to take shape. Peter smiled as he watched the ornately etched wooden body of the pencil appear in front of him. Peter looked up to Jamison and he nodded that it was okay to take the gifts. Peter reached up and took the book and pencil in his hand and held them close.

"Do you, Peter. Take Mary and Marshal as your parents?" Jamison said as he held the bowl of Giizhkaandok[27] cedar to Him.

Peter took a pinch of Giizhkaandok[27] cedar and walked to the fire. He took a deep breath, opened the book and began to write. The flames started to sputter and the letter "I" rose from the flame and into the sky. Peter's eyes widened as he wrote the words, "I

272

do". His mouth hung open as he looked at the words written in flames above the fire. In a mesmerized moment of awe, he tipped the Giizhkaandok[27] cedar into the fire and everyone clapped. Jamison looked down upon him with a smile and patted Peter on the shoulder and moved on to Chavo.

Jamison walked to the stone and set down the Giizhkaandok[27] cedar that Peter used and walked to Chavo and offered the plate of Mshkwodewashk[14] sage to him. Chavo took a pinch and shifted it to the palm of his left hand. He glanced up into Jamison's eyes to see them burn. Jamison's eyes met Chavo's and held his gaze. Chavo recoiled from the surprised vision for a moment then settled willingly in to see what was meant for him. The flames burned in Jamison's eyes and a sudden shift of vision caught Chavo's attention. He was captive, but he grinned because he was right where he needed to be. The flames consumed the world around him yet, he stood waiting with a smile. Chavo's face mirrored the one in the vision and Jamison jumped back surprised to feel Chavo's emotions. He rubbed his hand over his face to rid himself of Chavo's vision.

"Do you accept Mary and Marshal as your parents?" said Jamison as he waited for Chavo's response.

"I do." he said as he nodded. He glanced over to Mary with a smile.

Jamison smiled at the boy and nodded. He stepped aside to let the boy pass. Chavo walked to the fire and emptied his Mshkwodewashk[14] sage into the fire. The flame rose and licked at the Mshkwodewashk[14] sage as it drifted down into the embers. The fire's hunger hissed as it greedily ate the Mshkwodewashk[14] sage. Chavo turned and walked back to his spot. He stood tall and proud.

Jamison took a deep breath and held out his wand. He lowered his eyes to the ground and circled a white chain of smoke around Chavo. He laid his hand on Chavo's shoulder, and the ground began to quiver. Once the ground stopped shaking, everyone's gasp lingered in the moment as they took in the ancestors who came to witness the union. With a puffed chest, he looked upon Chavo with pride.

Wind Witch

An old man shuffled to the front of the ancestors and gave Chavo a toothless grin. He reached inside his vest and pulled out his whistle and blew a high-pitched sound. Soon, the night air brightened as a bird made its way to Chavo. The falcon circled the establishment a few times and landed on Chavo's shoulder. The old man set the whistle down on the ground and the spirit whistle took solid form. Chavo thanked him and he laid (A)Sema[15] tobacco on the ground before picking it up. The old man smiled and waved as he moved and melted in with the others.

Jamison gave a slight chuckle as he looked at Chavo's gift. The boy and the bird looked good together. Both are so strong and hunters. As curious as he was about the gift, he knew he had a job to do, and he turned to Sarah.

He walked up to Sarah and stationed himself to stand in front of her. Once again, the fire in his eyes began to glow. Sarah could see the red flames dancing across the wetness of his eyes. She turned her head to assess the flames. As she watched, the flames grew in Jamison's eyes, and she saw her arrow flying through the air. A huge light exploded, and the darkness was gone. Ruin was everywhere, but cheering rang loudly in the air. Her eyes went wide, and Jamison's eyes were as wide. In shock they stood together as they shared the vision.

Jamison shook his head and held his wand to the stars and a spray of light shot out from the end like a shower. At first, darkness and silence hung heavily then, a swoosh caused Lyra to scream in the distance. Mistress Raven's screams came next then Verna's. The ladies began flopping their arms around like lunatics. Sarah and Jamison watched with curiosity. Then, a swirl of brown bats began to loft in and were teasing the ladies. Sarah stifled a chuckle, for she knew they would not hurt them. She smiled for Sarah really loved Bats and she knew they were playing. Sarah's eyes raised in delight when black bats added themselves to the gathering. Sarah looked up and the bats' silhouetted bodies lofted up through the air and their clumsy dance made her laugh a bit.

In one big swoop the congregations of bats flew low to the ground, then the next minute, they all flew up into the sky leaving the ancestors behind smiling on the ground. Sarah looked at the ancestors, then the retreating bats, then back at the ancestors. Sarah marveled as each bat took a limb in a nearby tree. There were so many bats that the limbs of the trees bowed at the weight of so many tiny creatures nestled on the same limb. Sarah laughed for a moment as she took in the site.

Jamison's expression was one of confusion. He had never seen anything like that before. He was sure he would see other unusual things now that this partnership was in full force. He was just amazed as each person's ancestors presented themselves. Jamison looked around the glen at all the unusual things being shown here tonight. This may be his first ceremony, but it will not be his last. He shook his head and looked over to Jack who was chuckling and shrugging his shoulders. Jamison's eye caught movement behind Sarah and he leaned to look over her shoulder to see what was going on.

Sarah noticed Jamison's stare and turned to see what he was looking at. She looked over her shoulder to see the ancestors' shifting forms and she stopped to face them straight on. Sarah's mother and father began to walk towards her, and Sarah gave a weakly held smile to her parents. She mustn't cry, she thought and stood strong as her parents made their advance. Their smiles were wide, but they did not speak. They just slid aside to reveal a small form no taller than four feet began to take shape. The shape shifted and Sarah's eyes couldn't believe what she was seeing.

Jenny, Sarah's first friend in school, took shape in front of Sarah. She stood there sheepishly smiling at Sarah as she waited for Sarah to recognize her. After a moment, Sarah's heart broke and recognition fell over her face. Sarah fell to her knees and cupped her hands and let out a deep grieving cry. Deep sobs left her soul and after a purge, Jenny walked up to Sarah and lightly touched the downtrodden head.

Sarah looked up to her and said, "Aanii, I am sorry I couldn't save you. Jenny, I am so sorry."

Jenny lowered herself in front of Sarah, "You did the best you could Sarah. We were so little. How could you do anything?"

Wind Witch

[Flash] The two girls looked up from their chore to view the truck rolling down the driveway to the school. Two men exited the truck and began to yell for the Father. After a moment, the Father emerged from the school to greet the men. The men and father began to chat and laugh rather loudly. Sarah glanced over to the talking men and saw them hand the father some money. The Father stuffed the money into his pocket and waved his hands toward the girls. The men glanced over at Jenny and Sarah and turned to walk towards them.

Jenny rose and began running with Sarah in tow. They ran as hard as they could but the men caught them. The girls fought to no avail, they knew they had to fight or die. Little fingers against big men, are useless. One man dragged Jenny towards a shed and Sarah blacked out when the other hit her over the head for fighting. Sarah remembered waking up in Jade's room a few days later all beaten and bruised. [flash ended]

Sarah's eyes went wide at the emerging memory and broke down in tears. Jamison wrapped his arm around Sarah. With a wave of his wand, a small pan with burning coals appeared. He reached into his pouch and added Mshkwodewashk[(14)]sage to a little pan and held it to her to smudge the evil memory away. Jenny watched with great concern as Sarah began to settle herself and regained her composure.

"Sarah, Oh please Sarah. Stop Grieving." said Jenny as she attempted to wrap Sarah in a hug. "Please stop crying. I have good news!" Sarah uncovered her face to listen to Jenny. Jenny leaned in close to Sarah's ear and whispered, "I get to stay! Well, Kinda."

Sarah's face was riddled with confusion. 'Jenny can stay?' she thought. She looked over to the ancestors standing in front of her. Some of them waved and some of them nodded. With either response, Sarah knew that Jenny was telling her the truth. Sarah's eyes widened and she looked around at those at the fire then up at the swooping bats and back again to Jenny.

"How can you stay? Jenny, you're. dead?" Sarah looked upon her friend inquiringly.

Wind Witch

"Ya, No, we, we didn't have fires now did we? I just chose to stay. Now, I really get to stay because I have a job." said Jenny as she bounced around like a school girl.

"A job? Ghosts have jobs?" Sarah said as she walked up to Jenny.

"Well, Sarah, we have a job." she said with a smile.

"I guess so, seriously, these arrows and all this must be for something." grumbled Sarah.

Jenny skipped and hopped over to the ancestors, "We, us wind spirits, are at your service Miss Sarah." She gave a grand bow and as she did a little ball of flame came out of the fire and rest on her hand.

Jenny walked over to Sarah and laid the ball of fire in her hand. Sarah looked at the fire and it burst into a flaming bat, then turned into a regular bat in Sarah's hand. Its little black body flopped back and forth over Sarah's hand as it got its bearings. Sarah lifted its body to view it closer and give it a nice scratch on its head. With a quick flutter of his boney wings, he flashed into light then back again.

"See, your bat can understand you and spirit!" Jenny exclaimed as she danced around. "You will be able to always call me. There is a catch." Jenny said as she stopped dancing. "I can only come in times of need. The Council of Wind Spirits will tell me when I can come to help or visit. Oh, I hope they let me visit."

Sarah looked upon her friend with her almost laughing smile and queried, "Only in times of need? What if I need you tomorrow? Or at my birthday? You can't come when I want you to only when I need you?"

"Oh, my sweet sister spirit, the need here on earth is great. I will be around more than you know." Jenny said as she stroked the little bat in Sarah's hand. "Toby" she looked down at the bat, "Will know right where I am always hiding. Where Toby is, I am there too. Right little guy?" Jenny smiled up at Sarah and continued scratching.

Wind Witch

Low drumming began in the distance and Sarah turned from Jenny and back to Jamison. The young gentleman held out his hand and directed Sarah back to the fire. Sarah glanced over her shoulder and watched Jenny take her spot with the others. Jamison took a deep breath and shook his head to collect his thoughts and turned to Sarah with the bowl of Wiingashk[28] sweetgrass.

"Do you Sarah, Take Marshal and Mary to be your parents? As witnessed by all the ancestors here?" Jamison spoke firmly to the girl.

Sarah looked over her shoulder at Jenny then again to Marshal and Mary. She looked at her brothers and nodded, then to the group of gathered wizards, took a deep breath and took a few steps forward, and took a pinch of Wiingashk[28] sweetgrass between her fingers. With a quick glance to Jamison, she walked to the fire. She opened her hand and let the Wiingashk[28] sweetgrass fall into the sizzling hot coals. Like the others, the strands of medicine were licked up and consumed to seal the agreement.

Cheers and celebrations began again in the valley. Ancestors stayed amid the living and the children's eyes danced around the clearing at the celebration. Mary and the rest of the ladies conjured up a meal for the guests. Zaagishi-Geezis[13] Shining Sun prepared a spirit plate for the visiting spirits and set it in the fire so all the ancient ones could eat too. She sighed as she looked around the valley at the merriment of the union. Dead and alive cheered as Mistress Raven took her first steps as a Native American Maiden in the dance arena. Jamison watched with a smile for no sight like this one would ever be seen again. He was uncertain what was to come, but he knew it was time to get ready.

Jack lingered on the sidelines for a bit watching the night's activities. He sat back in his chair and folded his arms over his chest and thought, 'This is not how I thought this would all turn out.' His stomach growled as it digested its feast and he wondered, 'is there room for dessert yet?' He reached into his pocket and pulled out a napkin and unrolled a nice piece of pie. With an appreciative bite, his teeth sunk into the nice crispy crust, and he sighed as he swirled the tasty tart sweet cherries around his mouth. As he chewed, he watched Zaagishi-Geezis[13] Shining sun, walk up the steps to her cabin

278

and take a seat in her favorite rocking chair. She took out her pipe and pouch and began loading the bowl. With a strike of a match, a few puffs of the pipe, the clove smoke began to scent the air as it lofted to the heavens.

A warm wind began to blow through the valley, and she felt it toss her hair around like a leaf. Zaagishi- Geezis[13] Shining Sun took in a deep breath of fresh warm air and said to Jack, "It's about time. It is Nmebine-Giizis[50] May after all. Now Sarah can let spring come to our forest. These old bones need rest. Mino Dibikatken N'Wiijkiwenh[51] Good night my friend."

She knocked the hots out of the pipe and rose from her seat. She turned and entered her cabin and readied for her sleep. She glanced out the window as she turned out the light. She turned to face the darkness, and she thought, "It all starts with three, one more. We need one more." She smiled at their merriment, and she was happy for the new family. Such a good day. Such a good turn of events.

Jamison and Mistress Raven walked to the fire and looked around at the unusual events. Wolves howled as the children tried to find them in the dark. The adults sat in chairs talking with the ancestors. Old and New faces became friends as the night wore on. One by one spirits left the gathering and ventured off to their own world.

"Come, children! It is time to rest!" called Mary as she and Marshal turned and walked to the cabin.

The children ran past them and into the house. Verna stood in the kitchen and watched the children's celebration. Marshal and Mary stood outside peering through the window, just watching the kids rid themselves of their coats and boots. They smiled as Verna settled them down with a hot cup of calamine tea.

With a hug, Marshal said, "Honey, the kids are home. Let's go and celebrate with them."

Verna smiled as the couple walked through the door, and she said, "Welcome to your new family, Mr. and Mrs. Martin!"

279

Wind Witch

The couple stood beaming, "Family. What a wonderful word." said Mary.

The children stopped sipping their tea and rose from their chairs, and they walked up to Marshal and Mary. Peter handed a note to Marshal, "Family is a very good word!"

Chavo scuffed his feet and said, "I have a better word right now."

Everyone stopped and looked at him, and Mary said, "What word is that?"

"Miigwech[30] Thank you. Miigwech[30] Thank you." Chavo said with a nod that he had the right word.

Sarah said, "I agree. Miigwech[30] Thank you very much for giving us a family."

Peter closed his eyes, took a deep breath, and began to write, " Miigwech[30] Thank you.!" on his notepad. His eyes remained closed as the others watched each letter, red and burning, appear in midair. Peter opened his eyes and smiled when he saw his words burning in the air. He turned and smiled at Marshal and Mary.

"Well now," said Marshal as he looked at the burning word floating in the air and back to Peter. "Hun, I see now that our little man is showing us a good use for his fire." He looked at his wife, "This, I am thankful for."

Peter smiled and ran to Marshal, who grabbed him up into his arms. Mary and Verna beamed at the two and walked in for a group hug. Arms wrapped around Marshal and Peter, and everyone held each other for a brief moment.

Verna yawned, "What a perfect day! However, it is time for bed. So, you three, off to bed you go!"

With great disagreement, the children surrendered to their rooms. Sarah heard Marshal and Mary tuck the boys into bed. After a brief conversation, she heard them walk towards her room. The door opened, and the pair walked through the door. Mary sat on

280

Wind Witch

Sarah's bed, and Marshal kneeled on the floor and pulled the blanket up and tucked it under her chin.

"We thought you would like to have this for the night." Mary unfolded the piece of paper and handed it to Sarah.

Sarah looked at her name on the paper and smiled. She laid the paper on the table next to her and said, "Yes, thank you so much."

Marshal cleared his throat, "I may be rushing this a bit, but could you call me Father or Dad?" He shifted uncomfortably on his knees, "I mean, I hope you will feel as if I could be your father."

Sarah sat up in her bed and looked at her new parents, and said, "I would like that. It might take a bit to get used to, but, yes, mom, dad, thank you for wanting me to be your daughter."

With large smiles, Marshal and Mary gave Sarah a hug and tucked her into bed. The pair bid her goodnight and closed the door behind them. Sarah lay there looking at the adoption paper with her name beaming in the light for a moment. Her eyes closed as she saw Sarah Marie Shingwak-Martin shining in black ink on the white adoption paper.

Wind Witch

Made in the USA
Columbia, SC
28 October 2024

44829406R00154